Irregardless

MAIN

of Murder

A Miss Prentice Cozy Mystery

Irregardless
of Murder
A Miss Prentice Cozy Mystery

Ellen Edwards
Kennedy

ST KITTS PRESS ◆ WICHITA, KANSAS

PUBLISHED BY ST KITTS PRESS
A division of S-K Publications
PO Box 8173 • Wichita, KS 67208
316-685-3201 • Toll-free 888-705-4887 • FAX 316-685-6650
stkitts@skpub.com • www.StKittsPress.com

The name St Kitts and its logo are registered trademarks.

This novel is a work of fiction. Any references to real people and places are used only to give a sense of reality. All of the characters are the product of the author's imagination, as are their thoughts, actions, motivations, or dialog. Any resemblance to real people and events is purely coincidental.

Edited by Elizabeth Whiteker
Cover design by Diana Tillison
Cover illustration by Bob Ale-Ebrahim

First Edition 2001

Library of Congress Cataloging-in-Publication Data

Kennedy, Ellen Edwards, 1947-
   Irregardless of murder : a Miss Prentice cozy mystery / Ellen Edwards
Kennedy.-- 1st ed.
      p. cm.
   ISBN 0-9661879-7-0 (pbk. : alk. paper)
   1. Adirondack Mountains (N.Y.)--Fiction. 2. English
teachers--Fiction. 3. Women teachers--Fiction. I. Title.
   PS3611.E66 I77 2001
   813'.6--dc21
                                             2001001610

AEB-8803

Advance praise for
Irregardless of Murder

"...a delightful read. The characters are wonderful.
I'm looking forward to more adventures of
Amelia Prentice and her friends."
—ANNE GEORGE, **author of The Southern Sisters Series**

"It's got everything a great cozy story
needs—a charming and sympathetic heroine,
a colorful supporting cast...a little romance, and, of course,
a murder that challenges the reader..."
—SARAH SHABER,
award-winning author of *Simon Said* and *Snipe Hunt*

"...a wonderful debut mystery with a delightfully
appealing amateur sleuth. Ms. Kennedy's characters are so
well drawn, you can almost hear them breathe."
—JOANNE FLUKE,
author of *The Chocolate Chip Cookie Murder*

"Tight plot, fascinating characters and a tantalizing mystery.
I couldn't figure it out or put it down."
—ROSEY DOW, **best-selling author of *Reaping the Whirlwind***

"...a satisfying traditional cozy mystery with an interesting
cast of characters, more than a touch of romance, and
moments of brilliance."
—N.J. LINDQUIST, **author of *Shaded Light***

"...wonderfully refreshing. With quiet humor, Miss Prentice
follows her instincts, protects her students, and cautiously
opens her heart to an old love."
—B. LYNN GOODWIN, **Editor/Interviewer,
*Writer Advice Newsletter***

Dedication

Dedicated to Harold Kennedy,

Donald and Mary Lula Edwards,

my unflinching first readers:
Louise Sowa, Gayle Edwards, Anne Smith,
Jennifer Carver and Rosey Dow.

And, of course, to Nellie Ruth Lynn, of late beloved memory,
who said, "Put a little romance in it."

"*Irregardless*. Should be *regardless*. The error results from failure to see the negative in *-less* and from a desire to get it in as a prefix, suggested by such words as *irregular, irresponsible*, and perhaps especially, *irrespective*."

—*The Elements of Style*,
William Strunk, Jr., and E.B.White

Prologue
Thursday Night, 6:01 PM

Marguerite LeBow painfully suppressed a sneeze and watched the library's copy machine spit sheets into a neat stack. Her eyes were dry and scratchy, there was a relentless tickle in her nose, and an encore explosion was inevitable. Definitely time for another allergy capsule.

She squinted across the tiny room. There was just a little light coming from the stacks through the half-opened door. This place did double duty as a cloakroom. The staff's outerwear hung on pegs along the wall above a narrow bench with galoshes crammed underneath. On the floor next to the bench stood a tiny refrigerator. A new, roomier library building had been promised for several years now, but in the meantime, the staff made do.

Somewhere under all those coats was Marguerite's purse. Another tickle and a reflexive intake of breath. She fumbled in her pocket and pulled out a tissue just in time to catch the sneeze. Whew! She mopped her nose. That was a big one! It was better not to stop a sneeze. You could bust your eardrums.

She patted the coats along the wall, feeling for the familiar leather lump that held her essentials. Here was Miss Ingersoll's coat. She could smell the Estee Lauder Youth Dew even with her stuffed nose. And this squeaky parka that reeked of cigarette smoke had to be Brenda's. That girl was a chimney. But...

Marguerite smiled. *He* smoked. Lately, she'd come to *love* the smell of cigarette smoke. He was truly wonderful, just like she'd always dreamed. And so handsome. "Meet me at the restaurant," he'd whispered just now, then headed out the door.

Marguerite's eyebrows came together in a small frown, then lifted and relaxed. Mom was a problem, of course, but she'd come around. With God's help, everything would be all right. Father Anthony had said so himself.

She resumed her search. Ah, here it was. She plunged her hand in the bag and pulled out a small prescription bottle, rattling the contents and turning towards the copy machine to examine the capsules in the dim light. Only four, maybe five left. She'd have to get the prescription refilled.

The hum of the copy machine had stopped. Her task here was done. Miss Ingersoll wanted those copies right away.

Marguerite stood irresolute, medicine bottle in hand, while another sneeze began to rise behind her sinuses. Go ahead, she told herself, swallow the thing and get going!

But she couldn't. Not without water. Or some kind of liquid.

She looked down at the tiny brown box of a refrigerator. She'd long ago consumed the contents of her own lunch sack and thermos, but there was bound to be something else in there she could—borrow.

Heck, it wouldn't be the first time she'd done something questionable in a good cause. Marguerite grimaced as she fumbled around in the refrigerator. She'd hate for Mom to find out what she'd done lately, at least not right away. But soon, everybody would understand—when the time was right—and she, herself, would be a hero. And UDJ would be in trouble, big-time!

Here it was: a half-filled bottle of Evian. Well, she thought, shrugging and unscrewing the cap, nobody around here has cooties, I suppose. And I don't really have any germs. This is just allergy.

Placing the capsule on the back of her tongue, Marguerite upended the bottle and drained the contents. Then, she closed the refrigerator and dropped the empty bottle into the wastepaper basket next to the copier.

Marguerite sneezed again as she replaced the medicine bottle in her purse. She'd sure picked some great place to work. She hung the purse on a peg. This old library building must be a hundred years old. The mildew and dust were murder on the sinuses.

It'll take a little time for the medicine to kick in, she reminded herself, sniffing as she gathered the stack of copies. This allergy was a beast, all right. She felt really lousy.

Really, *really* lousy.

Holding the papers to her chest, she shuffled over to the bench and sat for a moment, panting. It was hard to catch her breath. The allergy doctor'd said she had a touch of asthma, too, but she'd never felt *this* bad. Her heart was pounding against the papers. This was kind of scary.

Marguerite swayed and the copies slid to the floor in a rustling cascade. This was awful! She wanted to throw up. Could she make it to the wastepaper basket in time? Would she ruin those copies by stepping on them? Why couldn't she *breathe?*

She crumpled to the floor with a muffled thump, every muscle in her chest straining to pull in air. As she writhed, now unmindful of the wrinkled and ruined pages beneath her, her lips formed words of distress, but there was no breath to propel them to listening ears.

To Marguerite, it seemed a long time, but it was only another agonizing half-minute before she lost consciousness, then, less than three minutes later, surrounded by a hundred thousand books and over a dozen well-meaning souls, Marguerite LeBow died alone.

Chapter One

"Miss Prentice? Can you hear me? Miss Prentice?" Someone was shouting very close to my face. Someone who had eaten garlic recently.

"Of course I hear you," I answered indignantly. That didn't sound quite right, so I repeated myself.

I felt curiously vulnerable. Where was I?

"Thank God!" someone said. Who was that? Sounded like Laura Ingersoll, the Head Librarian. But what would she be doing—ah, I remembered now. The Public Library. My usual Thursday evening of correcting English papers. But this situation didn't seem usual at all...

I seemed to be lying on a hard, flat surface. I opened my eyes and tried to close them again, but a thumb held them mercilessly open, one at a time, while a flickering bright light made the whole proceeding even more uncomfortable. It was Mr. Garlic-Breath.

"Good. Equal and reactive," he told someone. "Don't

worry, she's coming around."

"Thank God," Laura said again.

"Hello, Toby," I said.

My tormentor was one of my former students, Toby House, a paramedic. "Ello-hay, Iss-may Entice-pray!"

"Ello-hay, yourself, Oby-tay..." I began, and struggled to sit up. I fanned my face weakly. "Whew! Arlic-gay!"

He laughed squeakily. Toby had always squeaked when he laughed. "I'm sorry! We were in the middle of dinner when the call came in. Linguine with clam sauce. Probably good and cold by now," he added. At these close quarters, I could see that Toby had developed a slight double chin since graduation. Missing one meal probably wouldn't hurt him.

He turned away. "She's okay, sir. She's sharp enough to answer me in pig Latin. That's a good sign—whoa, hold on now, we're not through yet!" This last was directed to me, as I began to slide to the edge of the polished library table.

My skirt had hiked halfway up my thighs. I yanked it down decisively, embarrassment heating my face. I was unaccustomed to being seen in such a vulnerable position. Worst of all, I was surrounded by a small crowd, among whom I recognized my neighbor Lily Burns, the kindly and thankful Laura Ingersoll and, to my surprise, another former pupil, Police Detective Dennis O'Brien.

"Pig Latin?" said Dennis to Toby.

"Sure, didn't you have pig Latin way back when?" Toby seemed amazed. "You know—you'd be Ennis-day Oh-Ryan-bay, or is it, Oh-Bay—well, anyway, it's kind of silly, I guess."

"Yeah, mm-hmm," Dennis said.

Toby leaned towards me once more, covering his mouth in a thoughtful attempt to shield me from another blast. It didn't work, but I appreciated the gesture. I was feeling nauseated.

"Miss Prentice, you're probably going to have one heck of a headache tomorrow. Take some Tylenol and try to rest, okay? Don't forget to keep warm and drink plenty of water. And if you feel dizzy or have trouble with your vision or throw up—"

"I know, see a doctor," I interrupted hastily.

"And you're going to need to have that dressing changed tomorrow, okay?" he added, replacing his instruments in a black bag. I touched my forehead and was surprised to find a large bandage there. When had Toby done that? I couldn't remember.

Dennis stepped forward, carrying a small notebook. "Miss Prentice, we've got a few things we need to ask you about—" Dennis wasn't all that much younger than I—about five years—but he, along with many people who were decades older, insisted on calling me "Miss." It rankled a little, but I'd come to accept it as the occupational hazard of being an English teacher.

"Detective," Toby put in, gesturing in the direction of the copy room. "If it's okay, I'm—um—needed over there—"

Dennis nodded.

A man with a large camera entered the library and headed directly for the copy room. What on earth was going on?

"Eye-bay, Iss-may Entice-pray," said Toby, squeezing my hand. "Take care of that head." He'd always been one of my favorites.

Dennis directed members of the crowd around us to be seated at individual library tables. Then he stepped closer to me and ran one hand through his thick blond hair. He always did that in moments of sore agitation.

"Now, I want to ask you—" he began.

"Me? Ask me what? I mean, what about..." I trailed off, still addled. My head was really beginning to hurt. "I'm sorry.

What do you need to know?" I squinted at Dennis's face and tried to concentrate.

"What were you doing in the copy room?" he asked abruptly.

Why did he sound so hostile? Weren't we old friends? "That should be obvious—making copies!" I glanced back at the copy room and saw a flash of light. Were they taking *pictures* in there? Pictures of what?

"Anything else?"

"Else? What else, doing the tango? No, actually. Making copies—that's it." I could be abrupt, too, when the occasion warranted. This was getting irritating. I had been injured and here was Dennis, acting like a stranger. To my horror, I felt hot tears well up.

"Where's my purse? I need my purse." I swung my legs over the side of the table and slid to my feet. "I need to get home..." My knees buckled a bit, but Dennis caught me. The tears were flowing more or less freely by now in a humiliating betrayal of my bravest efforts.

"Easy now, Miss Prentice. You can go home in a minute. Just a few more questions, I promise. Then I'll get someone to drive you. Perkins?" he said, gesturing to a uniformed officer nearby. He reached in his pocket and pulled out a notebook and a handkerchief. "Here. Are you sure you can stand?"

"M-most assuredly!" How pompous I sounded! I accepted the handkerchief and blew my nose. "I'm sorry, Dennis. It's just that I'm so terribly embarrassed, you know."

Dennis looked up sharply from his notebook. "Embarrassed?" he said, frowning. "Embarrassed!"

"Yes, embarrassed," I said, a little surprised at his strong reaction. "Of course. To fall like that...and be found unconscious in the Public Library..." I spotted my neighbor, Lily Burns, seated at a nearby table, straining to hear our conversation. She held up my purse, then eagerly read my gestures and hurried over.

"Oh, Amelia," she said, "this is just so awful!" She embraced me and a cloud of *Toujours Moi* engulfed us both. "Now don't you worry about a thing. You can come spend the night at my house. I'll make cocoa and you can tell me all about it." She patted my hand and cocked her head sympathetically, but her carefully lined blue eyes sparkled with anticipation. Lily was a one-woman CNN.

"Mrs. Burns, I must ask you to step back to that table, please," said Dennis.

Lily was unruffled. "Don't worry, Detective. I'll only be another second."

"Lily, I'm afraid there's nothing to tell. I just tripped in the copy room and hit my head. Why all this fuss, I can't imagi—"

Lily gasped. "She doesn't know!"

Dennis began sternly, "Mrs. Burns, I told you to—"

"Don't know what? Dennis, what's going on?"

Dennis ran his hand through his hair again and opened his mouth to speak, but Lily cut in once more.

"It's Marguerite LeBow, Amelia. She's dead. On the floor in there." She pointed at the copy room. "It must have been her—her body that you tripped over." She gave a tiny hysterical giggle and fell uncharacteristically silent.

"What? But, I don't understand, Lily. I...I was just making copies," I tried to explain. At the time, it seemed important that everyone understand. "Sixty-seven copies—a woodcut of the Globe Theatre—you know, the one Shakespeare—" I looked down at my sleeve. "Oh! Dear God, blood!" It was a prayer. "Lily, there's blood on me!" I plucked at it frantically, pulling the stained fabric away from my skin.

"It's okay, dear," Lily reassured me. "It's yours. From that cut on your head. You must have bled like a stuck pig before Laura found you. They think Marguerite had a stroke or heart attack or something," she finished rapidly, casting a defiant eye at Dennis.

"That's enough for now," he snapped. "Perkins, see that Mrs. Burns gets back to her seat. We won't be needing any more of *her* input."

Perkins stepped forward, gripped Lily's elbow firmly, and steered her toward another table.

"Miss Prentice," said Dennis. "You need to get home to bed. Perkins will give you a lift and I'll be around later to ask you a few more questions."

I nodded dumbly. At the moment, however, Perkins was fully occupied, trying to persuade a protesting Lily to sit without resorting to his nightstick. In his place, I would have been tempted. Lily's arms were folded over her fashionably sweatered chest, and her small frame was rigid, tacitly daring him to use force.

Others at neighboring tables watched this whispered exchange with interest: gentle Laura Ingersoll, shaking her head slightly in protest at Lily's behavior; a girl from my third period class whose name often escapes me—Destiny? Serendipity?—staring frankly as she nibbled a cuticle.

Only my student Derek Standish seemed oblivious to the little drama. The boy had attained his impressive six-foot-and-then-some stature during a growth spurt last year and made an intimidating sight, even when seated. I remembered his English essay that I had corrected not an hour before. Derek loved disagreeable, creepy subjects: beheadings, witchcraft, monsters. Our very own Stephen King in training. Right now, he was hunched alone at his table, scowling darkly in the direction of the copy room and systematically cracking his large knuckles.

After a minute, Lily apparently capitulated, and Perkins headed my way. The assembled multitude resumed whatever nervous habits gave them comfort and waited to be interrogated.

"Ready, Miss Prentice?" said Perkins. He helped me into my coat, located my purse, and we headed for the exit. Just as I stepped through the door, someone pinched my elbow.

"Amelia, listen," Lily hissed, "I'll call you later—"

"MRS. BURNS," roared Dennis from across the room.

She glanced over her shoulder, not the slightest bit intimidated. "Can you believe it?" she whispered. "I remember when he couldn't hit our front porch with a newspaper and now they let him carry a gun! Coming, Detective O'Brien," she sang out, and winked at me.

Chapter Two

I was disappointed in the police car ride. As I slid into the back seat, I looked about for some remnant of the many fiends and felons who must have occupied this space, but, though a bit shabby, it was pristine. No grimy hand prints, no spent shell casings, no empty syringes. I sighed and pressed the unbandaged side of my face against the cool glass.

"No siren, either, I take it," I said aloud. I was getting a little punchy.

In the rear view mirror, the stone face smiled at last. "No, ma'am. Emergencies only."

It was still a beautiful October night in the Adirondacks, cool, but not bitter. I'd walked to the library tonight, enjoying the brisk wind gusts, sniffing the hint of smoke in the air. Lily Burns had broken the air pollution ordinance again and burned her leaves. I loved that smell. It had been a great evening to be alive...

Alive. A wave of guilt swept over me. I sat back in the seat and tried to think of nothing.

Inasmuch as my house was only around the block, it was a short ride, but I was grateful and told Officer Perkins so. I couldn't have walked back tonight. I hadn't felt this shaken up in years. It was a real tragedy, too, since Marguerite was her mother's only child. It was amazing how he had handled Lily, being so calm and all—

All these things and more I babbled to the ever-impassive Perkins as we navigated the long front walk and the porch steps. At the big front door, the dear, big, heavy, obstinate portal that had greeted me so many happy times in the past, Perkins cut to the chase and held out his palm.

"Oh, yes, of course." A tip. I blearily fumbled in my purse for my wallet until—

"Your key, please?"

"Oh! My *key*! Sure!"

Perkins unlocked and opened the door without any of the jiggling, thumping, and lip-biting that had become my ritual. Apparently, all the door needed was a firm hand. I marveled.

My farewell to Officer Perkins was effusive, as it always was when I was especially glad to see someone leave and felt a little guilty about it. Thank him so very much, he had been more than kind. Yes, I would be fine. No, thanks, I didn't need him to come in and look around for intruders. I'd be fine. Thanks again. I was the original brave little soldier, I was.

But once the big door was shut with a brassy jingle and I had driven the bolt lock home, all the starch drained from my legs and I slid slowly to the floor, right on top of my great-grandmother's heirloom oriental rug. Resting my head against the solid door, I closed my eyes and shut out the world.

"Sam?" I called into the darkness. It was futile, of course.

My parent's obese, beloved old cat barely tolerated my presence. Sam and I had had a kind of inter-species sibling rivalry that I'd never experienced with my own sister. The situation had only gotten worse after Dad and Mother died.

All at once, Sam's warm, furry bulk filled my lap and he was rubbing his head against my hand. Why he had come was a mystery. He had never once responded to me unless food was involved, but I wasn't one to turn away a miracle, especially not tonight. I wrapped my arms around him and sobbed into his fur.

I began to tell Sam about the night's events and to express my shock at the tragedy, but as my monologue progressed, it gradually turned into a prayer. Sitting on the scratchy wool rug in the entryway, clutching an unusually meek Sam to my breast, I told God how I felt about things.

It just wasn't fair, I told Him. Marguerite, poor ditsy mite of a girl, dying so young and so senselessly. And what of her mother, Marie, abandoned by her husband at nineteen with a tiny baby to raise by herself? Dear, earnest, hard-working Marie, who had experienced so much heartache in her life, now left totally alone.

I knew what it was like, I told Him. Hadn't I nursed both my beloved parents through the agony of cancer? I had survived somehow, thanks to His help, never once begrudging my sister, Barbara, her beautiful home in Florida, her handsome husband, or her four children.

And speaking of marriage, Lord, I was forty-five already. Was I ever—

The doorbell rang.

I froze. Sam struggled free of my embrace and bolted. The bell rang again. Slowly, I began to rise, first on hands and knees and then gripping the front doorknob, pulling myself painfully upright.

Squinting cautiously through the stained glass panels that framed the doorway, I fumbled with the bolt lock. I could see that my visitor was tall, but he wasn't familiar. I opened the door a tiny crack and saw a police car on the street.

"Yes?"

"Miss Prentice." A disheveled file was thrust through the crack. "You left your papers on a chair in the library."

"Oh, Officer Perkins, it's you. Thanks."

He bent over until his nose almost touched mine. I could have sworn he sniffed.

"You all by yourself, ma'am? I thought I heard voices."

"Nope, just me. I live alone—well, there's my mother's cat around here somewhere." I gestured back over my shoulder.

Perkins glanced over my head into the hall and gave me a skeptical look. "Um, did the paramedic explain that you're not supposed to have any alcohol? Just in case it's a concussion, you know?"

"Don't worry, Officer, I don't drink." I pulled myself straighter and fumbled in my coat pocket for the handkerchief Dennis had given me. "And I know all about first aid and—*honk*—things." I wiped the tears from my face and looked around, realizing for the first time that I was still wearing my coat and hadn't turned any lights on.

"I'll be going up to bed now," I announced and snapped on the porch light.

"Yes, ma'am, if you're sure you're okay."

"I am, I assure you." I jutted out my chin.

Perkins turned.

"Thank you for bringing the papers," I called after him. "I needed them."

As he sped away, I turned on the hall light. And the lamp in the front sitting room. And the light over the staircase. And the bedside lamp, as well as the one in the bathroom.

It wouldn't do to have the City Police Department thinking the English teacher was sitting alone in the dark, drinking. Such a thing could be all over town by sunup.

"Oh, this is useless!"

I sat up in bed. Only minutes before, I had been desperately exhausted, longing for sleep. Now, I couldn't turn off the movie that played inside my eyelids.

Why did I go to the library tonight? Was I really such a creature of habit? If I'd stayed and corrected papers here at home, my head wouldn't be hurting, I'd be able to sleep, and I wouldn't be wearing this huge bandage.

But Marguerite would still be dead.

Marguerite dead. I couldn't believe it. I closed my eyes, picturing that earnest child with the perpetually anxious expression on her pale face, the unruly brown hair tied at the back of her neck with a ribbon, and the long earrings that bounced as she trembled in uncontrollable enthusiasm over some silly thing or other. It was always something dramatic with Marguerite.

Pig Latin, for instance. To my other students, the silly language had been a brief amusement, a mental toy to enjoy and cast aside. Marguerite, as always, overdid it, writing her name in pig Latin on her books, circulating notes in it, and even doing her homework in it. So much enthusiasm, so much energy—and now she was dead. How could it have happened? She'd seemed so healthy.

I'd tripped over Marguerite in the copy room. I knew CPR. If I had been less clumsy, might I have been in time to save her? Maybe just a few minutes earlier...

"This has got to stop!" I declared aloud. "Any more of this

and I'll go crazy." I glanced around the room. "Sam? Come here."

From his curled position on Aunt Clarissa's hand-braided rug, Sam stared at me, his eyes reflecting silver in the moonlight. He tilted his head questioningly.

"That's right," I reassured him, patting the comforter beside me. "You can sleep up here. But just for tonight." I made a kissing noise.

Sam's leap was graceful, but his four-point landing caused the bedsprings to creak in protest. Even before he curved himself into a ball at my side, his motor-like purring had begun. I settled back, sinking into the sedative rhythm and whispering my gratitude to Heaven for the blessing of sleep. My eyes drooped, closed. There was no movie this time, just soothing blackness.

I awoke at 6:30 AM to an alarm clock-telephone duet. Sam had deserted me some time in the night, presumably to use the litterbox which I had banished to the back porch. In one fluid movement, I pounded the top of the clock with my fist and picked up the telephone.

"Miss Prentice?" That somber bass could only belong to our principal.

"Mr. Berghauser."

"I read about what happened in the paper this morning. Are you coming to school today?" That was Gerard B. all over. None of this "how are you" nonsense. Just get to the point.

"It's good of you to ask," I said, deliberately misreading sympathy into his question, "but don't worry, now, I'll be just fine. Just a bit of a bandage on my head."

"Bandage? A large bandage?"

I could hear the wheels turning. Such a spectacle might be

distracting to the students. Worse yet, there might be negative publicity.

"Oh, just average-sized, you know," I said vaguely, enjoying his discomfort.

"We have Coach Gurowski available to substitute—"

Oh, no, you don't! That cretin wasn't going to play havoc with my gradebook ever again! It took a week last time to straighten things out. "Thank you so much, but it's not necessary."

"Well. If you're sure, all right then," he conceded, adding, "I'm afraid I was right about the LeBow girl. A shame, a real shame, but then, she was never really stable, was she? And when it comes to these drugs—"

"Drugs!" I squawked. "There was no question of drugs! It was some kind of seizure or something."

"That's not what the *Press Advertiser* says." I heard the rattle of newspaper as he read aloud: "'Family sources revealed that drugs had recently become a problem and that such an outcome was no surprise to those who knew Marguerite.'"

What family sources? What did they mean, "no surprise"? *I* knew Marguerite, too! I'd read her journal, filled with tumultuous adolescent idealism. Marguerite was quite literally an open book, but a clean one.

I remembered her words: "It just isn't right!" she'd said, when I'd challenged some emotional comments she made during a classroom debate her senior year.

"I know, Marguerite, but there are better ways to get your point across without personally attacking your opponent. That's called an *ad hominem* argument, and it's, um, bogus," I pointed out, trying to use terms to which she could relate. "You make a better point attacking his logic, using facts to refute it, rather than calling him names."

"I'm sorry, Miss Prentice," she'd whispered, still quivering with emotion. I was reminded of a hummingbird. "I got carried away. It's just so, so...evil!"

The subject of the debate was the legalization of drugs.

"It's always drugs these days," Berghauser was saying.

Not always, I wanted to yell, but restrained myself. "Well," I managed to say through clenched teeth, "I don't know about that. But anyway, I'll be there right on time."

"Good," he said, and hung up.

Groaning, I climbed out of bed and headed for the dresser. The face in the mirror was pale, with an irritated, world-weary expression. I winced as I pulled away the edge of the bandage and squinted at the wound.

A tiny white butterfly-shaped adhesive held together the edges of the bulging cut, which was dark maroon and surrounded by purple bruising. No, I wouldn't be able to dispense with the big white bandage yet.

Sunshine streamed through the stained-glass panels in the entry way as I came down the wide old stairs. My sister Barbara had been married in this house, and descended this staircase, her long satin train rippling down behind her, just the way we had planned as little girls. The family had filled the house then, uncles and aunts, now dead; and their children, now far-flung and lost to one another. Still, it was a lovely memory and I smiled.

There was a brisk tap-tap-tap at the door announcing Lily Burns, a casserole in her hand and lively curiosity in her eyes.

"Isn't this doorbell working? I rang and rang." She stepped inside. "Now, Amelia, I'll take care of everything. Don't say a word." She swept past me into the kitchen. She didn't mean it, of course. She was hoping I'd say many words, all on one particular subject.

She opened the refrigerator. "I would have come last night, but that miserable Dennis O'Brien kept us at the library for hours. I almost came over irregardless. Did you know your porch lights were on all night?"

"'Regardless.' Yes, I did, but Lily, I can't—"

"Don't mention it. I was going to bring you the box of chocolates my broker gave me last Christmas. Tacky gift. But I know you like candy and it should be all right, because it was in the freezer the whole time. But I decided at a time like this, you should eat healthy." She held up the casserole proudly. "It's chicken divan. Not a thing unhealthy in it except a little butter and a touch of sour cream. Four hundred degrees for half an hour and it'll be all ready to eat. I'll come back at noon and fix it for you, if you like. I'd stay all morning, but today's Women's meeting at the church, you know, and I've gotta show up to plan the...what's that?"

Having finished his business on the back porch, Sam was pulling himself with some difficulty through his newly-installed plastic cat door. I was gratified to see him actually use it, but it didn't do much for his dignity. When he finally completed his struggle, his fur was sticking out in every direction and he had narrowly avoided stepping in his food dish.

"Why looo-oook," said Lily, stooping to stroke behind his ears. "It's Samuel! How is oo? Did oo wike the snack I weft for oo yesterday?" She smoothed down his fur. "I had some leftover beef stroganoff from the Covered Dish Supper and it seemed a shame to waste it," she explained, looking up at me. "Besides, Sammy woves sour cweam, doesn't oo, tweetheart?"

Sam arched to reach Lily's outstretched hand. As they caressed and whispered sweet nothings to one another, I realized that a mystery had been solved: how Sam remained solidly obese on a diet of expensive lo-cal cat food. If it was possible for a cat to have a double chin, Sam did.

"Now, don't look at me like that, Amelia. It's just that he's a dear widdle man, who takes such pleasure in his food, don't oo, tweetie?" Her words had a familiar ring. She had once used them to describe her late husband Darryl, a kind, patient, agreeably plump man who died of a heart attack at age forty-two.

Lily pulled something from her coat pocket. "Here's your paper, by the way. Don't read it, though. No need to dwell on the negative. Besides, the paper doesn't know everything, does it?" She paused, presumably for breath, and examined my coffee machine.

"Lily—" I began.

"Let's see, how does this thing work? Does it use a filter? Is this where you keep your coffee?" She pulled out the filter basket and began rummaging in my cupboards.

"Lily—" I said again.

"Say, how about instant? I always think the really good brands are every bit as good as the ground coffee. When I—"

Thwock! I slapped the rolled-up paper on the kitchen table. "Lily!"

Lily jumped slightly and stared at me, wide-eyed, like a startled deer wearing blue eye shadow. "Yes, Amelia?" She spoke softly and evenly, but I could tell I had annoyed her.

"I'm sorry. It's just—I mean, Lily, it's awfully sweet of you to go to all this trouble, but..."

"No trouble at all," she insisted frostily.

"I just don't have the time to visit. I have to be at school in forty-five minutes!"

"Amelia, you mustn't!" Lily put down the coffee filter and pointed at my bandage. "It could be a concussion! There could be internal bleeding! I had a great-uncle who hit his head on the edge of an anvil and a week later, he keeled over, stone dead." She snapped her fingers.

"Lily, I promise you, I'll be careful."

"And besides," she concluded, getting to the real bottom

line, "you'll make a spectacle of yourself, showing up at the school with that—" she pointed again— "big white thing half covering your face!"

"Lily, I'm just fine. Really. My head doesn't hurt but a little bit. You know, it's football season and there are half-a-dozen youngsters in school wearing casts and bandages. I should fit right in. Now," I said, reaching in the cupboard for the coffee can, "I've got to get going. Will you have some coffee with me?"

Lily pulled on her coat and gloves. "No, thank you," she said primly.

Sam and I escorted her to the front door. "Thank you for the casserole, Lily. You're a much better cook than I am." That was the truth, and we both knew it.

Lily waggled her head modestly and I could tell I was going to be forgiven. "It's just one of those things off a box of something. Oh!" she exclaimed. "Forgot to ask you—there's the sale at Peasemarsh this weekend. Wanna go?"

JJ Peasemarsh was a sportswear company with a factory outlet store across Lake Champlain in Burlington, Vermont. Their clearance sale was a yearly pilgrimage for us.

"I don't know why not."

"Great! I'll call to remind you later. So long, Samuel," she cooed, scratching him behind his ear. "No, no, dear, watch the stockings! Bye."

Risking backstrain, I picked Sam up to prevent his following Lily. The wretched cat had sold his affections for a dollop of sour cream.

Chapter Three

After Lily left, I had to scramble to get to school on time. Usually, I walked the five blocks and was glad to get the exercise, but as I stepped from the shower, the clock read 7:30, my usual arrival time.

I pulled on my clothes and considered one of my options: a seldom-used car safely padlocked in the garage out back. As I combed my hair, I tried to remember where I'd put the key. No use—my mind just wouldn't work under pressure this morning. Besides it was all I could do to lift that heavy garage door—on a good day.

"Ouch!" The comb pulled the hair near my wound. That did it. Plan B. I grabbed the phone and called Labombard Taxi.

Mrs. Labombard had read the morning paper. Yes, I told her, I was all right. No, I hadn't seen Marguerite's body, actually. Yes, it was very, very sad. Now, about that taxi?

Mrs. Labombard was glad I was all right. She'd send

somebody right over.

I had expected Mr. Labombard, a reticent soul who drove with incredible speed and sprayed his taxi with strong aerosol disinfectant after each fare. I was never sure whether it was a courtesy for, or an insult to, his customers.

This time, though, it was a brand-new cab operated by an unfamiliar driver: a lanky, blond youngster with a relaxed manner and an infectious smile. In striking contrast to his employer, he began talking the moment I climbed in.

"I know, I know, you expected Marcel, but he's not doing much driving these days. He's come up in the world. I'm number two in his fleet. It's brand new. Smells .w, doesn't it? Not like an operating room, like old Number One. What do you think?"

"Very nice, uh, Vernon," I answered, reading the permit form on the visor. It also informed me that Vernon Thomas was 6'3", weighed 188 pounds, and had been born just over twenty years ago.

"Vern, please," he said, twisting around and shoving a large, long-fingered hand within my reach. I shook it.

"And you're Amelia Prentice. Mrs. Labombard told me. Sorry about what happened last night. I'll see you get a nice, smooth ride. Now, where to?"

I told him. He turned back around, flipped the arm on the meter and was all business immediately. We arrived at the teacher's entrance in four peaceful, pleasant-smelling minutes.

"Vern," I said as I counted out the fare, "that was indeed a nice, smooth ride." I added a tip. "That's for you. Good luck on your new career."

"Thanks, but this is just temporary. I'm getting my Master's in Journalism. Gonna be a newsman, like my uncle. Maybe you know him—the editor at the *Press Advertiser?*"

"Gil Dickensen?" I knew him all right. We'd had dealings.

An arrogant, opinionated, smug, totally puzzling man.

Vern nodded.

"You're Carol's son? Of course!" Gil Dickensen's sister Carol had married a man in the Air Force. I'd heard she'd died about five years ago. "I went to high school with her—she was a lovely person."

"Yes, she was."

I looked carefully at his face. "Your mother's people all have dark hair. You must resemble your dad. There's a little of your mother in your eyes, but I wouldn't have known that you and Gil were related."

Vern laughed. "I'll take that as a compliment. Ol' Gil's a piece of work, isn't he?"

"Now, I never said—"

The taxi radio squawked.

Vern snatched up the microphone. "I'm on my way! See you around, Amelia," He put the car in gear and added, "I'll be sure to give Gil your regards."

He was gone. I stood thinking. Just how much did he know? What had his mother told him, if anything, about Gil and me? Not that it made any difference, though it was just a bit embarrassing to have ancient history dug up again. The bell rang and I consigned Vern, his uncle, and ancient history to the very back of my mind.

Much of the usual milling around and good-natured hijinx of Friday morning classes were missing today. My homeroom students filed in silently, exchanging knowing looks. What interaction there was, was accompanied by covert glances at my bandage. I ignored the questions in their eyes and examined the roll book.

"Is Stephanie Aarons in school today?"

My students were delighted to enlighten me: "Home. Sick!" came the yelled answer from the rear of the room.

"David Atwood?"

"He's sick, too."

"Caught it from Steffy!" someone else called out, and there was general merriment until I called a halt.

I scanned down the list of names. "Derek Standish—is he sick, too?"

Silence. A general exchange of glances.

"Derek's not here, Miss Prentice," said Hardy Patschke, entering, as was his habit, precisely one millisecond before the sounding of the late bell. He shrugged his plaid flannel shoulders. "Don't know why, though. I just heard 'em talking about him in the office." He handed me a folded slip of paper. "Berghauser sent this to you."

"That's *Mr.* Berghauser, Hardy." I knew the principal wasn't popular, but there was no use encouraging disrespect. "Thank you. Sit down, please." I slid the paper under my desk blotter and finished my notations in the roll book.

Precisely ninety seconds later, the class bell rang and my classroom emptied of homeroom students, to be immediately refilled with members of my eight o'clock English class. Derek Standish's seat was empty.

Serendipity Shea entered triumphantly, surrounded by an admiring clump of girls hanging on her every whispered word. I saw her gesture toward my bandage and tried to ignore the outright stares.

"Hurry and take your seats," I said briskly. "I've corrected your *Julius Caesar* papers and you need to finish up your Shakespeare folders. I had planned to hand out a picture of the Globe Theatre today, but there was a little problem with the copy machine."

The school day had begun.

Aside from an ache-all-over feeling that began to overtake me during second period, I managed to conduct business as usual rather well. Strangely, I found I didn't so much mind this kind of pain, but relished it as a secret badge of endurance. I felt terrible, but I was still here, still doing my job. "'Come what may, Time and the hour runs through the roughest day,'" I promised myself, rubbing my eyes and trying to remember which of Shakespeare's plays I'd quoted.

It was a relief, though, when the bell rang for my conference period. Every teacher had one sometime during the day. It was our *de facto* break time, though a parent with a gripe or a question could lay claim to those precious fifty minutes by making an appointment at the office.

As I tried to decide if I craved a cup of coffee enough to brave stares and questions in the teacher's lounge, I remembered the note Hardy had delivered. It took a minute to find it and decode the school secretary's unique shorthand:

"O'Brien spk w/U conf.pd./Tch Lng."

Dennis O'Brien hadn't forgotten me. He wanted to "spk"—speak?—with me. "Conf"—was that an "f" or a "j?" Conference period. "Tch Lng"—Teacher's Lounge.

As I threaded through the rowdy crush of adolescents, I smiled, remembering a meeting I had once had with Dennis O'Brien's mother. His failing grade in my class was about to lose him his place on the basketball team. I was in my first year of teaching, and June O'Brien's scowl was terrifying, but I was determined to stand up for myself in my first parents' conference.

I needn't have worried. Once his mother learned that he'd only turned in about half his homework and saw the proof for herself in the gradebook, Dennis's fate was sealed. After that, Dennis was, if not a model student, at least an adequate one.

The subject of my stroll down Memory Lane stood as I entered the teacher's lounge and shook my hand, adult to adult. His well-pressed suit, crisp shirt, and tastefully striped tie, all selected by his wife, Dorothy, gave him an air of authority.

"I appreciate this, Miss Prentice," he said and indicated a seat at one of the flimsy plastic tables. When he sat, his knees lifted the table, and I was momentarily reminded of the time Alice in Wonderland outgrew her house.

"Why don't we get some coffee and take it to my class-room? It's empty now and it'll be quieter there," I added, but I had other reasons. The lounge had been filling up with other faculty who were even more nakedly curious than my students.

"Good idea," Dennis agreed, and we left just in time to pass Gerard Berghauser. As the door closed behind us, I heard a whisper, "Who's that she's with?" Drat the man! He would most assuredly tell them.

"I was just remembering the time you were kicked off the basketball team, Dennis," I said as we climbed the steps to my room.

"Oh, gee, I'd forgotten that. Boy, was my mom mad after she talked to you. I'd been lying to her, you see, and she couldn't abide that."

"I hated to get you in trouble."

"Hey, it was the best thing that could've happened," he assured me, opening the door of my room. "It was kind of a relief to get found out."

"And you made it back on the team."

"Yeah, I did, didn't I?" He grinned, and I knew he was thinking about those three tall trophies in the case downstairs. We took two seats in the front row.

He coughed. "Look, Miss Prentice, we need to..." He reached in his pocket for his notebook and dropped his pen. I was given a close-up view of the top of his large head as he fumbled on the floor. At these close quarters, I noticed for the first time he had some gray hair coming in. More, in fact, than I had.

"Youth's a stuff twill not endure," as Shakespeare said, or, "Go figure," to quote Lily Burns. No one had ever seen a gray hair on *her* head, thanks to the miracle of modern chemistry.

The pen retrieved, Dennis began again, "We need to go over a few things about last night."

"I'll be glad to, but please—I mean, people tell me the paper said—"

He sighed. "Okay, okay. Here's what I can tell you: We have reason to believe—" he spoke slowly and evenly, as though repeating a memorized speech— "that the vic—that Marguerite's death was not accidental."

"You mean—suicide?"

"I don't mean any more than I just said, Miss Prentice. Just know that we're doing all we can to get this straightened out. Now, can we go over a few things?"

I folded my hands in my lap and squared my shoulders. "Of course."

"Do you remember falling over Marguerite Lebow?"

"Not clearly. I just walked in and fell. It was pretty dark in the copy room. It always is."

Dennis tilted his head and scratched it with the point of his pencil. "What do you mean, 'always'?"

"The library's an old building. The refrigerator and the copier tax the wires too much to put anything else on them. At least, that's what Laura told me. Besides, there's plenty of light from the stacks when the door's open."

We went over the people I had seen. "Anybody else you remember?" Dennis asked. "Somebody with Marguerite, maybe?"

"Well, she was talking to Derek Standish when I arrived. I didn't think anything about it because it's—it was— Marguerite's job to help people find things."

"Anybody else?"

"I'm not sure. I was quite immersed in my work. I found the word 'irregardless' in three papers."

Dennis chuckled. "Still harping on that one, are you?"

"It's still incorrect, Dennis. 'Irregardless' is a double negative and not even a real word. I always take ten points off for it."

He grinned and shook his head. "Miss Prentice, still torturing those poor kids." Then he sternly adjusted his expression. "Okay, back to the subject. Marguerite was—"

"Oh! I do remember somebody. There was a man I didn't know. Short, dark- haired—oh, my goodness!—he said something to Marguerite, then walked away. Could that mean something?"

Dennis shook his head as he scribbled in his notebook. "Couldn't say for sure. But any detail helps. Go on."

"Well, I saw Gil Dickensen talking to Laura Ingersoll at the front desk. He'd brought a stack of newspapers, I remember. And Lily Burns was there." I closed my eyes and tried to picture the scene. "Dennis, I remember something else: that dark-haired man bumped into Lily on his way out of the library. Made her drop her book."

"Would you recognize this guy again?" Dennis sat up and looked me in the eye.

I sighed. "No, I don't think so. I mostly saw the back of his head. Lily might, though."

"Okay. I have another question about the copy room. It says 'Library Staff Only' on the door."

"Yes, but Laura lets me make copies there and pay at the desk when I'm finished. She showed me how to use the machine. I make so many, it was less trouble for her this way."

"So you weren't there to meet Marguerite?"

I was surprised. "Oh, no. I didn't even know she was in

there."

"I see." He frowned and tapped his chin with the end of the ballpoint. I had seen him do that during tests. It meant he was stumped. He forged ahead anyway. "So you went in. Where did you see Marguerite?"

"I didn't see her. I just, well, stepped on her." I shuddered.

"That's how you fell. And you hit your head—how?" He indicated my bandage with his pen.

"I think I must have fallen against the copy machine. It's all I can remember."

He was nodding as I spoke. Looking at his notes, he said, "It ties in with what we found." He looked up. "What was it you were going to copy?"

"A picture of the Globe Theatre. For a class on Shakespeare. But I never got to do it, as you know."

"And that was all you were going to do in there?"

"No, Dennis, I was going to whip up a batch of fudge! We've been over all this before!"

"I know, but bear with me. How long have you known Marguerite LeBow?"

Another surprising question. "Well, about as long as anybody in this town. Since she was born, really."

"And you taught her in school?"

"You know that." This was getting tiring.

"What kind of student was she?"

I couldn't see how this had anything to do with the tragedy, but I assumed Dennis knew his business. "A pretty good one. She worked hard. Mostly B's and C's."

"But?" Dennis was good at this. He had heard the hesitation in my voice.

"Well, I guess you might say she was a little flighty. No, that's not fair. She was reliable and loyal. Just a little too imaginative, perhaps. Fanciful. Maybe even a little eccentric."

"A troublemaker? A liar?"

"Oh, no. I wouldn't say that."

He leaned forward. "You sure? She wasn't in the habit of making up stories?"

I shook my head. "Quite the contrary. She was scrupulously honest."

"How about mental problems?"

"What?" I was honestly shocked.

He waved his pen hand vaguely. "You know, delusions, that sort of thing?"

"Who told you that? You didn't know Marguerite, did you?"

He locked eyes with me for a split second before jerking his gaze down to his writing. "I'm not at liberty to say right now," he said quickly, tilting his eyebrows slightly by way of apology.

"Oh." Interesting. "I understand. But no, I don't think there was anything wrong with Marguerite. She just tried a little too hard and the other kids didn't understand her."

"But you did?"

I thought carefully. "Not really. But I didn't make fun of her, and I praised her when she did well. I was just doing my job and being decent to the girl, but she thought of me as her special friend. You'd be surprised how many students are starved for attention. Sad, really."

"It's very sad, Miss Prentice." Dennis stood, tucking the pad and pen in his pocket. "Well, I guess that's all for now. I'll call you if I have any more questions."

"Please do. And say hello to Dorothy and Meaghan for me. Is she still in nursery school at St. Anthony's?"

"Kindergarten, now, all day long," he corrected me, smiling. The class bell sounded and he departed as my fourth period class began straggling in.

"Hey, I know who that was," said Hardy Patschke, sliding into his seat. "He's a cop, like my dad."

"He's also a former student of mine, Hardy," I pointed out. Let him think it was some sort of reunion.

"No kidding!" The boy tilted his head and squinted at me. "How old are you, anyway?"

"I plead the Fifth Amendment on that one, Hardy."

"Huh?"

"Look it up, or better yet, ask Mr. Sweeny in Social Studies."

"Does *he* know how old you are?"

I smiled at him sweetly. "A question like that calls for another question, I think. Ten, in fact. Everyone take out a sheet of paper and number from one to ten."

The class groaned.

I'd planned a pop quiz all along, but they had no way of knowing that.

At noon, I called Marie LeBow from the pay phone just outside the lunchroom. She answered immediately, sounding much stronger than I'd expected. "I'm glad you called. I wanted to talk to you." Her voice was girlish and a little nasal, an echo of her daughter's.

"Oh, Marie, I am just so sorry."

"I know you are," she said wearily. "Thanks. I don't feel it yet, you know? Don't seem real."

"I know."

"The neighbors have been real nice. They brought food and everything. My sister's coming over to stay with me. People at the college give me a week off." Marie worked in the campus dining hall.

"That was good of them," I said, choking up a little.

"She didn't take drugs, Miss Prentice. She hated drugs. She didn't do what they said in the paper. You believe me, don't you?"

"Of course, I believe you, Marie." What else could I say?

"You were special to her, you know? 'Miss Prentice is my favorite teacher,' she told me."

"She did?" I was crying in earnest now. "She was special, too, Marie. She was a sweet girl. You did a good job with her."

"Yeah. Listen, I got something for you."

"What?" I was blowing my nose.

"Marguerite wanted you to have something."

"Oh, Marie," I protested, embarrassed. "That's not necessary. I couldn't possibly..."

"Nope," she said stubbornly. "I'm supposed to give it to you. Can I bring it to your house tonight?"

"Wouldn't you rather I came to your house?"

"No," Marie said, and paused. "I don't think so. I'll come tonight."

"You come whenever you like, Marie. We'll have a chance to talk."

"Yeah. We'll talk. Listen, one more thing: what's UDJ mean?"

"What is that? A radio station?"

"It's not important. Just something I was wondering about...wait, there's somebody at the door. I gotta go. See you later."

I hung up the phone, exasperated. I was just one of Marguerite's high school teachers; it didn't seem right for her mother to give me one of her only child's keepsakes. But Marie had been adamant. Maybe it would comfort her somehow. I well knew how comforting it was to be able to do something, anything, in the face of grief.

I stepped hesitantly from the telephone booth. When I made the decision to come to school this morning, I'd expected my bandage to arouse some attention, but surely the shocked stares were excessive. In the lunchroom, some of the students were downright theatrical in their reaction, turning away in mock disgust. Even the cafeteria ladies widened their eyes at me.

It was humiliating. I swept through the line rapidly, grabbing up a chef salad and an iced tea and signing my name to the lunch ticket as quickly as possible. Then I stalked briskly to the end of a long table in the back, looking neither to the left nor to the right.

I was shaking pepper on half a hard-boiled egg when Hardy Patschke stepped before me, a large wad of paper napkins in one hand and a sheepish look on his dark olive face.

"Um, Miss Prentice, I thought I'd better tell you—"

"What is it, Hardy? I'm trying to eat lunch here."

"It's your head." He waved a finger at me.

"I know all about my head! I had a little accident, in case you haven't heard. You already saw it in class. Enough clowning around. Please go back to your seat and finish your lunch."

The boy cringed, but stubbornly remained where he was. "But your head—"

"Kindly mind your own business, Hardy! My lunch period is almost over and you're becoming a nuisance!"

Hardy sighed deeply, then abruptly stretched out his hand and touched my eyebrow. The finger he brought back was red.

"Look. You're bleeding, Miss Prentice."

As if to reinforce his assertion, a red drop plopped in the middle of my egg.

I dropped my fork and sprang from my seat. "Oh! Oh, my goodness. Oh! Oh, dear! I'm so sorry, Hardy! I mean, I appreciate your—" I gestured helplessly.

"S'okay," he said graciously, and handed me most of the bundle in his hand. "Better see the nurse," he added, wiping his finger on another napkin.

"Good idea," I conceded and began gathering my para-phernalia.

"I'll put up your tray."

I mumbled repeated thanks and followed his advice as quickly as possible. While I still didn't relish the stares that accompanied my exit, now at least I understood them.

"Please be there, please be there," I muttered as I dashed down the hall, pressing the bale of napkins to my forehead. Judith Dee, the school nurse, had been working part-time ever since a budget cutback three years ago and I didn't know her schedule.

She was there, but she had purse and coat over her arm and was turning the key in the lock. "Miss Prentice! What's the matter?" she asked in a deep, Kathleen Turner contralto. Her voice was where the resemblance ended. Judith was blue-haired, dumpy, and definitely closing in on sixty.

I pulled the napkins from my forehead. "I guess I need a new dressing on this," I admitted.

"You sure do!" she agreed, turning the key and opening the door. "I heard about what happened. Come on in here and we'll see if we can't fix it."

It was a calming phrase, spoken quietly and implying com-petence. In many ways, Judith was perfect for her job. I knew from experience how desperately some of the youngsters at school needed mothering, and she seemed to relish the op-portunity.

I looked across the room at the bulletin board, layered with hundreds of wallet-sized photos of students past and present. I knew that if I asked her, she could identify almost every one.

"Sounds like you're over that chest cold," she remarked pleasantly. "Two weeks ago, I could just hear the phlegm when you talked. Mr. Simons—the math teacher?—he's getting it now. Have you heard him cough? Sounds like a Great Dane barking!" That was the one thing about Judith. She took a detailed and rather invasive interest in the physical ailments of everyone around her.

I sat on the low metal stool she offered and watched her pull on thin rubber gloves.

"It's the rule these days. No offense."

"None taken." I closed my eyes as she gently peeled back the dressing. She smelled of rubbing alcohol and baby powder.

"You've got quite a goose egg there."

"I know. Terrible, isn't it?"

"Actually, Amelia, it's a good sign. You want the injury to swell outward, away from the brain, rather than inward, and, well, you see what I mean."

"I never thought of that."

"It's true! This will hurt, dear," she warned as she removed the last portion of stubbornly clotted gauze, all the while making sympathetic hissing noises through her teeth.

It did. I winced.

"I'm so sorry. This is always the difficult part. I'm going to have to clean the wound a bit, but I'll be as careful as I can."

She pulled an extra-long cotton swab from a metal-topped glass jar and dipped it in antiseptic. She used a number of them, dabbing lightly and discarding frequently, as she carried on light conversation, mainly, I suspected, for purposes of diversion.

"I only heard a little about last night. How did you get this?"

I told her.

She clucked sympathetically as she worked. "And it must have been poor Marguerite you tripped over." She tore the paper wrapper from a gauze pad and applied it delicately to my forehead.

"You know, I didn't actually see her, but that's what I've been told."

"And she never called out or told anybody she felt bad?" Judith asked, intently laying adhesive tape over the bandage.

"No. Ouch!" She had pressed too hard.

"Oh, sorry," she said, stepping back and dropping the roll of tape. "Drat! Where did that go?"

"It rolled under there," I said, indicating a white metal chest of drawers.

"Never mind! I've got lots more." She pulled another roll from the cupboard and cut off a length of tape. "You know, it's very tragic and everything, but I can't say I'm all that surprised. Does it pull here?"

"It's fine."

"You've got something at home for the pain?" she asked.

"Yes, I think so."

"We can't give even so much as an aspirin in school, you know," she pointed out, disposing of my old bandage and putting away her equipment. "It's the law."

"What did you mean: you weren't surprised?"

Though we were alone, Judith lowered her voice to a near-whisper. "I thought everybody knew about Marguerite's, er, problem. Drugs, of course. Her mother was simply desperate about her."

Frowning, she appraised her handiwork. "All right, you're done. That wound shouldn't bleed much more, but be sure to let a doctor take a look at in a day or so."

"I will. But you know, I spoke with Marie a few minutes ago and she insisted Marguerite had nothing to do with drugs."

Judith shook her head slowly as she gathered up her coat and purse. "Poor Marie. In denial. Very common in situations like this." She escorted me out the door and locked it. "No wonder she had an ulcer last year. Nerves can do that to you."

She accompanied me down the hall, donning her coat as she went. "You know, I was driving by the library last night and saw the ambulance and all and wondered what it was. Marguerite LeBow, just imagine." She patted me on the shoulder and headed for the stairwell. "Well, take care of that head, now."

The class bell rang just above my head, making me jump. What was I doing here? There wasn't an inch on me now that wasn't stiff and sore.

Swallowing my pride, I threw myself on the mercy of Gerard Berghauser, who, while not actually speaking the words, "I told you so," allowed his mustache to twitch smugly as he called in the assistant coach to take over the remainder of my classes. It would mean an afternoon of unsnarling my roll book, but it was worth it. I dialed Labombard Taxi and wondered absently if there wasn't a lint-covered aspirin lurking somewhere in the bottom of my purse.

"Boy, what a small world," Vern Thomas said as I climbed into his cab. "This must be fate."

"What it is, Vern, is a small town." I groaned, leaning back and closing my eyes. "Home, James."

"Home it is."

He pulled up smoothly in front of my house in a matter of minutes. I paid him and was halfway up the walk when he called out, "Hey, you don't look so good. You want a little help?"

I was in the process of politely declining when I stepped off the sidewalk onto the leaf-covered ground and staggered slightly, prompting Vern to come running chivalrously to my aid.

"Whoa, now! Can't have the vapors right here on the sidewalk, can we?"

"Where did you ever hear about vapors?" I grumbled to hide my embarrassment.

"I don't know, British Lit, maybe? Lord Tennyson, Jane Austen, or somebody. Ever hear of those guys?"

"Somewhere in the dim recesses of my memory. I believe I studied all that around the turn of the last century," I said, mounting the steps slowly so as to not jar my head. "What kind of grad student are you? I mean, are you any good?"

"I'm gifted. All A's. Never study. Do all my papers at the last minute. It infuriates Gil. He says I'm arrogant. Think so?" He leaned against the doorjamb as I fished for my keys.

I paused and regarded him carefully. "I suppose it's a matter of semantics. I might call you naively impudent, perhaps, softened by just a *soupçon* of boyish charm, but not precisely arrogant."

He smiled. "You make me sound like a wine."

I turned the key in the lock. After a brief joggling of the handle, the door swung open.

He leaned forward, peering into my foyer. "It's a little dark in there. Wouldn't you like me to go in ahead of you and poke around for the boogie man?"

I sighed. He sounded like Officer Perkins. "It's good of you, Vern, but I just had the exorcist in last week, and he says everything's clean. Thanks so much." I began to close the door.

He grinned down at me. "Now I understand."

"Understand what?"

Vern was already galloping down the steps. He called over his shoulder, "Why Gil has never gotten over you."

Chapter Four

Waving half-heartedly, I closed the door. All at once, it seemed there was nothing in the world but my headache. I trudged upstairs and found some leftover painkiller of Mother's. Against all rules of caution, I took a half-dose and proceeded to the kitchen to make myself a cup of tea.

It was later, as I sat at the kitchen table sipping my tea, swimming peacefully in a happy haze, that Vern's parting comment came back to me. I shook my head, but gently. Vern couldn't possibly understand about Gil and me. *I* didn't understand about Gil and me. Vern was a nice boy, but he was, as I'd told him myself, a bit naive. If he'd witnessed the arguments, heard the angry words—well, he wouldn't have said what he did. Not for a minute. It was nice of him, though. He had his mother's kind heart.

On the floor nearby, Sam was bathing himself in that revolting leg-in-the-air way cats have.

"You know, Sam," I told him, "you're rather supple for a

fur-bearing bag of lard."

Hearing his name, he purred proudly and preened his whiskers, a much more attractive procedure.

Someone knocked on the door, long and hard. Sam disappeared. The knots in my shoulders that had begun to loosen immediately retied themselves, but my headache was gone. A slight, cheerful giddiness had replaced it.

"Oh, thank Heaven! You're here. The doorbell must not be working," cried Dorothy O'Brien as she rushed past me, five-year-old Meaghan hanging on to her hand. "We've been worried sick about you. You are all right, aren't you?"

"I'm just fine." Well, I was now.

Dorothy turned to face me. We had been friends a long time, sharing a love of history and the stories of PG Wodehouse. Her hazel eyes examined my face shrewdly. "Yes, I believe you are." She stepped behind Meaghan and put her hands on the little shoulders. "In that case, we have a tremendous favor to ask of you."

"Tree-mendous!" Meaghan repeated, her eyes wide.

"I'll be glad to do whatever I can."

"Well, you see," Dorothy began, "I'm a docent—"

"That's a guide!" her daughter interrupted proudly.

"I'm a volunteer at the Whaley-Stott House Museum." It was one of our more obscure, authentic tourist attractions.

"And a pipe broke!" Meaghan announced.

"Quiet, honey. Look, Miss Prentice. A pipe burst in the basement at St. Anthony's Academy. There's water everywhere downstairs, but no pressure for the, um, toilets and things, so school let out early today. Sister called me just as I was going out the door. I'd cancel, but I'm supposed take around a bunch of bigwigs from the State Historical Society..."

"And you want Meaghan to stay here," I finished for her.

"Yes, could she? You're absolutely the *only* human being

home at this hour of the afternoon." She frowned. "Are you sure you're feeling well enough?"

"Of course! And even if I weren't, Meaghan could be my nurse, couldn't you, dear?"

Meaghan nodded vigorously.

"Oh, Miss Prentice, you're an angel! I'll be back just as soon as I can. I'll talk fast and run their legs off." She held up a large, lumpy canvas sack adorned with a cartoon turtle. "Here's her toy bag. I'll never forget you for this!"

She glanced at her watch, pulled out her car keys, kissed her daughter, and was gone.

"Well, now," I said. I looked down at the little girl uncertainly.

Like her father had been, Meaghan O'Brien was a trifle tall for her age, with long, thin arms and legs, but her red hair and confident friendliness were her mother's. I had known Meaghan all her short life and liked to think we shared a mutual respect, but this would be the longest time we had ever spent together. How on earth did one entertain a five-year-old?

Meaghan regarded my bandage with frank interest. "Does that hurt?" she asked, pointing with a touchingly tiny index finger.

"Not right now."

"Can I look at it?"

"You mean under the bandage?"

She nodded.

"I'm afraid not."

Meaghan shrugged philosophically. "C'mon," she said. "Let's play." With great self-assurance, she led me by the hand to the front parlor and bade me sit on the floor before her.

After arranging my legs in a semi-comfortable position, I watched with interest as she rummaged in her bag.

"Turn around," she ordered. I obeyed and she began gently combing my hair.

"Meaghan, what are we playing?"

"I'm Miss Gladys and you're my customer."

I chuckled. Gladys's Glamour Spot was a popular beauty shop.

"My, my, my,"she said, quoting a famous Gladys-ism as she circled me, "You're late for a trim, all right!" Her voice had just the right bright, brittle tone. "Wouldn't you say so?" she added, bringing her face nose-to-nose with mine. Her tongue was purple and her breath smelled of grapes. Bubble gum would have been my guess. Or Kool-aid.

"Oh, yes, Miss Gladys," I answered, getting into the spirit of the thing. But when she reached in her bag for a bright pink pair of blunt kindergarten scissors, I had some delicate negotiating to do. We settled on a simple "wash and blow dry," without the scissors, and pantomimed the washing, rinsing, and drying with enthusiasm.

I enjoyed myself thoroughly. Entertaining Meaghan was turning out to be much easier than I'd expected. "That was fun, dear," I said, looking around for a chair arm upon which to hoist myself.

"But I gotta style it now," Meaghan insisted.

I settled back down.

Very delicately, with intense concentration, she combed the short waves from around my face down over my forehead. "Now you can't see your Bandaid so much," she declared, and handed me a two-inch hand mirror to survey the effect.

"Oh, Miss Gladys," I gushed theatrically, "it's just lovely! I'm going to pay you lots and lots of money for the good job you've done!" I squinted into the mirror again, then pulled myself to my feet to get a better look in the beveled glass above the fireplace.

I did look nice. I had worn the same hairdo for years, short and layered, parted on the left and combed straight back away from my face. With the bangs, I looked more up to date. And they did help to hide my bandage. I smiled at my reflection. "It's an improvement," I told it.

"Miss Prentice," Meaghan said, pulling reproachfully on my skirt, "we're not finished yet."

Meekly, I resumed my ungainly seat on the floor and Meaghan continued the transformation, using generous amounts of Li'l Lady Cosmetics. She obviously had the complete set, and if the colors were garish, they at least had fun, happy names. Meaghan chose Playground Peach lipstick, Robin's Egg Blue eye shadow, and Ring-around Rosy rouge. She worked enthusiastically and I submitted until she pulled out the Licorice eyeliner.

"Meaghan," I asked, my hand on hers, "when you color in coloring books, do you stay inside the lines?"

She nodded cheerfully. "Most'ada time!"

I applied the Licorice myself, while she held the tiny mirror. I don't think I did much better than she would have.

There was a knock at the door. My hand jumped, causing the piquant upturned line at the edge of my left eye to extend all the way to my scalp.

"I'll get it!" Meaghan shrieked joyfully and sprang to action. My efforts to restrain her were useless. My right foot had fallen asleep, and it was all I could do to stand up.

The metallic jingle told me that somehow Meaghan had managed the huge brass doorknob. I could hear the child's light soprano exchanging pleasantries with a deeper voice as I struggled alternately to walk and massage the tingles out of my numbed foot.

"We're playing. C'mon, we're in here," said Meaghan, the perfect little hostess, as she escorted Gil Dickensen into the parlor.

My appearance somehow lacked that wholesome dignity
that had become my trademark, and Gil's expression proved
it. His brown eyes widened, and the muscles in his jaw
twitched. He stroked his chin thoughtfully and stared. "Hello,
Miss Prentice. Am I interrupting anything?"

I let go of my foot, slipped my shoe back on, and limped
over to the mirror above the fireplace. "Not really, Mr.
Dickensen. We were just playing, as Meaghan told you." I
pulled a handkerchief from my pocket and scrubbed at my
face.

"What can I do for you?" I asked, my back turned to him.
All this scrubbing wasn't doing much good, not even with a
little surreptitious spit on the cloth. Apparently, Li'l Lady
Cosmetics required soap and water, if not turpentine, for re-
moval. I gave up and turned to face Gil.

"I wanted to ask you a few questions about last night," he
said, holding up a notepad and glancing down at Meaghan.

I picked up the makeup kit. "Let's clean this up, Meaghan,"
I ordered gently. To my surprise, she complied without an
argument, carefully replacing the cosmetics in their allotted
compartments.

"Why would you need me?" I asked Gil over her head.
"You were there yourself, weren't you?"

"Yes, but not the whole time. Just a few questions."

"Hand me that lipstick on the coffee table, Sweetie. All
right, *mais pas devant l'enfant*. Meaghan, would you like to
play that piano over there for a while?"

She eagerly climbed on the stool and began pounding tune-
lessly.

"Come on, I'll make some coffee. Or tea?"

"Oh, coffee, definitely. Black."

Gil followed me to the kitchen and took a seat at the table, watching silently as I bustled around. His presence unnerved me, as it always did.

Meaghan was attempting "Chopsticks," repeating the first two measures incessantly. I wracked my brain for a witty comment, but none came. In fact, neither of us said a word until I poured out the coffee.

"Well?" I ventured at last.

"Well, what?" He took a sip from his mug. His eyes, regarding me over the top, had more wrinkles around them than I'd remembered.

"Your questions?"

"Oh, yes. I guess I was just listening to the music." He smiled, patted his jacket, and extracted a pen from an inside pocket.

Meaghan abandoned "Chopsticks" and began what might have been loosely called a "Variation on a Theme from 'Mary Had a Little Lamb.'"

Someone rapped briskly on the front door.

"I'll get it!" Meaghan's excitement at another possible visitor could only have been exceeded by that of a particularly energetic terrier. Her tiny sneakers pounded across the foyer. This time, though, I was immediately behind her, just in time to be confronted by a red-faced Detective Dennis O'Brien, bellowing orders to his bewildered daughter.

"It's time to go. Get your coat."

Whimpering her objections, Meaghan turned and ran down the hall.

Dennis turned to me. "Where's my wife?" he barked. "And why isn't Meaghan in school?"

"Dorothy's guiding a tour at the Whaley-Stott House," I began, "and the plumbing at St.—"

"Never mind," he interrupted as Meaghan returned with her jacket and toy bag. "Let's go," he said, swinging the child and her bundles into his arms. Without another word, he was down the steps.

I stood, stunned, at the open door, watching him buckle Meaghan into a seat in the back of his car. Not until he drove away with a roar and a screech of tires did I close the door and press my cheek against the cool glass.

What had just happened? I covered my face with my hands, wincing as I touched the bandage. My eyes felt hot. I struggled with the lump that rose in my throat. It was too much. Black tears ran down my cheeks and onto my hand. I took my handkerchief from my pocket and wiped them up. Then I remembered. I wasn't alone.

I was frantically planning an escape to the bathroom upstairs when I heard Gil's voice.

"Amelia? What was that all about?"

I froze. I couldn't let Gil Dickensen see me this way. I turned to make my exit, but all at once, there was an obstacle: Gil's shirtfront. As his arms came around me, I gave up trying to escape, sagged against him, and let fly the sobs.

Nothing, not even the disturbing events of the last twenty-four hours, surprised me as much as finding myself in Gil Dickensen's arms again. But surprise or not, it was too late to stand on ceremony. I cried.

Not, I'm ashamed to admit, ladylike, hanky-dabbed-at-the-corner-of-the-eye crying, but a succession of uncontrolled whoops and hiccoughs the likes of which I hadn't experienced since I was ten. All the while, Gil held me, stroking my hair and murmuring meaningless words of comfort.

Once, briefly, the sobs abated somewhat, but the surreal quality of what was happening struck me again, and I was thrown into renewed spasms. Somewhere inside myself, I knew why. Because all this was as meaningless as the soft sounds Gil was making. He was merely being kind to a fellow human being in distress. Admittedly, it wasn't a role I had ever pictured him in, but there it was.

Gil lowered me gently into a chair and went into the kitchen to fetch a glass of water. More kindness.

"I'm sorry," I managed to gasp after a few sips.

He knelt beside my chair and smiled. "Don't be," he said. *Remember, Amelia, he's just being kind.*

His finger lightly tapped my bandage. "That thing hurt much?"

"Only when someone does that."

He pulled his hand back. "Oh, sorry."

"Don't be." I smiled wetly at him and blew my nose. "It doesn't really hurt very much."

He pulled out his handkerchief. "Here. Reinforcements." He pulled himself to his feet with a groan.

"Amelia," he said, pulling a chair over near mine. "Are you up for a little constructive criticism?"

I knew it. Here it comes. The zinger. "No, thank you very much. I don't need any cheap shots about hysterical females or—"

"Wait, hold it. Nothing like that." He shifted his weight in Mother's antique sewing chair and smiled a tiny smile. "I was just going to observe," he said slowly, "that you bear a striking resemblance to a raccoon." His smile was up to full candlepower now, and he turned it on me.

A muscle somewhere in my chest tightened.

His eyes searched my face speculatively. "No, I take that back. More like a Disney character. Something from Bambi, maybe."

Once again, I approached the mirror over the old fireplace and beheld my painted countenance. Despite the recent flood, there was still a considerable Li'l Lady residue, especially around my eyes, which had the added allure of being red and swollen from crying. "Meaghan's beauty treatment. It does look ghastly, doesn't it?"

Gil came and stood behind me. He spoke to my image in the mirror. "Until O'Brien showed up," he said softly, "I thought you looked kind of cute."

I looked down at the mantel's surface. Dust! I had just dusted there day before yesterday! I took a swipe at the surface with Gil's handkerchief. My hand shook.

"Amelia," said Gil, "I have a confession to make."

I ran the handkerchief over a figurine—a shepherdess—and replaced it on the mantel. "You do?" I straightened it.

"I didn't come here to get information for the paper."

"You didn't?" I reached for another figurine. A shepherd boy, this time.

"No, I came to see what Vern was carrying on about—would you cut that out and look at me?"

I set down the figurine and looked up into the mirror. His face, over my shoulder, had lost all traces of amusement. "What about Vern?"

"Well, his mother had told him all about you. I mean, about you and me, you know."

"Yes, your sister Carol, I see, go on."

"And he got this crazy idea that, well, anyway, after he met you today, he came home raving about this terrific—"

I turned around. "Home? Does he live with you?"

"Yes, sleeps on a camp cot in the kitchen, but only till he can find a place he can afford, which may be never, at the rate he's looking—look, are you going to let me finish?"

I folded my arms. "Finish."

"Vern kept telling me what an idiot I had been to let you go—"

"But—"

"I know, I know, he doesn't have the whole story. But he

was so darned enthusiastic, I just came by to see what kind of spell you had thrown over him."

"Spell?" For some reason, I felt stung. "Spell? Oh, yes, by all means. Let me go upstairs and look up the 'Vern Spell' in my book of spells. Something to do with eye of newt, I think, and..." My original intention was to stalk indignantly out of the room, but once again, Gil Dickensen short-circuited my plans.

He kissed me.

It was apparent from his technique that Gil had put in some practice since we had last done this. As for me, I had to rely on memory and trust that, just like riding a bicycle, it would all come back to me. I gave it my best.

Of course, I wasn't totally without experience of this sort. There was a time when I was in my thirties that everyone's eligible visiting nephew had taken me to whatever was playing at the Strand Theatre, but it had never led to anything substantive. Perhaps I lacked enthusiasm, or my attention was elsewhere, but when the moment for the goodnight kiss came, I either managed a skillful dodge, or made a lackluster response. I think somewhere in the recesses of my mind, I believed I was frigid, or whatever odious term current experts might use.

Now here was Gil, doing me the favor of showing me I had been absolutely, totally, and completely mistaken. I responded, all right. Responded my little heart out. It was quite a moment, and, if you want my opinion, could have gone on for quite some time, but the phone rang. We tried ignoring it, but almost immediately, there was a delicate rapping at the door.

Gil whispered an oath under his breath, then said, "Go on, answer that. I'll get the door."

It was Lily Burns. "Hope I didn't wake you, dear," she

began. I looked at the kitchen clock. It was 4:12. What kind
of sluggard did she think I was?

"No, Lily," I said, smiling to myself, "you didn't."

"Well, I just wanted to tell you I'll pick you up at 8:15
tomorrow morning. A little bit early for a Saturday, I know,
but I want to catch the first ferryboat."

"Pick me up?"

"You know, the sale at JJ Peasemarsh. Don't you remember?"

"Oh, yes, I do now."

"You can go, can't you? I mean, your head is all right, isn't
it?"

"It's fine. And yes, I suppose I can go."

"You 'suppose.' Don't do me any favors, Amelia."

"Oh, forgive me, Lily, but I've got company." I could hear
Gil conversing with someone out in the hall. The voice was
female. Probably Marie LeBow, I thought, remembering her
promise to come over.

"Company? Oh, really? Who is it?" Lily's ears pricked up
so fast, her earrings positively rattled.

"Uh, it's a long story. I'll have to tell you about it tomorrow." Surely I could come up with a plausible cover story by
then. You give people like Lily Burns and Judith Dee a couple
of sentences, they write a novel. "So if you'll excuse me, I'll see
you in the morning."

"Wait! There was something else. What was it? Oh—Marie
LeBow called me after lunch today and said she'd tried to get
you at school. They told her you'd gone home, so she called
you there, but no answer."

I must have been in transit in Vern's cab.

Lily continued, "She said—um, let me think—she said,
she couldn't come tonight, but she still wanted to give you
something important."

"Important? Did she say what it is? Did she want me to come to her house?"

Lily heaved a huge sigh. "Amelia, how on earth should I know? I'm simply passing on the message. Marie seemed to think you'd understand, poor woman. Maybe it has to do with funeral plans. She sounded a bit out of breath. Or maybe she was crying. Why don't you call her and find out for sure?"

"I will."

"Well, then. Tomorrow at 8:15."

I hung up and headed back into the entrance hall. "Gil, that was Lily—Gil?"

Nobody was there. I heard the faint sounds of conversation somewhere above my head. I followed the voices upstairs to my bedroom, where I found Gil together with Sally Jennings, the real estate agent. They were not exactly in a compromising position, but it was certainly a curious one.

Sally was standing, stocking-footed and on tiptoe, on Aunt Daisy's antique vanity chair, extending her arm high above her, tape measure in hand, apparently trying to determine the exact height of the ceiling. It was a pose that displayed her spectacular figure to best advantage.

Gil was leaning, arms folded over his chest, in the doorframe, watching.

"Give me a hand here, would you, Gil?" she trilled.

"*I'll* help you, Sally," I said.

Out of the corner of my eye, I saw what appeared to be a large gray fur pillow dead-center on my tapestry bedspread. Sam's eyes narrowed and challenged me to make something of it. I decided not to air dirty family linen. It was my own fault, anyway. If I hadn't relaxed the rules last night...

"Why, Amelia!" Sally seemed astonished to see me. What did she expect? It was *my* house. She retracted the flat metal tape with the press of a button and leapt lightly from the chair, then stepped into a waiting pair of three-inch alligator heels. Almost as a reflex, I looked down at my prim black flats. Next to Sally, I was a dweeb, I thought, quoting Hardy Patschke to myself.

"Oh, poor Miss Prentice. What a time you've had." She embraced me. She was wearing a cashmere sweater and smelled wonderful. The top of my head came just to her chin. She and Gil were exactly the same height, if she wore the heels.

And a shrimp. I was a dweeb *and* a shrimp. *Miss Prentice*, indeed. We'd graduated from high school together. Sally Dodd had been Head Cheerleader, Girls Swim Team Captain, and Queen of the Junior Prom. I was French Club, Chorale, and attended the Prom with my cousin Bob.

In every way that was possible to measure, Sally was one of life's winners: popular, beautiful, successful, rich, and married to Barry Jennings, the most sighed-over boy in the Class of '74. She'd done it all herself, too, starting from scratch, as it were, with no help from her widowed father. I had to hand it to her.

She held me at arm's length and surveyed my face with its bandage and the remnants of Meaghan's Li'l Lady makeover. "My, you do look all done in. We musn't wear you out."

I smiled bravely. "Not at all, Sally. I'm just a little surprised to see you. Why don't we adjourn to the parlor?" Ever so calmly, I led them downstairs.

"Now, Miss Prentice—Amelia—you musn't blame Gil," said Sally. "It's all my doing. I explained to him how we've talked about your selling this place—"

"*You* talked about it, Sally, not I." It was a running thing with us, practically the only foundation for our continued association.

I escorted them into the front parlor and turned on the ginger jar lamp that had always sat on Grandmother Lloyd's cherrywood drum table.

"Yes, but you did promise to think about it, now didn't you?"

It was true. I had—once—but only to get rid of her. "I have thought it over, Sally, and—"

"Wait!" She held up a slim hand.

I couldn't help staring at her gold bracelet, from which dangled a single large disk, bearing elaborately entwined initials. I had seen one in the Neiman-Marcus catalog last Christmas. A little seven hundred dollar stocking stuffer. (Engraving extra.)

"Before you say another word, let me tell you: I've found a buyer!"

Obviously, that clinched it for Sally. I opened my mouth to answer, but she went on, "A very *eager* buyer. One who'll pay handsomely for a house—" She paused and shrugged, shaking her head sympathetically. "You've got to admit it, Amelia—a house that's past its prime and in need of a lot of work." She waved her hands, inviting us to survey the wreckage. "For instance,"she added, "I noticed your doorbell's not working and a front step is loose."

"Sally, I'm sorry you went to all this trouble," I said evenly, "but this is my home. I grew up here and I'll probably—" I stole a glance at Gil, whose face was a blank— "die here. I have no intention of selling, ever."

"Now, Miss Pr—Amelia. I know you're not feeling a hundred percent this evening, so I'll give you just a little more time to think it over, okay? I'll be getting back to you later next week." She walked to the foyer where her camel coat was draped over the mahogany banister. "Uh, oh," she said, shrugging into the coat, "this wobbles a bit. Better have it fixed. Goodbye, dear, take care." She embraced me. When had we become such friends?

She paused at the front door and pulled on her kidskin gloves. She handed me a business card. "Here. Call me the minute you change your mind."

I read the card: "Ursula 'Sally' Jennings, Vice President, Jennings Real Estate." Barry, of course, was President of the firm, but it was common knowledge that she was its life and soul. A line at the bottom announced that she was a Gold Star Member of the Million Seller's Club, supposedly an intoxicating inducement to potential clients. Once again, Sally had come in Number One.

"You already gave me one of these."

"Keep it for extra." She looked around again. "You could retire on what you'd make from this place, Amelia. Better be thinking about that, too, you know. Coming, Gil?"

Gil, who had remained mute during this entire exchange, awoke with a start from his sleepwalking. "Huh?"

"I'm sure Miss Prentice is tired. We should let her rest. Come on, I'll let you walk me to my car." She took his arm.

"Um, well," Gil said.

"You can't leave just yet, Gil," I said. "We haven't finished with our—business."

Sally flipped a blonde strand out of her face and arched a doubtful eyebrow.

"Gil was helping me with my...newspaper...subscription," I improvised. "That is, I'm thinking of taking out a newspaper subscription for each of my students. We're studying journalism, you know."

"And she was trying to get me to give her a big volume discount," Gil said, shaking his finger at me as he shamelessly took up the lie. "Our Miss Prentice is a real horse trader, I'll tell you!"

Sally shrugged. "Whatever. Well, I'll see you later. Think about what I said."

As Sally's sleek foreign sports car pulled away from the curb, Gil said, "Thanks."

"No problem." Casually, I pushed on the banister, which was solid as a rock. "That's Our Miss Prentice, Horse Trader!" I waited for a playful reply from Gil, but got none.

He strolled, hands in pockets, back into the parlor, where he stared into the empty fireplace.

"By the way, that was Lily on the phone," I said. Casual, that was me. "We're going shopping at Peasemarsh tomorrow." Nice going, Amelia. Why on earth would he care?

I continued babbling. "I thought the doorbell was Marie LeBow. She was supposed to come here to give me something. I wish she wouldn't. It's from Marguerite and I feel—well, funny, you know? Gil?"

Gil shook his head slightly and blinked several times. "I'm sorry—what were you saying?"

"Marie, Marie LeBow. She was supposed to come here tonight."

"Why here? Couldn't you just go to her place?"

"I offered to, but she insisted on coming over. Lily just told me Marie couldn't come, but still wanted to give me something."

Gil's interest was piqued. "Odd."

"I wish I knew what she wants me to have that's so important."

"Why don't you just call and ask?"

"I was going to, but I was busy protecting my home from a hostile takeover. I'll do it now. Excuse me." I went to the kitchen, but was back in a minute.

"What is it?" Gil asked when he saw my expression.

I mopped my eyes with a tissue. "She had—I mean, Marie—the answering machine—the recording? It was Marguerite's voice. She was trying so hard to sound sophisticated. Oh, Gil, it's heartbreaking!"

"Did you leave a message?"

"Yes, but, could we, I mean, would you mind?" I tilted my head in the direction of the front door.

"You mean go over to Marie's? Right now?"

"Gil, I'm worried about her. Marie is the hardest-working, most reliable person I know."

Gil stroked his ear thoughtfully. "Well, you're right there. She delivered papers for us a few years ago. Did you know that? She had to be at the college dining hall to fix breakfast by six AM, so she picked up the papers at 3:30. Never missed a morning."

My eyes were tearing up again. "That's Marie, all right."

Gil grabbed his coat. "Come on. Let's go."

"Just a minute." I ran upstairs to the bathroom. It took two vigorous applications of a soapy washcloth to scrub off the residue of Li'l Lady. When I had finished, my skin felt tight and sore. I looked in the mirror. I was back to my old look now, shiny-faced, wholesome, and a little dowdy. I combed the damp bangs down over my bandage, applied some lipstick and spritzed cologne on my blouse. That was better, though without all the warpaint, I did look bland. I shrugged. That's me: a shrimpy, bland dweeb. Take me or leave me.

I looked down the stairs at Gil. He was jingling change in his pocket while he looked at his watch. He had done the very same thing in that very same spot more than twenty years before. We meant something to each other then, but the bitterness that eventually sprang up between us made our current *détente* something of a miracle. So, what was different about him now? Nothing, really.

Sure, we were united in concern for Marie and he'd been kindly comforting to me, but it was only a kiss and what was a kiss, anyway? Not much, in this day and age. I wasn't a young girl in the throes of infatuation any more, I reminded myself.

Just then, Gil looked up at me and smiled. "Ready?"

Blip. Something turned over in my chest.

Don't be too sure, Amelia.

"Ready."

Chapter Five

In the modest neighborhood of neat, well-kept cottages where Marie lived, hers was the neatest and best-kept. It was almost dark when we arrived.

"You said she didn't answer the phone?" Gil asked. "Her car's there."

"But look—no lights on in the house," I countered. "Not in front, anyway."

We made our way by the dim light of a street lamp and the glow from nearby houses.

"Look," I said as we walked up the sidewalk. I picked up a rake lying half-buried in a pile of leaves near her front porch. "She'd never leave something out like this. Now I'm really worried." I headed around the house.

Gil trotted up the front steps and rang the bell. I could hear it from outside, but there was no answering sound of movement in the house. No light in the kitchen window, either, but in the backyard, some clothes were hanging on a circular metal clothesline.

I felt a blouse. It was still damp. "Gil!" I called. "Come around here. Look at this."

I heard movement in the bushes of the side yard, walked toward the sound, then froze.

A dark figure rounded the corner, but it wasn't Gil. It was a much bulkier man, silhouetted in the pale light from next door, walking heavily, cautiously, and carrying a club of some kind.

Had he seen me?

Frantically, I ducked under the clothes on the line, and clung to the center metal pole. The laundry, blouses and socks, bras and dishtowels, formed a pitifully inadequate circular curtain around me, but there was no other place to hide.

The line turned in the breeze, creaking.

I could hear his footsteps in the dead leaves, coming closer, then stopping. A circle of light played over the clothing, then a large hand slowly parted the laundry.

"Gil!" I shrieked, backing out of my shelter. My left foot slid sideways, out from under me. As my other foot teetered on a lumpy, shifting fabric-covered surface, I realized a sickening *déjà vu.*

Am I falling over another body?

I landed heavily.

"Who's that?" a voice demanded. A bright light played over my face and on the obstacle that had tripped me.

Whimpering, I scuttled away from the thing on all fours, then looked back at it by the stranger's light. "Bulbs," I murmured, still trembling, "A sack of flower bulbs. Thank Heaven." I looked up and was blinded by a harsh, yellow beam of light.

"Amelia?" It was Gil, running around the house.

"What's going on?" the large stranger demanded. "What're you doing here?"

"Please," I began. My head had begun to hurt again. "I mean, we—"

"Look here." Gil stepped in front of my cringing form and stood protectively in the flashlight's glare. My hero. "We're just here to see if Mrs. LeBow's okay. We're friends of hers."

"That's right," I said as Gil pulled me to my feet. "We couldn't reach her, so we got worried."

The man slowly lowered the flashlight. "You don't know where she went either?"

"She's gone? When?" I asked.

"This afternoon. My wife saw 'er go." He waved the beam in the direction of a light blue bungalow some fifteen feet away. "We live next door, y'know."

"Bert?" a woman's voice called. The back porch light came on. "Everything okay?"

"Just fine, Hester. Go on back inside. Be there in a minute." He turned to us. "Look here. Why don't you folks come over to the house? Maybe we can figure this thing out."

Shivering, Gil and I agreed.

"I'm Bert Swanson. Groundskeeper over to the college. My wife works with Marie at the cafeteria." He held the back porch door open for us.

The Swanson house was a cheerful contrast to Marie's crisp neatness. Their back porch held a jumble of rakes, brooms, mops, buckets, and several huge jugs of cleaning products. At one end was a small chest-top freezer with a large padlock. Piled on top were a fifty-pound sack of dry dog food and a huge net bag of fragrant McIntosh apples.

The apple fragrance grew stronger as we entered the tiny knotty-pine kitchen. A stout, gray-haired woman in jeans and sweatshirt topped by a faded apron reading "Kiss the Cook" stepped forward in welcome, wiping her hands on a dishtowel.

Bert began the introductions, but his wife Hester interrupted.

"You the prowlers at Marie's?" she said, smiling. Her eyes sparkled. "I told Bert you were too noisy for burglars."

We all shook hands.

"You want pie?" Hester asked. "Just come out of the oven," she added temptingly.

"Sure they do, honey," Bert said, wrapping his arm around Hester's sturdy waist. "You won't find better, I can tell ya that. This little lady's the best baker in the county," he informed us, and obeyed the instructions on his wife's apron.

"Oh, shuddup," she said. "Get outta here."

Bert ushered us into a comfortably cluttered living/dining room. Every level surface was topped by bright squares of printed cotton material in stacks. A muted television played quiz shows without ceasing.

"Hester's doin' one of her projects," he said apologetically, and moved several stacks from the sofa. "This time of year, she makes quilts. That one over there won second prize at the State Fair." He pointed to an ornate example of Hester's craft hanging on one wall. "It's called the Wedding Ring."

. Bert's broad face shone with pride. He was a burly man, balding on top, but still handsome, with a deep dimple on one side of his mouth that he displayed frequently.

Over huge wedges of apple pie and steaming cups of excellent coffee, Gil tried to get down to business. "About Marie—"

"Marie's the one give me the recipe for this pie. It's really for a cobbler that serves a hundred, but I pared it down a little."

There was a pause while we continued to appreciate Hester's culinary skill.

Bert leaned forward. "Don't you get it?"

Gil and I looked up, chewing.

"Get whup?" Gil asked, his diction impaired by a mouthful of hot apple.

"The recipe—she *pared* it down. Pared, apples? It's a joke!" He slapped Gil on the knee and roared with laughter.

"That's pretty witty," Gil said.

"You bet it is!" Bert's admiration for his spouse seemed limitless.

Hester came out of the kitchen with the coffeepot. "Honey, I just figured out who this lady is," she said, refilling my cup. "You're the teacher, aren't you? The one who found Marie's girl. That must've been terrible."

"It was," I admitted, fingering my bandage.

Hester clicked her tongue sympathetically. "Tragic. Such a young girl. And poor Marie."

Gil took advantage of the moment to get to the point. "Bert told us you saw Marie leave today."

"That's right," she said, stepping into the kitchen to replace the coffeepot. She returned and sat in an easy chair in the living room, where she took up her quilting work. "Seemed odd to me."

"When was that?" Gil was in his journalist's mode.

Hester donned a pair of glasses and threaded a needle. "Right after I got back from work, so it would've been about, oh, two or so." A square of patchwork fabric, sandwiched around some white fluffy stuff, was stretched in a wooden hoop the size of a steering wheel. Hester held it level in her lap and plunged the needle dead-center. A second later, it peeked up from underneath, a millimeter from the point of entry. She pulled the thread taut, then dipped the needle rapidly several times into the fabric.

For a few moments, we sat transfixed, watching Hester's hands move hypnotically up and down with the precision of a machine.

"Did you talk to her?" Gil asked, his eyes still on the quilting. "Find out where she was going?"

Hester pulled the thread taut. "Heck, no! You won't catch me interfering with the police."

"Police!" Gil and I exchanged glances.

"Besides, I was having my own problems," Hester said. "I was taking Flippy, my dog—our dog—" Her voice broke. Her hands drooped over her work. She bowed her head and removed her glasses. When she looked up at us, she was blinking back tears. "I was taking our little dog to the vet's. For the last time." A sob escaped her, and she fumbled on a side table for a box of tissues.

Bert shook his head wearily. "Poor ol' Flippy. He was real sick. It was his time."

"He was like our baby, you know?" Hester looked at me as she dabbed her eye.

I nodded. I was lying, of course. I had no idea. I was never much of a pet person. Ask Sam.

"We were gonna do it ourselves. Kinda like pulling the plug or something. Bert's cousin—he's got a farm out in Chazy—give him some capsules."

"Honey," Bert protested, "they don't want to hear all this sad stuff."

Hester was not to be diverted. "Just put a couple down his throat like vitamins, he told us, and Flippy'd go to sleep." She ended the sentence on a high note of pain. "We were gonna bury him out in the yard with a little stone and everything."

"Honey," Bert said.

"We couldn't do it." Hester turned a shaky smile toward her husband and reached out her hand. Bert stepped forward and grasped it firmly. "This great big man has such a soft heart." She blew her nose. "Oh, I'm sorry. It just gets to me, taking our little baby to strangers."

"He didn't feel a thing, Hester," Bert pointed out gently.

"I know." Hester was resigned. She looked at Gil. "Anyway, I was just thinking I kind of knew how Marie felt when I looked over and saw her locking her front door and getting into a police car."

"Were they arresting her?" I asked. "I mean, did they have handcuffs on her?"

"Didn't see any." Hester donned the spectacles and resumed her quilting. "One of the cops was helping her carry a suitcase. She just got in the car and they drove off without a word to us." She shrugged. "Bert 'n I were gonna keep some of her out-of-town people here in our spare room. For the funeral, you know. Guess *that's* off."

Bert was gathering up our pie plates. "Maybe not. She might be coming back. You should've asked."

"Well, I wasn't going to embarrass the woman, right there on the street, with the police and all. Remember what a hoohaw there was over your dad—"

"That was years ago. Nobody wants to hear it any more. You folks like some more coffee?"

I declined, but Gil accepted. Apparently, the interview wasn't over yet.

"It was just for smuggling," Hester whispered while Bert was in the kitchen. "Whiskey out of Canada. Everybody did it, only his dad had to sample it, too. That's how he got caught." She broke off as Bert returned with Gil's refilled cup.

"Couldn't leave it alone, could ya, Hester?" Bert said goodnaturedly. "Careful there, Dickensen, you're gonna spill it. Trouble is, she never tells the end of the story: my dad was let off due to lack of evidence."

"It was all drunk up!" Hester said, and giggled.

Gil nursed his coffee through several more questions, but it was soon apparent that the Swansons had nothing else to tell us.

"Well, I'd better get Miss Prentice back home," Gil said at last. "She's had a tough couple of days, and she needs her rest."

Amid a flurry of thanks and return invitations, Hester pressed her apple pie recipe on me, and Bert insisted on walking us to the car.

"It's a sad business, Dickensen," he said as Gil slid into the driver's seat, "and Marie's a fine woman."

"You're right about that," Gil agreed. "Don't worry, we'll find out where she is."

"Not like that daughter." Bert scowled. "She was something else."

Even in the dim light, I could see Gil's eyebrows wobble with interest. "Really?"

"Played little games, if you know what I mean." He pressed his hands on the car door and leaned in. "Tried to make it look like a man was doing something he shouldn't. You couldn't believe a word she said."

"A tease, was she?" Gil asked.

I frowned in the darkness but kept quiet.

"Don't you know it! And then some—takin' sunbaths in the backyard and coming over all the time, borrowing things. Then gets all het up like a man did something wrong. Well, it just wasn't right, that's all. Couldn't believe a word she said," he repeated.

"Sad business all around," Gil conceded.

Bert sighed, and gazed at Marie's house. "That it is. Well, you folks have a good evening and come again." He slapped the top of the car affectionately and stepped back as Gil pulled away from the curb.

"And what was all that about?" I asked as we rounded the corner.

Gil grinned. "Oh, you mean Bert?"

"Yes, all that male-bonding, she-was-a-tease, the-devil-made-me-do-it stuff."

"I have my theory. What's yours, Miss Prentice?"

The sardonic tone was familiar. Oh, well. We were back to square one. "Well, my guess is that Bert made a pass at Marguerite. She probably rebuffed him, and he was afraid the whole thing would get back to Hester."

"Don't you bet there'd be hell to pay if it did?" Gil agreed.

"But Gil, can you imagine this is the first time this thing ever happened with a man like Bert? I can't buy that. I think an intelligent woman like Hester would be well aware of what's going on."

"And she puts up with it?"

"Look at it this way: when Bert and Hester married, Bert was probably the catch of the century. I'll bet she's been doing the Superwoman bit ever since, just to keep him. He's still a good-looking man—it must take a lot out of her."

Gil laughed. "Why, Miss Prentice, how perceptive, how downright *earthy* of you! You've been holding out on us all these years!"

"Not at all. I read about it somewhere. You know we spinsters live on soda crackers and ice water and never allow the word S-E-X to pass our lips."

We were stopped at a red light. Gil gave me a long, searching look. He accelerated, still watching me, as the light turned green. "I've missed you," he murmured.

"I don't know *what* you're talking about. I've been here all the time." I was tired of all these on-again, off-again games. And my head hurt.

"Forget I said that. Answer me one other thing about Hester: do you believe what she said about Marie? That the police took her?"

"Why not?"

"Didn't you see that big freezer on the back porch? What if Bert got too friendly with Marie, too? If Hester's the hard-headed woman you say she is—"

"Oh, come on, Gil."

"I mean it. Who was it took the dog for the Last Walk? Bert didn't have the heart, remember? Maybe he's a lover, not a fighter."

"I thought journalists only dealt in facts."

"This is investigative journalism. It sometimes takes imagination."

"So I gather, judging by your editorials lately."

"Ouch," said Gil, but he was laughing.

We pulled up in front of my house.

"You and Lily are going to have a busy day tomorrow." So he had been listening to me, after all. "Go get a good night's sleep. I'll use my sources to check out this police thing."

"And you'll let me know what you find?"

"Maybe. Or maybe I'll let you read about it in one of my editorials." He sped off.

As I trudged up the steps, I realized I was glad to be home. I felt terrible, tired and sore all over. I touched my bandage gingerly. I hadn't seen a doctor about this yet. Maybe I would sometime tomorrow.

Later, in bed, as I pulled the covers over my shoulder and settled in for the night, I thought about Hester and Bert. We had been pretty quick to judge them, and they had been nothing but gracious to us. I felt ashamed.

Still, I had to wonder: what had happened to the capsules that Bert had failed to use on Flippy? And were they as toxic to young women as they were to little dogs?

Chapter Six

I was just washing up my breakfast dishes when Lily Burns rang the doorbell. I looked at my watch. Eight-fifteen on the dot.

"Oh, no," I murmured as I went to open the door. I had forgotten all about our trip to the JJ Peasemarsh sale. My plans for the day, as I had outlined them over my morning cereal, were to include a little grocery shopping and a surprise visit to the newspaper office to see if Gil had learned anything.

"Come on, Amelia, get moving. The ferry won't wait for us, you know—ohhhhh, look, it's my tweetheart!" Lily had spotted Sam. Without even breaking stride, she changed her tone from brisk and businesslike to utterly idiotic.

"Pwesious kitty," she cooed, "is oo gwad to see me? Is oo?" She scratched behind Sam's ears and his answering purr needed no amplification to be heard all over the room. "Does oo know what Mama got here?" Lily asked teasingly, reaching into her purse. "Does oo want a widdle turprise?" she squealed, pulling out a tiny gray felt pillow and tossing it across the kitchen.

Sam, fat as he was, could move rapidly when he had a mind to, and today he did. He was a blue-gray blur, pouncing on the catnip mouse, rubbing his nose on it, wallowing on it, and batting it around the room in a decidedly pointless manner, all the while uttering the most uncivilized noises.

"For heaven's sake, Lily," I complained as we locked Sam in the house, happily alone with the object of his desire. "Was that necessary? He makes such a fool of himself over those things."

"He's having fun, isn't he? Give the poor ol' guy a break." As Lily unlocked the door of her big black car, the passenger door unlocked also. I slid in.

"I guess Sam does get some exercise that way," I conceded, "but it seems like we're robbing him of his dignity."

Lily turned on the engine and looked at me meaningfully. "You already did that some time ago." She pulled out into traffic.

"That's none of your business. Besides, the veterinarian recommended it."

Lily shrugged and changed the subject. "I noticed that you're wearing 'our' coat. I thought it was my turn today."

I looked down at my olive green trenchcoat. "That's ridiculous. So we both have the same coat? Who cares?"

"I do. We look like a couple of Girl Scouts."

"What do you know about Girl Scouts other than cookies?" I asked, smiling.

Lily gave me a frosty look.

I laughed. "Look, here's that scarf you gave me for Christmas," I said, pulling it from my coat pocket. "I'll drape it over my shoulder thusly and tuck it in here, *et voila*, we're twin Girl Scouts no more."

"And what about the shoes?"

"Shoes?" I looked at my feet. "Oh, no." I had originally dressed to see Gil, not to go shopping. I was wearing my high-heeled Sunday shoes which were surprisingly similar to Lily's.

"So, who're you dressing up for, Amelia, hmm?" she asked. "Gil Dickensen, maybe?"

"What are you talking about?" I said, too loudly, too quickly. "These are the kind you can wear to play basketball!" I hadn't actually tested out the claim myself, but the demonstration on television was fairly convincing.

Lily shrugged again. "It's no skin off my nose, of course. It just seems more than a coincidence: Gil Dickensen's car sitting in front of your house to all hours, then you get gussied up for no apparent reason. Reach in my purse and hand me a Salem, would you?"

I folded my arms and arched an eyebrow at her.

"Amelia, I said—" Her expression was blank, then the light dawned. "Oh, fudge!" she exploded. "I forgot."

"How long has it been?"

"Eight days—" Lily glanced at her watch— "eleven hours and twenty minutes, give or take, gloriously smoke free," she concluded with a grimace.

"Trust me, Lily, you'll be glad about this eventually," I assured her, rummaging in my purse. "Your food will taste better, your clothes won't smell, you'll be able to—"

"Yeah, yeah, yeah. Spoken like a true non-smoker. You and my doctor sing the same dreary song. Put a sock in it, will you? I'm doing this thing, but if I gain as much as an ounce, so help me, I'll—oh, thanks," she said as I handed her a stick of gum, "but back to the subject at hand: Mr. Dickensen's car." Deftly unwrapping the gum, she folded it into her mouth and slid her eyes over at me.

"Oh, that," I said glibly. "He just came over to work out a program of newspaper subscriptions for my students. They use them for research papers."

Lily looked doubtful, so I played my trump card. "For instance, did you see that article on the Lake Champlain Monster last week? There's been another possible sighting. It was fascinating."

"Hmpf!" The rhythm of her gum chewing speeded up abruptly. "I'm telling you, Amelia, it's a hoax!"

I peeled myself a stick of gum and relaxed. Lily was off and running and would be good for a five-minute soliloquy.

"I've lived here for—well, all my life, anyway—and not once in all those years did I ever hear word *one* about that stupid monster!"

"But the scientists say—" I put in wickedly.

"Scientists, my Aunt Fanny! Snake oil salesmen, all of them! Especially that nut, what's-his-name Alexander? Now there's a scientist for you—about ten ants shy of a picnic, parading around everywhere in that yellow slicker, looking like an ad for frozen fishsticks!"

Really, this was too easy. I decided to pour a little more fuel on the fire. "I don't know, Lily. I've read his articles in the newspaper. It was fascinating stuff. He has doctoral degrees in marine biology and—"

"Don't give me degrees! Some of the stupidest people I ever knew were up to here in degrees!" She indicated how high on her forehead. "All I know is, my father and his friends fished every *inch* of this lake, winter and summer, since before the Depression. They could tell you all about it—all the history, all the Indian legends—and never, not *once*, did any of them ever mention one word about any old monster!"

I looked at my watch. It hadn't been five minutes, but as the Bard said, "'Twill do, 'twill serve." Her mind was off Gil. "Well, Lily, you're probably right," I said soothingly.

"You bet your bippy I am!" Lily said, getting a tighter grip on the steering wheel and glaring at the road ahead.

Bippy? I must have really upset her.

Ever mindful of highway safety and fearful of elevating Lily's blood pressure any further, I kept my mouth shut for the last few minutes of the drive and enjoyed the gorgeous view. People paid big money for bus trips just to see beautiful leaves like these: red, orange, and shimmering gold in a glorious symphony of eye-music, breathtaking even under overcast skies.

"Speaking of being right," Lily began after a few more miles of riotous foliage slipped past, "wasn't I right about that Abbott woman and the mailman? Didn't I tell you?"

For the next few miles, she filled the time with choice bits of information and speculation about the personal lives of various friends, enemies, and distant acquaintances. I let most of it float over my head until I heard a familiar name.

"...and sure enough, it was Sally Jennings," she said, reaching for the pack of gum and sliding out a fresh stick.

"Wait, explain that again. Sally Jennings what?"

Lily sighed and spit the chewed wad into a wrapper. "I told you, Amelia, it's not that complicated. They want to turn the houses into specialty shops and restaurants. You know, antiques, crafts, ye olde tea shoppe?" she said, pronouncing the final *e*'s. She handed me the little paper-wrapped gum pellet. "Here, stick this in the ashtray for me, would you?"

"What houses?"

"Amelia! Pay attention! Some of those big old mausoleums on your street! It was supposed to be a deep, dark secret, but Barry Jennings got to drinking over at the Elks Club the other night and it all came out. I swear I've never seen that husband of Sally's lift a finger except to hold a cocktail. I bet he hasn't shown one house in ten years, while you see *her* everywhere. She runs that whole company, poor girl. Anyway, it seems some millionaire from Montreal is bankrolling this Jury Street deal." Lily knew nothing about real estate and less about banking and finance, but she was remarkably adept at picking up jargon.

"So that's it," I said, remembering Sally's enthusiasm and her "very eager buyer."

"That's it, all right. Sally's going to want to kill Barry. The rest of those places are gonna go for top dollar now. And of course Nate Scolari's going to be steaming when he hears."

"Why?" Nate and his wife, Sophia, lived at the other end of my block.

"Because he's already gone and sold his place, that's why," said Lily with firm assurance. Her sources were nothing if not reliable. "And Sally had Nate believing she was doing him a favor! Of course," she said, tilting her head significantly, "I did hear that Nate's place was simply falling apart."

Lily signaled for the turnoff to the ferry dock. "You might say it served him right, though, telling everybody how anxious he was to move to Oregon." Leaving our hometown for greener pastures was a cardinal sin to Lily. She had never really forgiven my sister Barbara for moving to Tampa.

I shivered. The car was warm enough, but this information gave me a sense of foreboding. I tried to assess what it could mean. Surely they couldn't force me to sell my house. Or could they? There was such a thing as eminent domain. I had seen the state university condemn whole neighborhoods as it expanded.

Lots of people wanted my house, too. "You live at the old Prentice place?" they would say. "How lucky you are!" And I would smile and nod and keep silent about the property taxes, the antique plumbing, and prehistoric wiring I was going to have fixed just as soon as I could afford it, never mind the shortage of teenage boys willing to mow lawns and shovel snow.

But those things didn't matter, any more than it mattered that Dad had stuttered occasionally, or that Aunt Beatrice wore a wig to hide her thinning hair. You excused these things in someone you loved.

And I loved that place. It was more than a house. It was a part of my identity. My birthright. Why couldn't people understand that? My family had lived there. My parents had died there, and I would probably die there, too.

Gil had said as much in the heat of our last big argument all those years ago. "You're wasting your life in this place. You'll end up like that miserable, shriveled-up woman—Miss what's-her-name—in *David Copperfield!*"

"Shh, keep your voice down!" My parents were upstairs. "And if you mean Miss Havisham, that was *Great Expectations*," I said coldly and turned away from him.

"Whatever you say. But when I come back—"

"*If* you come back," I snapped over my shoulder, though tears were filling my eyes. Gil's unit was shipping out to Vietnam within the week. "Look, Gil, this is not the time to get married. I'll be in college next year. Mother and Dad need me here, now that Barbara's married. Besides, if we were married, and you were—" I broke off.

"All right. Have it your own way. *If.* I'm warning you: *if* you don't marry me now and *if* I come back, things just won't be the same!"

We had both been right, in a sense.

The fresh-faced, earnest young man I loved died in the frantic scramble to evacuate Saigon, and a hardened cynic had returned in his place. Things were certainly not the same. Since he hadn't answered any of my letters, and apparently had no interest in re-establishing any old ties, we had settled into an uneasy truce. Until recently.

"That'll be fifteen dollars, for car and passenger," said the man in the window.

I blinked and snapped out of my trance. We had arrived at the ferryboat dock.

While Lily fumbled in her purse for her half of the fare, I reached across and handed the man mine.

The sky above Lake Champlain was overcast, a common occurrence in October, and a wind was whipping up little whitecaps, but a good crowd of cars had gathered for the first crossing of the day.

Lily pulled her car into line behind the last vehicle and turned off the engine. She waved a hand at the gray expanse of lake. Our destination, the Vermont shore, was easily visible from where we sat. Near the dock, seagulls bobbed patiently among the waves. "Look at that, Amelia. You've lived near that lake all your life. Can you tell me you ever heard one single tale about any dumb sea monster until the last few years?"

I had more important issues on my mind, but I obediently searched my memory. "I guess you're right, Lily."

"Oh, no!" Lily grabbed my arm and squeezed hard. "Speak of the devil," she whispered through teeth clenched in a rigid grin.

A wide, smiling face, bristling with salt-and-pepper whiskers and topped with a battered tweed fedora, appeared in her open car window.

"Why, ladies, what an unexpected pleasure!" said a cheerful tenor voice.

Lily cringed. She always had the same reaction to Professor Alexander Alexander, marine biologist, historian, and monster hunter.

Lily and I held diverse opinions of the Professor. While she found him irritating, even repulsive, I harbored an amused affection for him. It seemed to me he was a cross between Don Quixote and Captain Ahab, with just a touch of Mr.

Rogers.

"Dr. Alexander," I cried delightedly.

"Please, Miss Amelia, you agreed to call me Alec, remember?"

"Of course—Alec."

He beamed at us. For the past decade, with the aid of an apparently limitless foundation grant, he had been conducting field research on his all-consuming life's work: the Lake Champlain Monster.

Depending on who was doing the talking, the monster was either a mysterious aquatic dinosaur, occupying the darkest depths of North America's own version of Loch Ness, or a shameless fake, dreamed up to promote tourism and dupe empty-headed dreamers such as the amiable, hymn-whistling Professor Alexander.

I was squarely and fearlessly on the fence on this issue, though I couldn't help but appreciate Alec's chivalrous friendliness and good-natured persistence in the face of frequent ridicule. No matter how much one might doubt the existence of the monster, no one ever questioned Alec's sincerity, so his efforts were tolerated in our community, however loony they might appear.

"What brings you to the lake, ladies?" he asked as a pair of binoculars and a camera suspended from his neck bumped against the side of Lily's car.

"We're going shopping in Burlington," I answered. "How about you?"

Lily turned her face toward me and widened her eyes in exasperation.

Alec tugged his beard thoughtfully. "Oh, the usual, y'know. Weekdays, I'm in my boat using the sonar, weekends, on the ferryboat. Not much luck, though last week I did get a wonderful shot of a significant row of ripples." His face brightened, and he held up his camera. "I have it here somewhere. Would ye like to see?" He patted his slicker pockets.

I had never been sure if it was just my imagination, or if the Professor did indeed have a faint Scots burr, but after hearing him roll the 'r's in "row of ripples," there was no doubt. I tried hard not to picture all that hairy bulk dressed in a kilt.

"Oh," he said sorrowfully, "I must've left it in m'other coat." He sneezed loudly, several times. "Forgive me, ladies," he said, repairing the damage with a ragged handkerchief. "It's allergy. Never know when it'll hit. Got some dandy capsules for it, though," he added, smiling. His good spirits seemed indomitable.

"Well!" Lily said suddenly, turning back toward the open window and Alec. "We musn't keep you, must we? There's probably a *lake*ful of ripples out there today!" She accompanied her statement with a tinkling laugh that had an hysterical edge to it.

"Oh, right you are," Alec murmured, trying to untangle his camera cord from Lily's side mirror. He succeeded at last and straightened up. "*Bon voyage, mesdames*," he concluded with a surprisingly good French accent. "Good shopping!" He lumbered away, whistling "Amazing Grace" under his breath and rearranging his gear.

"And good riddance,"said Lily, pressing the button that automatically locked all four doors, then the one that raised the windows.

"I don't see why you dislike him so much," I commented as we watched his distinctive yellow form move through the maze of cars towards the ferry. "He's just colorful. He brings in tourists, you know."

"Maybe." She sniffed. "But what kind of tourists? Tabloid readers and curiosity seekers, that's what! Used to be, people would come here to go swimming or fishing, or to see museums and learn about the history of the place. It was dignified. Now, it's like a circus side show. 'Pay your quarter and see the freak,'" she chanted. "We may have lost the Air Force base," she said, referring to the stringent defense cutbacks that had set our town's economy reeling, "but we're not as desperate as all that!"

Just then, I glanced over my right shoulder where a grotesque visage, its features distorted, was pressed against the glass of my window. Even as I jumped in fright, I recognized the face.

"Vern!" I said, opening the window. "You nearly gave me a heart attack!"

"Sorry," he said. "It was immature of me. Gotta be careful with people your age," he added with a wink.

"What are you doing here? Where's Gil—" I began, forgetting who was with me.

"Who's this?" Lily interrupted.

"Lily Burns, meet Vern Thomas," I said, as he thrust his long arm past my face for a hearty handshake. "He's Gil Dickensen's nephew. Carol's son."

"Oh, really. I see." Lily gave Vern her fingertips. "He probably wants to talk about another newspaper subscription," she said pointedly, arching a carefully plucked eyebrow at me.

Since the cat was already beginning to struggle its way out of the bag, I decided to go ahead and satisfy my curiosity. "Where *is* Gil? I called him three times this morning."

Vern shook his head. His straight blond hair flopped into his eyes. "Don't know. He was up and gone before me. I think he was going to see—um—" he paused and looked over at Lily.

"You mean the PHS all-time champion center?" I asked, taking a chance that Vern might have heard of Dennis O'Brien's stellar basketball career. Lily couldn't tell a basketball from a cantaloupe.

Vern's faced lit up with admiration. "Hey, yeah, that's right!"

"Well, good. I'm glad to hear it. Tell Gil I'll need forty-five subscriptions," I added.

"Huh?"

"Student subscriptions. He's arranging it for me, didn't he tell you?" I said urgently, trying to communicate with facial expressions and hoping the story was plausible enough to Lily's ears.

"Well, yes," Vern agreed tentatively. Abruptly, the gears in his head engaged. His eyes widened and his eyebrows assumed a knowing angle. "Oh, yes! Just let me make a note of that. Forty-five, was it? Where's my pencil—"

The end of his sentence was drowned out by a deafening blast from the ferryboat horn.

"Excuse us." Lily punctuated her interruption by turning on the ignition. She pointed to the line of cars ahead of us. "We're going to have to move now."

"Oh, sure. Well, see you later, Amelia. Maybe in the coffee shop." *Without Lily*, his expression said.

"Maybe—" was all I had time to answer. The car jerked forward unceremoniously, then crept down the graveled incline toward the ferry.

Wearing white windbreakers emblazoned with the company initials in dark blue, a team of young men guided the cars as they rolled over the metal grid onto the deck of the two-story ferryboat. With the elaborate boredom of long experience, they directed each car into tight formation, enabling approximately two dozen vehicles to be crammed aboard before they indifferently gestured "stop" to the next car and pulled a huge chain across the open end of the boat.

I watched with interest as a tall, broad-shouldered crewman passed between the rows, ramming a wooden wedge under a rear wheel of each car. That dark, shaggy head looked familiar, but I was never able to get a good look at his face. If he was avoiding eye contact, it wouldn't have been the first time. Occasionally, a student would try to steer clear of me because of some imagined slight or even out of simple shyness.

The boarding portion of the ferryboat ride always turned Lily into a white-knuckled nervous wreck, so I kept my own counsel during the process. It wasn't until after a good deal of heavy clanking, another ear-splitting blast from the horn, and a slight shudder indicated that we were under way that she heaved a deep sigh, turned toward me, and said, "Now what was that all about?"

"What was what all about?"

"Don't you play dumb with me, Amelia Prentice! That business with that boy just now."

I pulled my scarf from my shoulder and tied it around my head. "You heard. I'm getting some newspaper subscriptions for—"

"For your students. I know, I know. At least that's the party line. Come on, 'fess up to Aunt Lily: doesn't that heart of yours still go pitty-pat for Gilbert Dickensen?"

"Really, Lily! You're being revolting!" I opened the car door and set one foot out. "Are you coming?"

"Not unless you're going directly upstairs." She patted her coiffure. "I have no intention of getting wind-blown and soggy." She opened her own door. "Just so you can get all sentimental over the salt spray—"

"It's an inland lake, Lily, fresh water, not salt."

"Whatever." She slid out and slammed the door. Without another word, she turned and wound her way briskly between the parked cars to the narrow metal staircase which led to the ferry's observation level. The wind blew her stiff blonde hairdo to one side and it was obvious that her narrow high heels gave her a little trouble as she climbed the grated steps, but she made it, head high and dignity more or less intact. With one last disdainful glance down at me, she disappeared into the shelter of the enclosed observation deck.

I sighed. I had irritated her, maybe even hurt her feelings. Well, I told myself as I made my way to the bow, I couldn't help it. Lily didn't play fair.

"She can dish it out, but she can't take it," I quoted aloud, remembering an expression from my childhood. Lily Burns could wait, for the moment. It was my time to commune with the lake. I strolled to the bow.

The ferryboat was open at both ends, and during its many daily excursions, only a heavy chain, each link the size of a man's fist, separated the cars on the deck from the cold, blue-black depths of the lake.

It's no wonder they put wedges under the wheels. I leaned against the sturdy chain and watched the water slip away under the boat. Though we were moving at a relatively slow speed, there was a brisk breeze blowing against my face. I noticed, to my relief, that my head wasn't hurting. I inhaled deeply.

Those of us raised in what we call the North Country have lived along Lake Champlain, ridden upon it, splashed in it, and gazed across it, often without realizing our good fortune. It was not until I traveled away from home and lived for a short while in a lakeless area that I realized how much I could miss the healing, exhilarating qualities of the water and its nerve-soothing rhythm.

I stood there for a time with my feet planted wide apart while my scarf whipped sharply in the wind, relishing the rocking of the boat against the growing waves, soaking up the thin, cloud-veiled sunshine. It was curious, the pleasure I took in the lake in all its moods.

If I believed in reincarnation—and I don't—I might have been a sea captain in another life. No, I amended myself, not on the sea—boundless stretches of water extending to the horizon are a little disconcerting. Besides, I wasn't much of a swimmer. Perhaps a bargeman on a canal, or a riverboat pilot. I smiled. The thought appealed to me. Amelia Twain.

The first raindrop hit me on the nose. The next plopped in my eye as I looked up. I turned quickly and collided with one of the taller crewmen, wearing his hood. He grunted, spun around, and hurried about his business while I headed for the stairs, walking carefully in my higher-than-usual heels. A crowd of other passengers had gotten there first, so it was several damp minutes before I burst through the door of the observation deck, stamping and shaking off rainwater.

"Amelia!" said a familiar voice.

"Hello, Sally," I said. I took off my scarf and shook it. "Are you going to the sales, too?" I asked, hoping she wouldn't bring up the subject of real estate again.

"The sales? Oh no. I'm here on business," she said, pulling a cigarette from her pocketbook. She indicated a short, dark, well-dressed man at the counter buying coffee. "As a matter of fact, there's someone I'd like you to—"

"Uh, Sally, excuse me. Lily's calling me." It was true. Lily was waving frantically from a small booth across the room. I also noticed that she was about to be joined by the ubiquitous Professor, carrying two steaming Styrofoam cups.

"Talk with you later," I promised Sally, not wanting to be out-and-out rude. She nodded and turned her attention to her companion, who joined her just in time to light her cigarette.

I'd been riding on this ferryboat for years, and this coffee shop always made me think of the little car favored by circus clowns, capable of holding large numbers of people. Today, roughly three dozen passengers were milling around, buying souvenirs from a counter at one end of the enclosed deck and ordering snacks at the other.

Huge raindrops slammed against the large plate glass windows. The weather was denying us one of the ferry's chief attractions—an unobstructed view of the fabled Green Mountains of Vermont—but people were finding other ways to pass the time.

Lily, for instance, was glaring into her cup. As was her habit on these trips, she had snatched one of the much-coveted booths and set up camp there for the duration, formerly fortified with cigarettes. It was clear from her body language that this time she was considering the merits of making a run for it.

"Here I am, Lily," I announced, sliding in beside her. "Alec, I'm glad you could join us."

The Professor sighed and shook his head. "I shouldn't, you know. I should be out there. Shouldn't let a little rain deter me, but when I saw what charming company was inside, well..." He trailed off, allowing us to form our own images of his struggle with temptation. He removed the teabag from his cup, added a generous stream of sugar from a glass dispenser and stirred. "Soo, I decided I could spare a wee moment." He winked.

I could feel Lily stiffen beside me.

He began to stand. "But you must let me fetch you a cup—"

Abruptly, Lily pulled her purse on her shoulder and slid towards me. Clearly, she wanted out of the booth. I stood.

"Amelia," she said, buttoning her coat, "may I borrow that scarf of yours? I left something in the car."

"Of course." I pulled the balled-up wad from my pocket.

"It's kind of wrinkled," I admitted. "Are you sure you need to go down there? It's awfully wet outside."

Alec nodded agreement.

"I'm sure." She tied a knot under her chin. "Real sure. And please drink that coffee up for me, will you? I haven't touched a drop. Musn't let it get cold. 'Bye."

For about sixty uncomfortable seconds, I stared at the table and Alex whistled "Stand Up, Stand Up for Jesus" under his breath.

"She has to take some medicine, I think," I said.

Alec smiled gently. "She isn't the first person to think me a humbug, you know."

"But you're not—I mean, nobody..." I trailed off.

He ran a large, badly chapped hand over his head. His hair was cut in a strange variety of crewcut, with various tufts of salt-and-pepper hair sticking out at odd angles. His eyebrows matched, looking thick and wild, as though stray bits of hair had slid down from above. His scraggy, broad beard completed the ensemble perfectly.

"It's all right. I'm accustomed to skeptics by now. Better be." He took another speculative sip. "Actually, I welcome them. Keeps me fresh, on my mettle. Especially a fine woman like Miss Lily." He tapped his forehead. "She's shrewd. Won't buy a pig in a poke, as they say. I admire that."

I smiled back and sipped my coffee. Here was another thing I liked about Alec: he was generous to his detractors. Lily had an admirer, albeit an eccentric one. She could do worse, I thought, watching him wave greeting to a couple of passing crewmen.

"I like those new lads," he remarked as two crew members passed through the *Crew Only* door. "They're so young and eager, even though they've only just come on. Reminds me, though—" He pulled his yellow slicker hood over his head.

"Duty calls, dear lady," he said, taking my hand and bowing slightly over it. So courtly was his manner that, for a moment, I actually feared he was going to kiss it.

"Good hunting, Alec," I said.

He smiled, rearranged his binoculars, squared his shoulders, and charged through the crowd after his fellow sailors. I thought I heard him whistling "Nearer My God to Thee," but with the noise of the engine, it was hard to be sure.

I tasted my coffee again. Pretty bad. I poured a touch of sugar in it and wondered where to find some creamer.

"You'll rot your teeth with that stuff," Vern said, sliding in across from me.

"How do you know I don't have false ones?" I shot back.

He leaned forward. "Your left canine is just the slightest bit crooked. Never happens in the fake ones. Yee?" he said, demonstrating in his own mouth. "Open up, I'll show you."

"Don't be disgusting!"

"Sorry. You asked, though. Where's your friend?"

"In the car. Alec gets on her nerves."

"Too bad. He's kind of a neat guy." He pushed back his hood and shoved a damp blond lock of hair off his forehead. "I heard him lecture at the College. He was fascinating."

"So you don't think he's wasting his time looking for this monster?"

Vern wiped spilled sugar onto the floor. "Well, lots of people around here claim they've seen the thing. The Professor said there've been more than 240 sightings. I know a guy, he swears the Monster nearly sank his fishing boat."

"Did he say—" I began, but was interrupted by a loud blast of the ferryboat horn. Vern and I looked at one another.

"We can't be there yet," said Vern. "Can we?"

Just then, the *Crew Only* door slammed open, and Alec came barreling through, roaring, "Man overboard!" He disappeared out the exit and down the stairs to the lower deck.

A kind of genteel pandemonium broke out in the room as confused passengers shouldered one another in an effort to descend the stairs to their cars.

"C'mon," said Vern under his breath. He grabbed my elbow and steered me toward the *Crew Only* door.

"But—but—" I sputtered.

"Shut up, Amelia," he growled. "This tub could be sinking or something. Can't you feel it? The engine has stopped."

He was right. There was no longer that rhythmic bass thumping that had dominated all other sounds on the ferry. I would have stood longer, testing for vibrations, but Vern yanked my arm.

"C'mon," he repeated urgently.

I obeyed.

The *Crew Only* door led out onto the walkway that circled the observation deck. A thick rope, draped across the railing rather like the gentlemanly barricades one finds in banks, was the only indication that we were in a restricted area. Behind us, a ladder bolted to the wall led upward to the tiny bridge.

For the moment, the rain had stopped. I looked around. I could see why Alec had chosen this place as his vantage point. The beautiful, rolling Green Mountains lay dark and impassive in the distance while the inky waters of Lake Champlain lapped into high, foamy waves in the foreground. It seemed unlikely that the Professor's chronically shy monster would choose to make an appearance in this busy stretch of water, but if he did, Alec would surely spot him.

"The life jackets are over here," said Vern, pointing to a metal chest.

"Wait," I called to him. "Look down there." We had a bird's eye view of the action on the deck.

Vern joined me at the railing. "They've let down someone

with a raft," he told me. "Look, they've got something!"

A burly crewman was bending over the rail to receive a sodden, greenish-brown bundle, which he carried tenderly to an empty spot among the cars, out of our view. He laid his burden gently on the deck and, as he stood to bark some instruction to someone nearby, I stood on tiptoe to get a better look.

The crewman stood back and held out his hand to take a wadded piece of cloth which he shoved into his jacket pocket. It was an insignificant movement, over in two seconds, but my eyes had just enough time to catch a glimpse of a familiar maroon-and-olive green pattern. It was my scarf.

My mind whirled. "Oh, dear God! Oh, no! Vern," I gasped, "that's Lily!"

I looked around for the fastest way to the lower deck. The only stairs I could see were crowded with passengers, eager to get to see what was happening. I looked down again and toyed with the idea of sliding under the railing and taking my chances on the eight-foot jump, when an alternative came to me.

With Vern close behind, I ducked under the rope and barged shamelessly through the crowd to the top of the tightly-packed staircase. Then I squeezed under the railing and made my descent on the outside, the toes of my high heels making contact with the narrow strip of steps that extended beyond the rails.

It was an outrageous thing to do, of course. Only a month ago, the same stunt performed at the high school had earned one of my students two weeks in detention. It was effective, though. Within seconds, I was on deck, hurrying toward the knot of people that surrounded Lily. Later, Vern told me everyone was shouting at me, but I didn't hear a thing as I desperately threaded in and out among the cars.

I was only a few cars away now.

"That's Lily Burns, isn't it?" I asked the white-jacketed young man who barred my way.

He nodded once, then held out his hand. "Stay back, ma'am, and let him work."

"Let who work?"

There was no answer. The crewman's attention seemed elsewhere, but when I attempted to squirm around him, huge hands gripped my shoulders and restrained me.

"He knows what he's doing, ma'am," he kept repeating. "We gotta stay back."

"He?" I stood on tiptoe and caught sight of a flash of shiny yellow. No one was talking now. The only sound was the whipping of the wind in my ears.

All at once, I heard a cough, then a retching sound. A happy collective murmur spread through the crowd. There was a smattering of applause. The crowd parted, and I stepped forward to see Lily's small, crumpled form stirring once more to life.

The one who had revived her sat back on his heels, scratched his scruffy head, and beamed at me.

It was Professor Alexander Alexander.

Chapter Seven

"It was Providence, dear lady," Alec insisted. "The poor mite was out there, flailing away desperately when I caught sight of her. I knew right away who it was. She must have just gone down for the third time, as it were, when the lads fetched her out." He waved away my gratitude and smiled down at the stretcher where Lily lay, shivering and unnaturally quiet.

"Gracious Providence," he repeated, rolling his *r*'s gently. "There's just no other explanation. I was tempted, remember, to remain in your pleasant company, but something compelled me to go out at that moment and scan the waves." He shrugged and ran a knuckle under one eye. "Providence," he murmured again and ambled away.

It was just a few minutes to the Vermont side, where an ambulance was waiting. As I began to climb in the back with Lily, she crooked a trembling finger at me. I leaned close to her face.

"Don't look so worried. I'll be all right," she said hoarsely.

"You go on to the sale." Her hand, very cold and still a little damp, patted mine.

"No, Lily! I'm going with you." I pulled the blanket down at the end of the stretcher. One of her stockinged feet had been sticking out. I hoped it was just my imagination that it looked a bit blue.

"Nonsense!" she snapped, and my heart lifted a little to hear the spirit returning to her voice. "Come back up here where I can see you!"

I obeyed and her voice dropped to a raspy whisper. "You need to drive my car off that boat and I'm going to need a nightie. They're taking me to the hospital." She looked around her. "Where's my purse?" she wailed weakly and grabbed my arm. "Oh, no! It's at the bottom of the lake!" She tried to raise up on one elbow, but an attendant restrained her.

A long arm, bearing the bag in question, was thrust in the ambulance door. "I found it on the deck," said Vern. "Dry as a bone." He withdrew back into the crowd.

Flat on her back, Lily fumbled in the bag for her car keys and a credit card. She handed them to me and, clutching the bag to her breast, ordered, "Run along now." Her voice was gaining strength with use. "Come see me at the hospital in a little while once I've gotten cleaned up. And tell that tall kid thank you. Remember," she called as I backed out of the ambulance, "pale pink. Size eight, petite. Or small. Whichever they have—" The ambulance door slammed shut.

"Don't worry, ma'am, your friend'll be okay," the attendant assured me. "We see all kinds in this job, and this one's a keeper."

"Did they find her shoes?" I asked. "They're alligator and—"

"Sorry." He shrugged. "Must have come off in the lake." He climbed in the front seat and the ambulance pulled away.

Poor Lily. She loved those shoes.

Vern walked up to me, snapping his fingers impatiently. "Need the keys. We gotta get her car off the ferry. They can't load up for the return trip till we do."

I handed them over and he bounded away.

I found a bench near the ticket booth and waited, shivering, for Vern to return with the car.

Someone walked up and stood before me. "Miss Prentice, how is Mrs. Burns?"

I looked up at Sally Jennings. "She's going to be fine, we think."

"Oh, what a relief. I was just telling Steve—Mr. Tréchère, would you come over here?" She waved over her dark-haired companion from the ferry. "This is the lady I've been telling you about."

Steve Tréchère looked down at me where I sat, switched his cigarette to his left hand, and reached out to shake my right. His overcoat was draped jauntily over his shoulders and he wore a chunky diamond pinky ring and an expensive-looking watch. *Suave* was the word for Steve Tréchère. With his curly dark hair and chiseled cheekbones, he reminded me of an abbreviated Louis Jourdan.

Though he looked me straight in the eye, I sensed that his mind was somewhere else. "Good t'know you," he said, with a slight French-Canadian accent.

"Steve's from Montreal," Sally explained, "but he's got some business interests locally. I'm just introducing him around."

"Oh, ah, yes," I said. Then this was Sally's Very Eager Buyer. The Millionaire from Montreal. Sounded like an old Betty Grable movie. He was probably going to try to persuade me to sell my house.

I looked around helplessly. Where was Vern?

Tréchère glanced at his watch. He turned to Sally. "Look,

I'm afraid we gotta—" he began, just as she began to sympa-thize with me. "You've been through the mill, lately, haven't you, Amelia?"

Her solicitude caused me to touch my bandage. My head wasn't hurting, I noticed with relief.

Sally patted my shoulder. "First finding Marguerite LeBow like that and now this."

At the mention of Marguerite's name, Tréchère whirled back in my direction and fastened a piercing look on my face.

"What's this? Who'd you find?" he demanded, his dark brows tightening over his eyes.

"Just a local tragedy, Steve," Sally explained. "Drugs are a terrible curse in this country," she said and sighed. "I'm sure it must be better in Canada, right?"

"And you're the one who found this person?" Tréchère asked. His scowl was unnerving.

"No. Actually, I fell over her." I shuddered. "It was ter-rible. If you don't mind, I'd rather not—"

"Oh, of course, Amelia," Sally cut in. "We'll get back with you later. Steve? Are you ready to go? Our appointment at the bank is in fifteen minutes."

Tréchère continued to stare at me. I looked away, but as I did, I had a fleeting thought. The night of Marguerite's death, Lily had collided with a short, dark-haired man rushing out of the library. I hadn't gotten a very good look at him. I won-dered if Lily had.

"Steve?" Sally asked again.

"Eh? Ah, yes. Excuse us, please," he said to me, and his face relaxed. "It is very important, this appointment." He smiled, and the sense of menace faded immediately. He was charming, no doubt about it. And familiar, somehow. Prob-ably because I've seen him—or his taller, older brother—in the movies. As he backed away apologetically, I found myself wanting to tell him he was wonderful in *Gigi*.

I watched them climb into Sally's sportscar. Steve Tréchère was an attractive man, but if he was interested in buying my house, I wasn't anxious to meet him again soon.

Lily's car swung around the corner and halted with a jerk. "You ready, Amelia? Hop in!" Vern leaned out and opened the passenger door. "Where to, the hospital?" he asked as I complied.

"Not just yet. I need to go to JJ Peasemarsh first. It'll be a mob scene, but Lily needs a few things. I know the way."

"That's good. I don't know my way around this town all that well."

"Then why were you riding the ferry?"

He grinned. "To keep an eye on you. Boss's orders." He pulled out into traffic.

"Gil?" I wasn't really surprised. In fact, I was very pleased. "But you said you didn't see him."

Vern shrugged. "Forgive me. I fudged a little. He left me a note in the kitchen this morning. Said to look after you."

"And just why would I need looking after?"

"I didn't know at first, but now I do." He pushed his hair off his forehead. It fell back over his eyes immediately.

"You do what?"

Vern stopped for a red light. "I know that what happened to Lily wasn't any accident. And that you were the one supposed to fall overboard." He punctuated his words by poking my shoulder with a long forefinger.

"That's ridiculous!"

"Think about it. You were both wearing the same color raincoats. They look alike, you know."

"They are identical," I agreed.

"And you gave her your scarf. It must have looked like you climbed the stairs, then turned around and came back. And, no offense, Amelia—" The light turned green and he moved the car forward. "But one small middle-aged lady in a raincoat and *babushka* looks a lot like another one."

"I don't know, Vern. After all, the deck was wet, and Lily was wearing high heels. She could have—"

"Not with that high railing along the side, she couldn't've! Not without help. Okay, sure, if she was standing over by the chain at the bow, but—"

I gasped. "I was standing by that chain!"

"I know. I was watching you. In fact, I was so close, I could have pushed you overboard myself." He braked suddenly and rebuked another driver, "Easy, easy! There's room for everybody, buddy. Whew! This traffic's getting wild."

"But, Vern, it doesn't make sense. I don't know anyone who would want to hurt me. Or Lily, either."

"Gil thinks it has something to do with Marguerite. After all, Marie's disappeared, hasn't she?"

I hadn't an answer for that one. I kept picturing myself falling under the front of the moving ferryboat. If I were to be sucked into the wake of the propeller, even Alec couldn't revive what was left of me.

"Who was that you were talking to at the dock?" Vern asked. "He looked familiar."

"Ever see *Gigi*?"

"See who?"

"Never mind. His name's Steve Tréchère. The Millionaire from Montreal, so-called. Sally's been taking him all over town this week," I said. I explained what Lily had told me about the proposed plans for the houses on my street.

Vern seemed impressed. "Could be a good thing for the community," he said. "You going to take him up on it? It might mean a nice little hunk of cash. You could get yourself one of those cool condos over behind the Mall. Careful, lady," he warned, braking suddenly for an unwary pedestrian.

I explained to Vern in no uncertain terms what I thought of trading my ancestral home for a condo, however "cool" it might be. He held up a hand defensively. "Hey, it's none of my business. Gil *told* me you're a little obsessive on the subject."

"I have no doubt Gil told you a good deal about me," I said, bristling. "I suggest you reserve judgment until you know it all."

"Hey, I'm cool." Vern grinned at me. His ability to change moods on a dime could be irritating. "Y'know what I'm gonna do?"

"What's that?"

"I'm going to reserve judgment."

"Good."

"Until I know it all."

"Even better," I said dryly, watching for the next turn street. I tried not to smile.

All at once, a familiar figure in a green and yellow jacket emerged from one of the shops and began walking rapidly along the sidewalk, away from us.

I grabbed the steering wheel and pounded desperately on the horn with my left fist. "Vern! Stop the car! Turn around. It's Marie LeBow! Did you see her?"

At the sound of the horn, Marie glanced vaguely over her shoulder, but continued walking. In a few seconds, she would be out of sight.

Vern exploded with a brief, blasphemous phrase. "Don't ever do that again! You nearly killed us both!" He was shaking with anger.

"But it's Marie! I saw her over there!" I insisted, pointing to the spot where she had melted into the crowd. "Pull over! Do something! I've got to catch up with her!"

"In all this traffic? Are you out of your mind? All I can do is turn at the next corner and go around the block."

I agreed meekly. Vern was too angry to press further.

Traffic was as congested on the side street as on the main thoroughfare. Everyone, it seemed, had the same idea about shopping at JJ Peasemarsh.

We were fortunate that Vern had had some heavy-duty driving experience. Even so, it took at least five minutes and some aggressive merging to get around the block and approach the spot where I had last seen Marie.

"Look for a green and yellow parka," I instructed Vern, pointing. "She was headed that way."

Cruising along the street at five miles per hour, jammed in traffic, and scanning the ever-shifting crowd, we spotted perhaps six green jackets and at least four yellow ones. There were many other color combinations as well, but the only green and yellow coat we could find was on an infant in a stroller.

"Unless she's a master of disguise," Vern cracked, his good spirits returning, "I don't suppose that could be Marie."

We were nearing the JJ Peasemarsh parking lot. I sighed. "Come on, Vern, let me run my errand, and we'll head on over to the hospital."

Finding a parking space at JJ Peasemarsh was tricky at the best of times, but the Annual Giant Pre-Halloween Fall Bonanza Sale was always widely advertised and heavily attended.

"There's one!" I cried, pointing to a space just ahead.

"No, it's not," said Vern, "there's a car in it."

"But look, that woman's about to get in and drive away."

"You think so?" Vern put on the brakes and we waited for a harried-looking shopper to drop her burdens, paw through her purse for keys, load up, climb in, and back out of the much-coveted space.

"Come on, come on," Vern muttered.

Behind us, the logjam of increasingly irritated drivers moved forward as we turned in the empty spot. I could almost hear the grumbling behind the rolled-up windows.

As I emerged from Lily's car, I caught another glimpse of green and yellow through the front door of the store. I slammed the car door and set out briskly towards JJ Peasemarsh. As I did, it occurred to me that I was getting awfully tired of walking among parked cars.

"Hey! Wait up!" Vern called.

"I saw her again!" I said over my shoulder.

"Then don't lose her!" he called back.

Marie, if that's who it was, had disappeared into the store. I was two car rows away from the entrance, moving rapidly with Vern close on my heels, when a car door opened in front of us, effectively blocking our way. I stopped abruptly, and Vern slammed into my back, causing a mild contusion to my ankle and no doubt an irreparable hole in my hose, but there was no time and no room to examine the damage.

We were about to turn around and take an alternate route when a blue-gray head emerged from the driver's seat.

"Why, Amelia," said Judith Dee, smiling in her warm, grandmotherly way, "are you here for the sales, too?"

Vern snorted impatiently. I poked him with my elbow and greeted her in what Dad used to call Mother's Sunday Dinner Voice. "Hello, Judith. Yes, we are."

Judith stepped forward, lifted my bangs, and examined my bandage. "Any better?"

I smiled and nodded. "Getting there."

Suddenly, she grabbed my wrist and lowered her voice to a whisper. "Did you hear what happened to Lily Burns?"

"Yes, I did." I tried to rearrange my purse on my arm so she would let go, but her grip only tightened.

"There was a bulletin on the radio just now. How do you

think it happened?" Judith glanced over both shoulders. "I've heard she likes a drink now and then," she suggested. "Her father had that liver, you know."

"No way!" Vern said in outrage. "It wasn't even nine AM and all she had was a cup of coffee!"

Judith's hand went limp and slid, snakelike, off my arm. Her eyes widened as her attention shifted to Vern. "Were you *there?*"

"Er, um, well," he said. "You know? I've got a really important call to make. Excuse me. Catch you inside, Amelia." He loped away towards a phone booth in front of the building.

"Vern and I both happened to be on the ferryboat this morning, that's all. We didn't really see it happen." Which was true, as far as it went.

"Have you heard any more about what happened to poor Marguerite?" Her eyebrows knit together sadly.

I shrugged. "No. You know as much as I do."

"You taking good care of that wound?"

I laughed and waved vaguely at my head. "Trying to."

"Well, let me know if you need anything for pain."

"Sure will."

How on earth was I going to get away and continue my search for Marie? Should I enlist Judith's help? Right away, I discarded the idea. It would take up too much time in explanation, for one thing. And Lily wasn't the only one in town to enjoy a good gossip.

I began my departure speech. "Listen, Judith."

"I'm sorry, dear," she said, patting my arm. "I'm going to have to run along now. I've got a long shopping list." She patted her purse and walked away.

"What is this place, anyway?" Vern asked as I joined him at the front of the store. We joined the line at the entrance turnstiles.

"It started out as a factory outlet store for Peasemarsh Brothers of Boston. You know, the suit manufacturers?" I asked. I had to raise my voice over the din of the crowd.

Vern shrugged.

"It was before your time, I supppose. Well, they're out of the suit business now. Anyway, they started with just men's suits, but later began carrying seconds from all kinds of companies: work clothes, lingerie, even shoes and formals. At least half of the evening dresses at our high school prom come from here, though the girls would rather die than admit it.

"There's someone I know," I said, spotting determined-looking Hester Swanson in line several rows over. "I'll bet she knows where all the real bargains are." I waved.

She frowned in my direction, then smiled weakly.

"Don't remember where you've seen me before, do you?" I muttered. I turned back to Vern. "As I said, everybody comes to this sale!"

Vern worked his way through the turnstile ahead of me. "It's a mob scene, all right. What does this Marie look like again?" He stopped and scanned the crowd from a superior height, then stooped to hear my answer.

"You'd probably recognize her if you saw her. About my age, a little over five feet, curly black hair, round face. Rather pretty, but looks a little apologetic around the eyes."

"And a green and yellow jacket, I know. Hey, doesn't she work at the University cafeteria?"

"That's right."

"Well, I know her, then. Listen, you go get—" he waggled his fingers vaguely— "whatever for Mrs. Burns and I'll scope out the place. See ya!" He plunged into the milling crowd. I could see his head bobbing above the rest.

I sighed, hitched my purse a few inches up my shoulder,

and made my own dive into the mass of bargain-hungry humanity. The aisles between the racks of clothing were filled, but not yet jammed, and the usual sense of polite New England reticence among strangers still reigned, at least for the time being.

"Excuse me," said one woman whose arm jostled mine.

"I'm so sorry," said a man who had backed into me.

Later, things would be different. I knew this from hard experience. The last few hours before closing on Sale Day, the law of the jungle went into effect, and if one was determined to remain until that hour, I strongly recommended helmets and knee protectors.

In all the years JJ Peasemarsh had existed, its basic floor plan never changed: ladies' clothes to the left, men's to the right, shoes in the center. Sizes were numerically arranged, by racks, curtained fitting stalls stood along the right and left walls, and checkout counters were at the front and rear exits. A highly effective, time-tested system. Neat but not gaudy.

I made my way to the left on tiptoe, so absorbed in trying to spot Marie, I completely bypassed the rack of nightgowns in Lily's size. I had to turn around and retrace my steps.

"Excuse me. I'm so sorry." I was making the apologies this time as I made my way upstream back to the size eights.

"Hello, again!" Judith Dee called fleetingly as we passed each other in parallel rows of lingerie.

I smiled and made a great show of examining a piece of nearby merchandise, which turned out to be an extremely provocative brassiere.

"Hmmm. Purple with black tassels—it's so YOU," Vern said in my ear. "Sorry. No luck so far."

"I'll be finished here in a minute, Vern," I said. "Why don't you look over there at that row of stalls and see if she comes out of any of them."

"Will do." Vern saluted and was gone.

The selection of size eight nightgowns in any shade of pink had already dwindled. I was forced to choose between a garish floral print that resembled something in a Tennessee Williams play and an old-fashioned, high-necked flannel number. I had just decided that Lily would rather be Blanche DuBois than Laura Ingalls when Vern interrupted me once more.

"Come on! I found her! She's over here! Hurry!"

Vern plunged ahead, moving so rapidly that I was hard-pressed to keep up. In desperation, I parted hangers, plunged directly through a rack of designer jeans, and popped up in the middle of a French-speaking family group.

"*Excusez-moi,*" I said, backing into a bin of garter belts and nearly falling in.

Vern reached out a hand and steadied me. "Look!" he said, pointing to a curtained stall. "Isn't that her jacket—on the floor?"

I could see what he meant. The sleeve of a familiar green and yellow parka poked out from just beneath the hem of the stall's curtain.

"Well, what do we do now?" Vern whispered.

I stepped forward. "Marie?" I called softly. "Marie LeBow?"

A dozen faces turned my way, and several heads popped curiously from behind other curtains, but there was no answer from inside the stall.

I leaned closer to the curtain and called again, "Marie? It's Amelia. Are you in there?"

Still no answer, though the curtains twitched slightly and the telltale sleeve disappeared from the floor.

Vern and I looked at one another. He shrugged.

"Marie, yesterday you wanted to talk to me," I whispered into the curtain. "Won't you come out?"

Still no response. I frowned at Vern. If it wasn't Marie in there, surely the occupant would have poked her head out to correct my mistake. We were stymied. People were staring at us suspiciously.

Vern pulled my arm.

I retreated, but only for the moment.

"It's not her," Vern whispered to me behind a tall rack of feather-trimmed peignoirs, his eyes still glued to the curtain in question.

"She."

"Huh?" he asked, his eyes still on the stall.

"'It's not she.' Your grammar—oh, forget it. That's Marie in there, Vern! I can feel it."

"Well, whoever it is hasn't come out yet." He stifled a sneeze. "Drat these feathers! I haven't taken my eyes off that curtain for a second."

"What can we do?" I whispered desperately. "We can't just barge in there!"

"I know! We'll do a stakeout!"

"You mean, like the police?"

"Sure! We'll wait her out. You stand over there, and—omigosh! She just flew the coop!"

Vern sprang forward in hot pursuit. As best I could, I followed his blond head through the crowd until it abruptly disappeared.

Where was he? Had he caught up with Marie, I wondered as I shouldered my way through the crowd. How could we detain her once we found her? After all, she wasn't a fugitive, and, stakeout or not, we definitely weren't the police.

Several rows ahead, there was a strangled cry and a muffled crash.

Just beyond a rack of terrycloth bathrobes, Vern's long form was stretched out on the floor.

"Should I call 911?" a man in the crowd asked.

"No, thanks," Vern said, slowly rising to all fours. "I'm okay. Just tripped, is all. Ouch!" He rolled over and winced at his bloody left knee.

He looked up at me balefully. "I'm sorry, Amelia. She's gone. I lost her."

Some minutes later, as I pulled Lily's car out of the parking lot, heading to the hospital, Vern speculated on what caused his downfall. "It was probably one of those hanger things. My feet seemed to get all tangled up, and boom!" He groaned with pain as he shifted in the bucket seat. "Look at that. What a mess!" The torn, bloodstained denim material had been cut away from his wound, leaving a large hole in one leg of his pants.

I reached for my purse. "Don't you want a pain pill? That's what Judith suggested." Fortunately for us, Nurse Dee had materialized from behind a bin of men's sweater vests and applied her medical knowledge and a stout bandage to Vern's knee.

"Nope. Even aspirin makes me sleepy. I hate that. I'll just tough it out." He lifted his knee to a more comfortable position with both hands. "What really gets me is we lost Marie. It really was her. I saw her!" He punched the dashboard in disgust.

"It's all right, Vern. Obviously, she didn't want to see me, after all. I can respect that. Marie's just lost her daughter. She's entitled to act a little strange. Now that I know that she's all right, I can let it go."

Vern smiled. "Well, anyway, they gave you that nightgown thing and I got a free pair of jeans."

"It was nice of the Peasemarsh people, wasn't it? I suppose they're just hoping we don't sue them. You're not badly hurt, are you?"

"Naw," he said jauntily. "It's just a little scratch. My knee's a lot tougher than your head. Look, I wish you'd let me take over. You drive like Mr. Magoo."

"And just what is that supposed to mean?"

He hunched his back. "Well, you kind of lean over the wheel like this, see? And squint at the traffic. And you're only going about—" he tilted his head to regard the speedometer—"twenty-eight? C'mon, Amelia, pull over. At this rate, it'll be midnight before we get there. My driving leg's okay, see?" he said, lifting a huge sneakered foot and waving it over the dashboard for my inspection. He was limber, that was for sure.

"But I know the way," I began to protest. "Oh, for heaven's sake, all right!" I said, pulling into the parking lot of a fast food restaurant. "All this griping has given me a dreadful headache," I added unfairly.

My feelings were hurt. "I've never even had a ticket," I muttered under my breath and opened the car door. "Wonder if you can say the same."

"Welcome aboard," Vern chirped as I marched around the car and he slid gingerly behind the wheel. "Make sure your seat belt is fastened, and thank you for choosing Vern Airlines."

"Oh, shut up." He wasn't going to jolly me into a good mood this time.

Once inside the passenger seat, I grabbed the door handle to give it a vigorous slam, but someone stepped in the way. Someone in a green and yellow parka. A pale, round face with an apologetic expression appeared at my right shoulder, and Marie LeBow asked in a hesitant voice, "Miss Prentice, can I talk to you?"

Chapter Eight

Marie was apologetic about the scene at JJ Peasemarsh. "But you scared me to death, y'know?"

She was sitting with us in a booth at the fast food restaurant, holding with both hands the hot chocolate Vern had bought her. She sipped it hesitantly, as though we would ask for it back at any moment. She had declined the offer of a sandwich, but Vern and I, realizing we had missed lunch, were sampling the place's highly touted hamburgers.

"I mean, when I left yesterday, they told me not to talk to anybody, especially not you, Miss Prentice." She nodded in my direction. "They—well, it was Dennis O'Brien, really— he seemed a little mad when I told him I'd called you. Told me to spend some time over here at my sister's. Wouldn't even let me take my car. Maybe he thinks somebody wants to get me, I don't know. We did have a couple of hangups on the telephone since I been here. Was that you?"

"No, of course not, Marie. I didn't know where you were

until just now."

"That's what I thought, but Dennis was real strong on me not talking to anybody. So when you started saying my name in the store like that, well, I just didn't know what to do!" She bowed her head over the chocolate and allowed herself another small sip.

Thus fortified, she continued, "So after I left the store, I started feeling bad about running away."

She looked directly into my eyes. "This 'not talking to you' stuff, that's crazy. You were always so nice to my girl, so I just made up my mind. I know there's no harm in you, Miss Prentice—"

"Please call me Amelia."

"I mean, Amelia—and if the police don't like it, well, too bad!" She set down her cup firmly, splashing a few drops on the table. A dark curl fell down over one eye, and she pushed it back angrily. "It's still a free country!"

She pulled a paper napkin from a dispenser and mopped up the spill. "I was supposed to stay out at the farm with my sister Valerie, but then I remembered the Peasemarsh sale was today. I never miss that sale, y'know," she told Vern. "I go every year. So Val drove me into town this morning. After she gets through paying bills and doing some grocery shopping, she's supposed to meet me here."

"Mrs. LeBow, what did you want to see Amelia about?" Vern asked abruptly. "Does it have to do with Marguerite?"

Marie took in a sharp breath and looked at him. Her dark eyes filled with tears.

"Maybe it hasn't sank in yet. I for—forget, sometimes, you know?" she said in a wobbly voice. "Then, all of a sudden, something reminds me. It hurts a lot. A whole lot."

She filled her lungs deeply several times, then wiped her eyes with a napkin. "Okay. I'm okay now," she said firmly.

She turned her attention to me. "Marguerite had this book for you. It was like a diary or something, tied shut with a ribbon and everything. She said you got her started writing in it."

"A journal," I said unsteadily. "I have all the seniors keep one for a month. You mean she still wrote in it?"

"That's right. Of course, I never bothered it 'cause it was private." Marie pulled out another paper napkin and began pleating it as she spoke. "But yesterday morning, I was going through her stuff for—for—" She broke down, sobbing into the napkin.

I slid into the seat on her side of the booth and wrapped my arms around Marie.

For several minutes, none of us said a word. Then, all at once, Marie's courage returned to her. With impressive resolution, Marie pulled herself gently from my embrace with a faint smile, cleaned up her face, and continued the story.

"I was hunting for a little daisy ring of hers. It was the only thing she had from her father. Just a little tiny opal thing shaped like a flower," she said, framing an imaginary ring on her finger. "That's what he called her. *Marguerite's* French for daisy, you know. It wasn't expensive or anything, but, oh, it mighta been one of those Elizabeth Taylor rings, she thought so much of it."

She blew her nose and added, "To tell the truth, her father—Étienne, his name was—wasn't all that much to write home about, y'know?"

Vern squirmed in his seat. I recognized the symptoms: male discomfort at female confidences. "Excuse me, I'm going to get a refill on my drink. Anybody want anything?"

Marie gave him her empty cup to refill. He slid out and took his place in line at the counter, limping slightly.

"Oh, Étienne was handsome, y'know, and real romantic.

All '*Marie cherie*' this and 'darling' that, let me tell you! I loved him a lot, and he loved me back, he really did, but after a year of bills and then the dirty diapers, I guess he couldn't take it any more." She shrugged apologetically.

"I wake up one morning and he's gone. Never seen him again, and good riddance. But I always made sure my girl knew her daddy had loved her. He didn't leave me much, but at least I got Marguerite out of it." She stopped speaking abruptly and looked at me, the painful realization returning.

With what must have been an incredible feat of will, Marie squeezed her eyes closed for a moment and went on with her explanation, nodding with determination.

"Anyway, what I'm trying to say is, I found the ring in her dresser drawer and with it was this diary thing. I knew right away what to do with it, because Marguerite told me, 'If anything happens to me, I want Miss Prentice to have it.' I says, 'What d'you mean? Nothing's gonna happen to you.' But she says, 'You never know, Mom,' and I guess she was right. Anyway, you were real important to her, Miss Prentice."

She smiled, a wide, sparkling smile, her eyes bright with tears. Marie had been beautiful once, and there were times when she was still.

My barely-eaten hamburger had long since become stone cold. I wrapped it up with shaking fingers. "Marie, I am honored to receive it."

"But you can't have it!" Marie said.

"Can't have what?" Vern asked, returning with the drinks.

"The book," said Marie, looking back and forth between us. "Not yet, anyways. I mailed it to you this morning. It should get there in a day or two."

It was silly of me, but I was deeply disappointed. "That will be fine," I said, then remembered something. "Marie, what did you mean by those letters you mentioned? UDJ?"

"Oh, them. That's nothing. Just something Marguerite wrote on the telephone message pad. Your name was there, too. That's why I asked." She waved away the question. "She was always talking on that phone. Anyway," she added, taking a big swig of her cocoa, "I decided. I'm going back tomorrow, police or no police. Miss, um, Amelia, what's going on with that Dennis O'Brien? He seems awful mad at you. Did you have a fight or something?"

I shook my head. "Honestly, Marie, I have no idea."

Marie said, "Well, I'm going home whether he likes it or not. I got lots of things to see to, and it's not making me feel any better by sitting over here, stewing and hiding out. Val'll drive me home. The funeral's on Tuesday. Can you come?"

I took Marie's hand. "Of course I can."

When she arrived, Marie's older sister Valerie turned out to be a stout, no-nonsense woman who regarded Vern and me with undisguised suspicion. She took in Marie's puffy eyes and glared at us accusingly.

"You're not supposed to see anybody from home," she scolded in French as Marie gathered up her purse and her parcels.

"*Mais c'est important,*" Marie began to protest, but Val was brooking no argument.

"*On y va*! Let's go!" she said sharply and, suiting her action to her words, hurried her sister to the battered van in the parking lot.

Marie waved to me from the window.

"Is she going to be all right?" Vern asked as they pulled away.

I sighed. "She's had it hard her whole life. She's a survivor. At least, I hope so."

"Well!" Vern took a last, loud pull on the straw in his soft drink. "Now that we've consumed this sumptuous repast, shall we hie ourselves to yon hospital?"

"Vern," I said.

"What? Too much?"

I patted him on the back. "Just a little, but I love you for it. Come on, let's go."

Chapter Nine

"Aren't you hungry?" Vern asked as we headed down a hall to Lily's hospital room. "You hardly ate a bite of your burger."

"Not really." Just the thought of that greasy thing made me feel sick, especially now, surrounded by medicinal smells.

"You sure? I could use a little something, myself."

A nurse frowned at us.

"Shh! Remember where you are. How could you think about food now?" I whispered crossly.

The corridor leading to Lily's room was a long one, and each open door framed a human tragedy. In one room, an oxygen tank was connected by tube to a mask covering a pale face. In another, a woman leaned solicitously over the bed, gently stroking a trembling hand. Each successive patient's plight seemed graver than the last. I felt oddly reverent.

As we neared Lily's room, we saw two men standing just outside, bowing their heads as people will when speaking in hushed tones. Gil and Alec.

The sight of Gil Dickensen as he looked up and smiled at me caused another lurch in my chest. Well, if I was having a heart attack, this was the place to have it.

Gil wore a sailing-style windbreaker over a polo shirt in blocks of primary color, identifying it as the latest style in casual menswear. I didn't know when he'd abandoned his signature dirt-brown corduroy jacket with leather on the elbows, but I liked the change.

Whoa, now, Amelia, I told myself. This is just adolescent-style infatuation. You've had the symptoms before. You dealt with them then, and you'll deal with them now.

I smiled at Alec. The Professor was looking almost dapper in a plaid sport coat, his hair partially slicked down and his beard combed. He carried a gift-wrapped parcel, which he was showing to Vern, who nodded and smiled.

Gil stepped forward, gently grasped my elbow, and pulled me aside. "Are you all right?"

"Fine, thank you. What are you doing here?"

"Vern called me from Peasemarsh. I took the ferry over right away, on official business, of course. Assigned myself to the story. What happened to the kid?" he asked, pointing at Vern's knee. I explained.

Gil looked hard at me. "Are you sure *you're* okay? The head and everything?"

"Don't worry about it," I said briskly. "Your nephew has done an admirable job of protecting me. Only he was protecting the wrong person."

"Not necessarily. Look, you want some coffee?"

I hesitated, looking down at the Peasemarsh shopping bag I carried. "I need to see Lily."

"You can't."

I gasped. "She's not—"

Gil guffawed so loudly and suddenly it caused hospital

traffic to pause for a split second and frown at our little group. Chastened only slightly, Gil leaned over and growled in my ear, "Mrs. Lily Burns is under a self-imposed quarantine, having to do, reliable sources tell me, with the state of her appearance. Even as we speak, a terrified little hospital volunteer is on the telephone trying to find a hairdresser who makes housecalls. Film at eleven."

"Whew! I better get in there!"

"Not till the doctors get through. They brought in a bunch of interns to study her. She's the center of attention, probably having a wonderful time. While we're waiting, how about that coffee?"

I followed Gil to a waiting room at the end of the hall. It was newly remodeled, clearly with an eye to the soothing quality of dusty-toned pastels. Soft, misty prints graced the walls, and a silk flower arrangement shared the coffee table with an assortment of ragged magazines. The only jarring note was the metal rolling table bearing a large electric coffee maker and a stack of Styrofoam cups.

Gil poured himself a cup of black liquid. It looked a bit thick for coffee.

"So you haven't seen her yet?" I asked.

"Nope. Had to rely on an informed source—the aforementioned volunteer. Want some?" he said, gesturing with the pot in his hand.

"Is it any good?"

"It tastes like battery acid. Just the way I like it. Mmm." He took a loud sip.

"And you take it black, of course?"

He replaced the pot on the burner and grinned. "You remembered. I'm touched." He gestured around the room. "Besides, do you see cream and sugar anywhere?"

"Guess I'll pass, then," I said and settled down on a sur-

prisingly firm settee. The pale violet linen-textured fabric, I
learned, was actually plastic. Padded with cast iron, I surmised,
and shifted my weight uncomfortably.

Gil shoved aside the silk flowers and a pile of *People* magazines and perched on the edge of the coffee table, almost knee
to knee with me.

"You look all right," he said, studying my face.

"So do you."

"No, I mean after all this." He jerked a thumb in the direction of Lily's room.

"Oh, you mean the...accident," I said deliberately and
waited for Gil to contradict me.

He didn't. "Yes. Tell me how it happened." He pulled a
pad and pencil from his pocket and leaned forward attentively.

So I told him, in no small detail, including the hunt for
Marie and Vern's fall. As he had been the night before, Gil was
a rapt and satisfying listener, hanging on my every word and
interrupting only to clarify a point of interest.

"Then Marie's sister came and picked her up," I concluded
and sat back, waiting for his reaction.

He tucked the pen and pencil back in his jacket pocket.
He had only used it once or twice. Apparently a good memory
is a vital tool for a reporter.

"It's quite a story," he said, reaching for his coffee cup.

"'Quite a story?' Is that all you have to say?"

"What do you mean?" He took a sip of coffee and grimaced. "Gechh. Cold."

"No speculation? No conspiracy theory? No fiendish vil-
lains lurking in the corner? Who was Vern supposed to pro-
tect me from, then?"

Gil set down his coffee hard, spilling some. He muttered
an oath as he tried to mop his pants leg with a handkerchief.
"That kid should learn to keep his mouth shut."

"Oh, *chill*," I said casually. I had heard a student use the expression and mentally filed it away for just such an occasion. "Together, Vern and I have survived the annual sale at JJ Peasemarsh. We have no secrets from one another," I said. "Besides, why shouldn't I know if I'm in some kind of danger?"

"Because it wasn't necessary. I'm not sure of anything yet. No use getting you all upset over nothing."

I sat back luxuriously, linking my hands behind my head. "Do I look upset?"

Gil smiled. "A little around the eyes."

I sat up straight. "Well, it's only because I hate being left out of something that directly affects me."

"All right, all right. But I can only tell you what I've been able to confirm."

"Commendable journalist's ethics."

He slapped his knee in irritation and stood up. "Are you going to let me tell you?"

"Sorry."

He picked up his half-filled coffee cup and gently lowered it into a nearby trash can. "The police think Marguerite LeBow was murdered."

"That's no surprise."

Gil held up an index finger. "But this is." He came over and sat next to me on the couch. "Guess who was at the top of the list of suspects?" He folded his arms over his chest and leaned back. "Or is it 'guess whom?'"

"You were right the first time," I said absently. "But tell me, please. I'm no good at guessing."

He swung his arm up and around my shoulders. "Let me put it this way: I now understand why O'Brien hustled his kid out of your house yesterday."

For some time, I sat staring at the opposite wall, thinking.

Suddenly, I jumped. "Gil! You mean *me?* The police suspect *me?*"

"Bingo."

"But that's impossible! Dennis O'Brien has known me for twenty years!"

Gil shook his head. "It won't wash. The neighbors probably said the same thing about cute little Teddy Bundy. But don't blame O'Brien. He was in hot water because of that very thing."

"Because of me?"

"According to my source, who has reason to know, O'Brien went ballistic when someone wanted to put your name on the short list. He stood up for you and got it in the neck for his trouble."

"What happened?"

"Somebody said he'd been treating you with kid gloves from the word go and maybe he didn't have enough objectivity. Suggested he be taken off the case. O'Brien managed to contain the problem, but—"

"—then he found me babysitting his daughter, which would *prove* he was partial to me! Oh, poor Dennis. No wonder he overreacted!"

"It might mean getting passed over for promotion—or worse," Gil agreed.

"But I don't understand why they suspect me in the first place."

Gil shrugged. "That I couldn't find out for sure, but I can guess. One: you were at the scene of the crime, so to speak. Two: you did help Marguerite get that job at the library."

"Gil, I felt sorry for the girl. I've done that sort of thing for dozens of my students."

"There's one more thing. My sources are sketchy on this, but the word is, Marguerite had been in touch with the police recently."

"'In touch?' What does that mean?"

"Remember, I got this off the record." Gil glanced over his shoulder guiltily. "Seems Marguerite offered to go undercover for the police. Become a 'narc.' She used that very term."

"Oh, Gil, they didn't—"

"No, no, of course not. They took her statement, which was pretty incoherent, thanked her kindly, and held the door open politely. She didn't take it well. She left in tears."

"She must have been crushed!"

Gil shrugged. "Probably. You knew her better than I did."

"Oh, Gil, this whole thing just breaks my heart! And to add to it all, I'm a suspect."

"If I were you, I wouldn't worry about that." He stood and extended a hand, pulling me to my feet.

"Why on earth not?"

He handed me my purse and the Peasemarsh bag. "Because the bloodhounds have been called off. I saw your 'tail,' Officer Perkins, on the ferry heading back across the lake about a half-hour ago."

"So I've been cleared?"

"I think so. At least, I hope so." He wrapped his arms around me, purse, parcel, and all, and leaned forward. "I'd hate to think I was about to kiss a murderess."

To tell the truth, there was a part of me in total accordance with Gil's suggestion, but my sense of propriety was deeply offended. I wasn't in the habit of necking in public, no matter what the temptation. And I wasn't about to start at this late date. What if one of my students saw us?

"Cut it out, Gil," I said, ducking under his arms and backing away. "We're not a couple of randy teenagers."

"We're not?" He put one hand in his pocket and rubbed the back of his neck with the other. "No offense intended, I'm sure, Miss Prentice."

"None taken, Mr. Dickensen."

There was an uncomfortable silence.

Gil walked over and leaned out the door. "Well, it looks like the medicos are leaving Mrs. Burns's room. By all means, Miss P, step into the breach as you always do."

He moved aside and allowed me to pass.

Halfway down the hall, I had to fight an impulse to turn around, run back in the waiting room, and throw my arms around Gil's neck. But I didn't. A person has to keep her dignity.

Chapter Ten

Lily was sitting up in bed filing her nails as I entered. She didn't look up, so I stood silently for a moment, taking in the spectacle.

Her face was now innocent of all makeup, except for a gray smudge under each eye, and she was very pale indeed. She was clad in a faded, mud-colored hospital gown which exposed her upper arms, something Lily would have never allowed under normal circumstances. An intravenous tube led from the crook of one white, freckled arm to a bottle of clear liquid hanging at the head of the bed.

Saddest of all, the expensive coiffure she had so carefully guarded on the ferry ride was now a matted blonde bird's nest, tilting comically to one side. I had the impression I was gazing at the ruins of a burned-out house.

As if she had read my mind, Lily suddenly dropped her hands in her lap. "Are you *quite* through staring at the Wreck of the Hesperus?"

"I'm sorry," I said, stepping forward to embrace her.

"Ouch! Careful of this tube thing. I can't really blame you, though. I'm a horror, all right."

"Not at all," I said hastily, "It's just that I can't remember when I last saw you without makeup. You look—" I groped for a word— "younger."

"I look like *crap*," Lily said, vainly trying to smooth her hair, "but it's sweet of you to try to spare my feelings, which is more than I can say for a bunch of so-called doctors I just met." She held out a trembling hand. "Look at that! I'd kill for a cigarette right now. Amelia, would you do me a favor?"

"Sorry, I don't bootleg cancer sticks." I located her purse on the bedside table, dropped her keys and credit card inside, and closed it with a loud click.

"Don't worry, Elliot Ness, I wouldn't ask you to break any rules. Just go down the hall to the nurse's station and see if you can find a girl. Oh, Kimberly, there you are!"

A tall, buxom teenager in a gray, well-starched parody of a nurse's uniform slid sideways through the door. She tiptoed to Lily's bedside and cleared her throat uncertainly.

"Tiffany," said the girl.

Lily blinked rapidly. "What?"

"My name is *Tiffany*, Mrs. Burns."

Lily waved her hand. "Oh, yes, I knew it was something to do with jewelry. Well, how'd you do?"

"Well, um, I called five places." Her eyes shot to the ceiling as she counted on her fingers. "Four of them said they had too many customers already and one said it would be at least sixty-five dollars for a wash and set away from the shop. Want that one, or want me to call some more?" She twirled a curl nervously.

"Well—" Lily began.

"Never mind, Tiffany," I interrupted, patting her crisp,

gray shoulder. "I think I can handle things now."

Tiffany wasted no time. She flashed me a pathetically grateful smile and was gone.

Lily was indignant. "Why'd you go and do that? I needed that girl to—"

"You just need somebody to boss around. Why boss around a stranger, when you have me?"

Lily shot me a wounded glance. "That was uncalled for, Amelia."

"You're right. I'm sorry. What I meant was," I amended brightly, "why call a hairdresser and pay a fortune when I'll be happy to do it for free?"

The word *free* got her. "You're right!" Lily smiled for the first time since my arrival. "What have you got there?" she asked, pointing to the JJ Peasemarsh bag.

I showed her and happily took her eager criticism of my taste in lingerie as a sign of recovery. Getting her into the gown was no small task, and neither was washing her hair, but we managed with the help of a cooperative nurse who temporarily disconnected the IV.

"Is this really necessary?" Lily asked plaintively as the nurse plugged her in once more. "I thought they said I was going to be all right."

"You are, Mrs. Burns. This is just precautionary."

"Will you look at that!" Lily said to me as the door closed after the nurse. She held out her arm to show a large red bruise inside her elbow. "They made that looking for a vein! I look like a junkie or something."

"What do you know about junkies?" I asked, gently combing her damp hair.

"Not as much as you, obviously. I mean, you probably teach dozens of them, don't you?"

"No. At least, I don't think so. They're not all that easy to spot. It can be pretty subtle." I sectioned out a small piece of her hair, wound it into a curl and fastened it with a bobby pin I had fished from the bottom of Lily's purse.

"You mean, you can't tell when a kid is on drugs?"

"There are signs, of course." My answer was slightly garbled by the half-a-dozen bobby pins I held between my lips. "Dennis O'Brien gave a talk about it at the PTA," I added, wistfully remembering a happier, less suspicious time.

"Don't they have bruises?"

"Well, sometimes. But injection isn't the only way to take drugs." I finished another curl and anchored it with a pin.

"There are pills."

"Right. And alcohol."

"What?" Lily was surprised.

"It's a drug, too, you know."

"So now you're saying I'm a junkie just because I like an occasional cocktail."

"Of course not. Lily, we've run out of bobby pins here. I'll just run down to the gift shop and get some. Anything else you need?"

As it turned out, there was quite a list. "Don't lose my credit card," Lily instructed as I left. "And don't let anybody in here yet. I'm Typhoid Mary for at least another hour!"

I was writing the last item on the list when I encountered a large whistling obstacle smelling strongly of aftershave.

"How is poor Miss Lily?" asked Alec, breaking off his softly whistled rendition of "A Mighty Fortress Is Our God." "Can she take a bit of company now?" His voice held a trace of impatience as he anxiously fingered the gift box.

As briefly as possible, I explained Lily's schedule for receiving visitors and was surprised to see his face break into a wide grin.

"Excellent idea," he agreed heartily. "A most practical

woman, Miss Lily. Makes sense. She wants to look her best. We must admire a woman like that."

I nodded, puzzled. Lily had certainly afforded Alec little opportunity to appreciate her virtues, but perhaps all the exquisite care she took with her appearance had not gone unnoticed. I took another look at the well-scrubbed Alec. Sincerity shone from his eyes.

"Excuse me. I'm headed downstairs to the gift shop," I said.

"Miss Amelia, could you stand a companion? This hall lacks for entertainment and that waiting room isn't a very cheery place. Even the coffee is foul. Of course, I'm a tea man myself."

Was Gil still in there, I wondered. If he was, I hoped he hadn't taken out any irritation with me on the Professor.

"I'd enjoy your company, Alec."

"Perhaps I can find another newspaper. I've read yesterday's cover to cover," he said, opening his large sportcoat and showing me the inside pocket where an entire folded copy of the *Press Advertiser* had been crammed. "It was full of that poor girl's death, Marguerite LeBow. I knew her, you know, though I'm afraid she wasn't one of my admirers." He stood aside to allow me to enter the elevator.

"Really?" I was surprised. I'd have thought an imaginative girl like Marguerite would find Alec's quest incredibly appealing.

"G for Ground floor, I presume," he said, pressing the button. "Yes, she wrote me a letter not so very long ago. It wasn't a very nice letter, and it disturbed me deeply."

"Why would she write you?"

He shrugged. "Can't imagine, I assure you. I'd only met her once at a library function. She was extremely cordial then. Asked me any number of questions about m'work."

"Now that sounds like Marguerite."

"Several weeks later, I saw her slipping a letter in the slot in my office door, then slinking away like some thief. And when I read the letter, well, I was shocked, I can tell you. The rubbish she wrote in that thing!" His wild eyebrows came together and his eyes hardened. The gift package he was carrying crumpled in his grip and I began to feel just a little bit frightened of big, hairy Alec.

"I'm sure it was just one of those pranks the students like to play," I assured him hastily. "I've gotten dozens of silly notes. I could tell you—"

"Lies, they were!" he sputtered. "Libelous lies! The *terrible* things she said. And cowardly—wouldn't even sign her name! I tore it up on the spot! The thing was actionable! I might've sued if—well, if this tragedy hadn't happened." He wilted slightly, his outrage spent.

"It's so strange, Alec," I said. "So unlike Marguerite."

He scratched the top of his head. "I didn't really know the girl well, so I couldn't say, but if I'd had the chance, I'd've had it out with her, I was that angry. Ah, here we are."

The elevator doors opened.

Shrugging off his anger as quickly as he had donned it, the Professor made himself useful in the gift shop, consulting my list and scanning the shelves for Lily's two dozen vital toiletry items. Clucking sadly at the wildly inflated prices, he watched as I handed over her credit card.

"Miss Lily doesn't stint, that's a fact," he said, whistling over the exorbitant total. "But I like a woman who takes care of herself," he added. "I don't mind telling you, something in me turned over when I thought she might be dead. And when she once more drew breath, it was like the rainbow come out." He hefted the bag and we headed back toward the elevator.

"Well, she has you to thank for that, Alec," I said.

He shook his head vigorously. "No, it was Providence, as I said. And don't forget that gallant lad who fished her oot." It might have been my imagination, but his burr seemed more pronounced. "I was just thankful to play a small part."

Alec and Lily? Was it even possible? Curiouser and curiouser.

I left him in the hallway, whistling "In the Garden."

"About time!" Lily snapped as I entered. She clapped her hands impatiently. "Get in here and get to work! I feel like Quasimodo."

"Well, I guess that could make the Professor your Esmeralda," I put in wickedly. "That's the kind of weird pairing that's perfect for an afternoon talk show."

"What? You mean that refugee from *Brigadoon*? Is he out there?"

"Waiting patiently for the unveiling."

Lily groaned and rolled her eyes.

"Let's not keep your public waiting any longer, shall we?" I set to work finishing up the pincurls.

Lily began pawing through the bag of merchandise. "*Black* mascara? Didn't I specifically say brown?"

"Sorry, that's all they had." I shrugged and drove another bobby pin home. "Listen, Lily, I need to ask you a favor."

"Go on, I'm listening." She pulled out the deodorant and snorted. "Roll-on? Really, Amelia."

I decided to ignore her whining. "Are you going to be out of here any time soon? Or are they keeping you overnight?"

"Didn't I tell you? The doctor came in while you were gone and pronounced sentence. Said he didn't like the look of my blood pressure." She dumped the remainder of the products on her lap. "I told him to take a surprise dip in thirty-degree water and see what *his* blood pressure did." She held up a tiny tube of toothpaste. "Gel. Good. At least you got *that* right."

I was becoming impatient with her nit-picking. "So when do you get out of here? Did he say?"

She shrugged. "They're going to check me tomorrow—Heaven only knows what that means—and then decide. It may be a couple of days, he says."

I sighed. "Well, I have to teach Sunday School tomorrow. It's too late to ask someone to take my place. I need to borrow your car and get home tonight."

"Amelia, don't you get enough of those slimy adolescents during the week?"

"No," I said, "not at all." And with a flash of pleasure, I realized I meant it.

"What about you and the Boy Reporter? I thought the Happy Couple might take this opportunity to elope."

I scowled and put several more bobby pins in my mouth.

"So that's how it is, eh? A lover's quarrel?"

"Lily—may I take the car or not?" I finished the last of the pincurls and sat heavily in the bedside easy chair.

She reached in her purse and tossed me the keys. "Go ahead. Leave me in this hell-hole with escaped geezers pawing at my door."

I pocketed the keys. "That 'escaped geezer' may have just saved your life, you know. Give him a break."

"Yeah, right. You're trying to tell me that fat old man jumped in and fished me out?"

"Fat old man" struck me as exceedingly unkind.

"No, that was one of the deck hands, but Alec's the one who did the Boy Scout act." I paused for effect to let Lily's imagination take over.

"Boy Scout act?" Lily spread makeup base under her eyes and around her lips. "What do you mean?"

Lily's making up process was fascinating. Her techniques were not at all like Meaghan's. I was reminded of a recent

National Geographic special on the Japanese Kabuki theatre. "You know," I said casually, "got you breathing again."

Lily powdered her face vigorously, then paused to look at me over the top of her compact. "Was I *that* far gone?"

I had begun telling her the story in an attitude of mean-spirited fun, as a kind of payback for her crankiness, but the memory of Lily's poor wilted body lying on the deck brought me up short.

"Yes," I said, and shivered. "We thought you were dead for a minute there."

"So? What exactly did he do? The Professor, I mean," Lily went on, flicking mascara on her eyelashes with a short, jerky wrist motion.

"Just some first aid stuff, you know," I mumbled. I had lost the desire to bait her. "Look, it's getting late. Would you mind combing out your own hair?" I fished in my purse. "Here's your credit card. Got to get going."

"Wait a minute! Oh, no, you don't—" Lily said, dropping her mascara wand and grabbing for my wrist, which she missed. "You're going to explain that last. Come back here!"

"I'll call you tomorrow, Lily," I said, fumbling with my coat. "And I'll be back to get you when you're discharged."

"I want to know what exactly a Boy Scout *does*!" she called after me as I rushed through the door. "You don't mean mouth to mouth—" Her voice, which carried a panicky tone, was cut off when the door closed.

I patted Alec's arm. "Give her fifteen minutes and go right on in," I said and headed down the hall to the elevator.

She'd be in good hands. After all, he'd saved her life.

Chapter Eleven

It was quiet in the hallway. No one was at the nurse's station as I passed. I turned into the elevator alcove and pressed the down button.

"Miss Prentice," said a deep voice from just over my left shoulder. "I gotta talk to you."

I turned and looked up at my student, Derek Standish.

He frowned, and I noticed something that had never struck me before: he was a full head taller than I. He took a step closer, and I glanced around nervously for a nurse or orderly, but there was no one. "Derek! I'd heard you were sick. Are you all right?"

"Never mind that. Come on over here. I need to ask you something," he said, indicating the door marked "Stairs."

"I'm sorry," I said. "I'm in a hurry. Why don't we talk about it in school Monday."

The elevator doors opened and I stepped inside. "Goodbye," I said cheerily.

He followed.

"Look, Derek," I said, fumbling for the "Door Open" button. I pressed it and kept pressing, refusing the doors permission to close around me and leave me alone with great, big Derek Standish. "What is it you want? I'm busy, and I don't happen to have my gradebook with me."

He heaved a long sigh and muttered something under his breath. His arms hung straight at his sides, and his hands were knotted in huge, tight fists. As he thrust them abruptly into the pockets of his white windbreaker jacket, a tiny trickle of fear ran down my back.

This is ridiculous. It's just the Standish boy. I went to high school with his mother. I boss him around in school all day. What on earth is wrong with me? Still, I couldn't take my finger off the button.

Derek shifted his weight from foot to foot. He glanced uneasily out the door, then said, "Mrs. Burns. She's okay, right? I mean, she didn't drown or anything, right?"

"No, Derek, they say she's going to be fine. It's very nice of you to be con—"

"Listen, mistakes can happen, right?" Derek's eyes widened.

"Of course they can. Derek, why don't we go over this in school—"

He stared at his large sneakers. "Listen. I might'uv made a big mistake."

"What? What do you mean? If it's about your absences—"

He hit the wall with his fist. "It ain't—I mean—it's not that. I mean..." He trailed off and glanced over his shoulder into the still-empty hallway.

Down the hall, an amplified woman's voice informed a Dr. Merritt he had a telephone call on line C.

Abruptly, Derek turned back toward me and his expression darkened. "But then, maybe I *didn't* make a mistake. You see, I just don't know everything that's goin' on—not yet, anyways."

"Going on? Derek, I don't understand."

"Yeah, that's what *you* say." He leaned down, his face inches from mine. His bass voice cracked. I saw, to my amazement, that his eyes were filled with tears. "Just tell me this—"

"Are you going down?" someone asked. It was a nurse, pushing a woman in a wheelchair.

Derek whirled and ran, slamming through the stairwell door. I could hear his heavy sneakers thudding on the steps.

"Is everything all right?" the nurse asked.

I nodded, smiling weakly, and released the button.

By the time we reached the ground floor, I'd decided that my nervousness was sheer imagination. By the time I got to the hospital entrance, I'd resolved that, first thing Monday morning, I'd refer Derek to the school counselor. The boy was clearly troubled. I tried to remember his home situation and was ashamed to come up blank.

Poor Derek, I thought, remembering the tears in his eyes. The young are so vulnerable, no matter how big they grow.

"Amelia! Wait up!" It was Vern, sprinting in my direction, and Gil, sauntering in his wake with the amused air of someone out walking an exuberant pet.

A golden retriever, perhaps, I thought as Vern stood before me in the chilly evening, panting in steamy gusts, his blond hair flopping over his eyes. Or a sheepdog.

"How's the knee?" I asked.

"What? Oh, that! Just a little sore, is all. You should have come," he chided. "You missed Wink's!"

"I beg your pardon."

"Wink's Delicatessen," Gil informed me coolly, jerking

his head towards a storefront across the street. "You'll have to excuse Vern. He's never been there."

"Neither have I."

"Too bad." Gil shrugged. "I didn't think you'd be interested."

"You could be right. I'm probably not a deli sort of person."

"See there, Vern? Didn't I tell you she wouldn't want to come? Too many *randy teenagers*, perhaps." Gil glanced at his watch. "I've got a call to make. You coming?" He wheeled abruptly and headed toward the hospital.

"In a minute,"said Vern over his shoulder. He dropped his voice. "What did you say to him? He was like that all through dinner."

"I don't know that I had anything to do with it," I said vaguely, scanning the parking lot. "I have to get home tonight. Where'd you park Lily's car?"

"Come on, I'll show you." He strode forward quickly, and I was hard put to keep up. "See, over there," he said, indicating a short flight of stairs leading to a parking deck next to the hospital. "Tell you what—how about I ride shotgun? I'll just go tell Gil, and be right back."

"I don't need a nursemaid, Vern."

"Yeah, but maybe *I* do," he said, grinning, as he loped back towards the hospital. "Meet me at the entrance."

There were two ways to get home. One was to go back the way we came: on the ferryboat. The other was to circumnavigate the upper portion of the lake by car and bridge, a much longer, but dryer, process. This time, we would go home by land.

Dusk had already fallen, and despite a light bulb here and there doing its feeble best, the parking deck was dark. Lily's car was easy to spot—large, dark, and shiny, a four-door luxury sedan with all the options, lovingly purchased for her years ago by her husband. It bore a bumper sticker: "Shopping is my life."

The car was totally automatic: gear shift, radio antenna, seats as well as door locks that opened in a four-way stereo clunk as I turned the key. I slid in behind the wheel and took a few seconds to place my purse on the floorboard.

I was thus occupied, leaning at an angle over the passenger's seat, when I heard several fumbling thumps. Someone was trying to get into the car!

The locks! Hurry! I struggled to right myself, wrestling with a now-uncooperative steering wheel and shoulder harness, but just as my hand reached the automatic lock switch, the passenger door behind me swung open, letting in a draft of cold air and the intruder.

"Don't!" said a rough whisper as I craned my head to look behind me. Something cold pressed against my neck. "Start the car!" the voice ordered.

I had seen countless television programs about situations like this: a woman, abducted in a car, never to be seen alive again. I had long ago resolved that, should the situation arise, I would struggle, scream, wreck the car, do anything except passively drive away with a murderous stranger.

"Start...the...damn...car," the voice said steadily and the cold, metallic something jabbed hard into my neck with each word.

I did as I was told.

With trembling fingers, I turned the key in the ignition and the powerful engine sprang to life. I switched on the headlights. A light on the dashboard warned me the hand brake was on.

Where is it? I fumbled frantically. *It's left of the steering wheel in my car.* No luck. *Maybe there's a switch near the floor pedals.*

"I said, *get moving!*"

I could feel myself begin to hyperventilate. "I'm not familiar with this car."

"Do it!" The pressure on my neck increased.

I found the release just under the dashboard and pulled it, gasping with relief.

My knees were shaking so hard, it was all I could do to operate the accelerator, and we backed from the parking space with a violent jerk. I slammed on the brakes and the tires shrieked.

The pressure on my neck stopped momentarily, but returned, more urgent than ever. "Let's go!" said the voice. It sounded unnatural. He was trying to disguise it.

"L-look," I said as I continued backing out. "You've scared me. And I'm doing what you said. But I can't drive with that—thing in my neck. I might run us into a wall or something."

The pressure let up, but only a little.

Willing my arms and legs to work, I drove among the rows of parked cars—swearing to myself that if I lived through this, I would never go near anything automotive again—and hoping that somebody, anybody would see us. I might be able to communicate my plight. But I saw no one. Where were all the people who owned these cars?

"Turn here," said the voice as we neared a sign marking an exit.

Quickly I turned and realized—too late—that I had gone in the wrong direction. We were heading back into the parking deck.

The voice called me a shocking name.

"I'm—I'm sorry," I said. "I'm nervous. I've never been in this place before."

My body was shaking as violently as ever, but a cold, calm thought flashed into my head: *keep playing dumb.*

The parking deck was built in several levels, stacked in a spiral so that one could drive in circles, avoiding the exit chutes, until he reached the top, then spiral back down to street level. My plan, conceived in this instant, was to do just that, hoping to buy time to think of a better means of escape.

I accelerated and sped past another exit sign.

The voice growled an oath and the pressure on my neck tightened.

"Oh, no, did I miss it again?" I asked.

We continued to circle.

"You know," I observed, trying to sound reasonable, even friendly, "we're wasting time here. I could let you have my purse and my watch and you could get away right now. I'll even let you have the car—though it's not mine—"

"*That's* not what I want," the voice said.

I snapped my mouth shut. I didn't want to think about what he *did* want.

The voice continued, "I just want to know something."

"Kn-know what?" I passed another exit sign, but he didn't seem to notice.

He pressed his weapon into my neck so hard, I gagged. I couldn't drive like this.

As smoothly as possible, I applied the brake. The car rolled to a stop. I could feel the breath of my assailant in my ear, tickling. He had been drinking.

A hand came around my throat and tightened. The voice spoke slowly and deliberately. "I want to know—what's UDJ?"

"What?" I mouthed. Breath enough to speak was hard to come by.

"*You* know!"

"No," I said soundlessly, "I don't." A frantic laugh was bubbling within me. I stifled it.

My gaze flew about wildly. I tried to make out a face in

the rear-view mirror, but the headrest obscured my view.

"If you don't tell me, I'll kill you!"

"Please," I croaked, "I don't know what it means!"

Miraculously, the hand loosened and the cold weapon was withdrawn. In the corner of my eye, I caught a glimpse of white sleeve.

Throwing the automatic shift into park, I slumped in the seat, rubbing my neck and taking gulping breaths. My heart was beating visibly against my breast, or so it felt. I knew who it was, now, but dared not reveal the fact.

"You better not be lying," the voice warned me, "'cause if I find out different..." The voice, deep as it was, cracked.

The next moment, Derek Standish had thrown down the tire iron and was out the door and gone.

"What kept you?" Vern asked as he hopped in the car a few minutes later.

I had already decided to give myself a little time to think about what had just happened. "I'll tell you about it in a minute. I'm awfully tired. Would you mind driving?"

Vern was a good chauffeur. He didn't try to fill the time with useless conversation, which gave me a chance to think.

I was certain my assailant had been Derek Standish. He'd returned to finish our interrupted conversation, his anger fueled by alcohol. Those last few words, spoken in the cracking bass, along with the quick glimpse of his white jacket sleeve, had given him away. Pinning down who it was made me feel much better, because I couldn't believe Derek would have actually harmed me. However—I stroked the side of my bruised neck and remembered his last English paper, filled with gruesome, torturous executions—I could be wrong.

And that question: "What is UDJ?" The same one Marie

had asked me. She had dismissed it as trivial, but clearly it wasn't.

What *is* UDJ? I asked myself. Well, it indicated a connection of some sort between Marguerite and Derek. Could Derek have been responsible for Marguerite's death? *Of course not!* my heart said. *Maybe,* countered my head, which had begun to ache once more. I laid my head back, closed my eyes, and did my level best to think of nothing at all.

I remained that way until we had put a good deal of road behind us, then, my eyes still closed, I asked Vern, "What would you think the letters UDJ stood for?"

"Isn't that a Jewish ladies organization? Or maybe something to do with organized labor?"

I sat up straight and frowned at him. "I'm serious. Are you positive you've never heard of it before?"

Vern shrugged. "I don't think so. Where'd *you* hear it?"

Hesitantly, and keeping my suspicions about Derek to myself, I told Vern what had happened in the parking garage. He reacted exactly as I had feared, insisting that we turn around immediately and report the incident to the police. After considerable wrangling, I managed to persuade him to let me wait until I got home.

"Okay, Amelia, but only because you look so lousy. You need to get home."

"Thank you, I think," I said, peering at myself in one of Lily's deluxe lighted car mirrors. "Ugh! You're right."

It was well past nine o'clock when Vern pulled up in front of my house, but the motion-activated exterior lights were blazing away, front and back.

"Someone's there!"

"Stay here!" Vern ordered and sprang from the car.

I couldn't let him face the intruders alone, so despite a headache and a case of acute trepidation, I emerged from the car and did my best to follow where Vern's tall, striding form had disappeared behind Grandmother Prentice's lilac bushes.

Halfway across the front lawn, I heard voices and laughter—a woman's.

Then, Vern's deeper tones, questioning.

Another laugh, and Real Estate Saleswoman Extraordinaire Sally Jennings came strolling around the house on the old driveway, reduced over time to little more than a faint footpath, with Vern and Steve Tréchère in tow.

"—but we didn't mean to alarm you," Sally was saying. "We were just pacing out the lot. By the way, I don't like the look of those evergreens over there. They may be sick. Oh, hello, Miss Prentice," she said, deigning to take note of me. "You've met Mr. Tréchère, haven't you?"

"Of course. And this is my friend, Vern Thomas."

In the dim light, the two men shook hands amiably.

Sally put a hand on my arm. "Miss Prentice, we've been admiring your house. Mind if I show Steve around inside?"

"I'm sorry, Sally, but it's been a long day, and I'm not exactly up to company."

"We'll only be a—" Sally began, but was interrupted by Tréchère.

"Not at all. It's not necessary to bother this lady so late," he said, with that slight trace of French accent. "We will say good night now. Perhaps later." His dark eyes were level with mine.

"Thank you for understanding," I said. He was a charming man, and it was tempting to invite him in, if only to hear more of that smooth voice, but my head was sore, my neck hurt, and I was bone-weary.

He nodded and turned away.

To my surprise, the pair headed back behind the house. Vern and I were on the front porch, jiggling the key in the lock when Sally's red sports car roared around on the old driveway.

"Wha'd'ya know?" Vern said, "They parked around back. Think they were trying to break in?"

The front door jingled open at last. I shook my head. "Not in the criminal sense, no, but maybe just to look around. I wouldn't be a bit surprised if they hoped I'd forgotten to lock up. Sally's bound and determined to get me to sell this place." All at once, Sam appeared on the front porch, mewing. I laughed.

"What's the joke?"

"I was just picturing Sally trying to crawl through Sam's cat door. Say, Vern, are you hungry?" I asked. "Because all of a sudden, I am. I just remembered, I haven't had dinner. How about coming in for an omelet?"

I knew the answer before I asked the question, and within ten minutes I was measuring out instant coffee while Vern tended the eggs.

"I'm all out of the ground kind," I told him.

"Hey, the caffeine fix is the same," Vern said, grinning as he deftly slid an omelet onto a plate. "Here. This is yours. By the way, you're looking better."

"I feel better. I must be getting my second wind."

"I'm glad you took that bandage off. Your bump doesn't look as bad as I'd expected," he said, waving a finger at my head.

I leaned over and examined my reflection in the toaster. "Well, the swelling *has* gone down some and the wound seems to be healing. I wish the bruise wasn't so dark, though."

"Just pull your bangs down over your forehead," he suggested, gesturing clumsily.

I pulled down a few strands. "Like this?"

"Terrific! It's almost invisible!"

"Well and tactfully said, sir. You have now truly earned your dinner."

Minutes later, as he was mopping jelly from his plate with the last scrap of toast, Vern looked up suddenly. "That's it!"

"Finish chewing and say again—*what's* it?"

"I know where I've seen that guy before. That Steve guy. Omigosh!"

"Calm down. Where was it?"

"You know that Japanese restaurant on Montcalm? The dark one with all the booths?"

"The Mikado. Yes."

Vern took a gulp of coffee and continued. "Well, I was there Wednesday, picking up some takeout for Gil. I paid up front, then they sent me to the kitchen to pick it up, 'cause they were short-handed—"

"Go on," I urged impatiently.

"And I saw him—Tréchère—in one of the booths. But Amelia, he wasn't alone. He was with Marguerite LeBow!"

"Marguerite? What were they doing?"

"Having lunch, if I remember right," Vern said. "I didn't pay much attention at the time. I mean, live and let live, right? If a girl wants to have lunch with an old guy—hey—" he held up his hands defensively, "that's none of my business."

"Was it a date, do you think?"

"That's the way it looked to me. They seemed pretty chummy. Holding hands and stuff." Vern got up and spooned more instant coffee into his cup.

"This is so strange," I began thoughtfully. "Everybody seems to have a different image of Marguerite. Berghauser and Judith Dee think she was a junkie, Bert Swanson called her a Lolita, the Professor says she was a poison pen, and now this. And if things aren't confusing enough," I added, "it seems she tried to become a volunteer narc, if that's the right word for it." I explained what Gil had told me. "What do you think she was up to?"

Vern returned to the table with his coffee. "Well, judging by what happened to her—nothing good. But I can't help feeling that she was more of a flake than anything else—no, I mean it!" He shook off my disapproving look. "I think we ought to follow the money. Do you know anything else about this Tréchère dude?"

"Just what Sally's told me: he's a successful businessman from Quebec and he wants to invest in real estate here. The Millionaire from Montreal, she calls him."

"And how did he make his money? Drugs are lucrative. Amelia, what if Marguerite was blackmailing him or something?"

"I don't think—"

"And you said *I* was naive! Maybe Marguerite needed money for college. This guy looks pretty well fixed. He could have paid somebody to knock her off. It all fits!" He slapped the table decisively, rattling the crockery.

"I think he was in the library Thursday night," I agreed, righting the salt shaker.

Vern stood abruptly. "And I'll bet you Marcel's little yellow taxi the answer's in that stuff Marie mailed to you!"

"I forgot *that*!"

Together, we ran to the mailbox, a small wrought-iron container affixed to the house just right of the doorbell.

"It's a package, isn't it?" asked Vern impatiently as I groped for Saturday's mail. "Is there one in there?"

"No," I said, and sighed. "Just these." I held out a stack of envelopes. "Bills, mostly."

"Rats. Oh well, it'll come next week. Hey, look there," said Vern, pointing to a colorful envelope. "You may have won four million dollars!"

"I wish."

There was a snapping sound from the side of the house and the crunch of gravel.

"What's that?" Vern whispered. Before I could stop him, he tiptoed to the end of the porch and leaned around the railing. He looked back at me and shrugged.

"Probably nothing," he told me at the door. "It's too dark to see. Just keep your door locked."

I deposited the mail on the hall table and we trudged back to the kitchen, where I proceeded to prepare two more cups of coffee.

Vern and I talked until well past two AM, going over our theories about Marguerite's death and what part Steve Tréchère may have played. We also covered the topics of Lily's accident and the Professor's courtship before Vern remembered to scold me about what he called "the carjacking."

"It's too late to call the police now, Vern."

"The station is open all night—come on, now," he insisted, extending the telephone receiver toward me.

"But the man didn't steal anything," I protested, "and he didn't hurt me, really. He just wanted to ask a question."

Vern was adamant. "Doesn't matter. It's still a crime. Kidnapping or something. Here—call!"

I put the receiver back on the wall. "This is my business, Vern. I've got to do it my way. You're making me sorry I confided in you." And darned glad I didn't tell you who it was, I added silently.

Vern assumed an injured expression. "All right, I can't force you, but—"

"And don't you say a single word to your uncle about this, either!"

He smiled. "Now that," he said, "is *my* business. I make no promises." He stood. "Look, I gotta go—" He consulted his watch. "Ohmigosh, it's 2:30!"

I followed him to the door.

"I'll bring back Mrs. Burns's car tomorrow," he promised wearily as he left.

"*Please* don't mention you-know-what to Gil," I called out as he descended the steps. "He has nothing to do with this, and I won't have—"

Vern paused and turned around. "You're wrong." He came back up the steps, scowling intently. "He has *everything* to do with this. If anything happened to you, he'd be destroyed."

"Now, Vern, don't confuse a flirtation with—"

He returned to the doorway and stood, shaking his head. "Don't you get it, Amelia? Gil's not flirting. He's dead serious!"

"That's ridiculous."

"It's cold out here—can I come in and explain?"

Vern continued his filibuster in the entry hall. "Take a look at the evidence: Friday, he put a down payment on the Field house over on the lake shore. How long has he lived in that rathole apartment of his? Ten years? In a couple weeks, he's moving to a three-bedroom bungalow, *with* a white picket fence."

"I'm happy for him, but—"

"Wait, hear me out! Yesterday, in the space of one hour, he maxed out his charge card at Bailey Menswear. Haven't you noticed how he was dressed today?"

"Some people would call that midlife crisis," I said dryly.

"Yeah, but in just two days?"

"*Sudden* midlife crisis." I sat down heavily on a lower stairstep and yawned.

Vern joined me. "Okay, but what was he doing pricing diamond rings at Statler's?"

"The jewelry store next to Bailey's?"

"That's the one. Convenient, huh?"

"How did you learn about this shopping spree? Were you with him?"

"No, but I know a girl who works at Statler's. She called me this morning to find out what gives, so I checked it out. There were a half-dozen bags from Bailey's in his bedroom and I found the sales slip in his trash can."

I massaged my forehead. "Quite a detective, aren't you? And the house?"

"Oh, Gil told me about that."

"Well, did Gil tell you exactly why he was doing all this?"

"Not in so many words,"Vern admitted. "But it all adds up, doesn't it?"

"Maybe. I don't know." I was dead tired and becoming confused. I humored Vern out the door with a promise to think about what he'd said, then trudged up the steps to bed.

As I brushed my teeth, I glanced at the clock. Three AM. "I'll never get to sleep after the day I've had," I told Sam, who was already drowsing on the rug.

As is frequently the case, I was wrong.

Chapter Twelve

Sunday School went fairly well. The lesson was on Jesus' first miracle at the wedding at Cana, and the class entered eagerly into a discussion of its significance.

The girls, for their part, were generally agreed that the passage illustrated God's endorsement of marriage. Some of the boys, on the other hand, tried earnestly to assert that it demonstrated His approval of alcoholic beverages.

While conceding that people in the Bible did drink wine, I tried to point out the passages condemning drunkenness.

"Sometime soon, you may be offered alcohol—" I began my little impromptu sermonette.

"Try last night!" Gavin Porter said, snickering.

"Yeah!" chorused several other of the boys. Knowing grins were exchanged along the back row.

I sighed. Life was being thrust upon them earlier and earlier.

"You say you saw some drinking going on last night?"

"That's right, '*saw*,'" several agreed, establishing themselves as innocent bystanders, all the while poking one another with gleeful elbows. Many of the girls were giggling now, too.

"And the ones you 'saw' drinking—how did they act?"

"Stupid!" Gavin said with a snorting laugh.

"Beat a guy up!" a smaller boy said in awe.

"Then puked his guts out!" Another boy added to the hilarity. "Lucky it happened, or Bob'd be dead by now."

"No way—Bob's just a wimp," boasted Gavin. "I'm not afraid of Derek—" he broke off and looked wide-eyed at me.

I pretended not to notice. "Tell me something," I asked the boys who were now scowling reproachfully at one another. "Did this—drinking person—look handsome?"

Quizzical looks all around.

I continued. "Did he look attractive? Did he appear intelligent?"

Heads shaking.

"Do you think God would approve of the way he was acting?"

Light bulbs came on around the room.

"No, ma'am," said Janet Smythe, the class idealist.

"Can you see the difference between serving a little wine at a wedding and getting knee-walking drunk?"

Several involuntary barks of laughter, in surprise that I would use such an expression, then unanimous nods.

"Good." I looked at my watch. "It's almost time for church, so let's pray. Martin, would you please?"

The class broke up quietly, and I proceeded to wipe off the blackboard and collect the lesson books left on the seats. I was stacking them in the storage closet when several of the boys returned to the room.

"Great! There's doughnuts left!" one of them said.

"Hey, dork, what's with spilling your guts about the party

last night?" said another.

Clearly, they didn't know I was there.

"Don't worry, Miss P's cool, she won't tell," he answered, his voice muffled by doughnut. "Besides, we didn't say anything much. Gimme one of those chocolate ones."

I have learned from long experience that eavesdropping is sometimes a helpful tool, if used in moderation. I stood very still in the closet and listened.

"No way! You said Derek's name. He'll kill you for that!"

"No, he won't! He's all tore up about that girl that got killed. Said he's looking everywhere for who did it, even in Vermont! Said when he finds 'um, he's gonna kill 'um."

"He will, too!" piped a shaky tenor.

"Come on, hurry. Church is starting. My mom'll kill *me* if I'm late!"

More sounds of the wax paper sack rattling. Presumably, they were filling their pockets for the long ordeal of the eleven o'clock service.

I stood thinking for a while. Right after church, I resolved, I'd better call Dennis O'Brien.

The unexpected chance to gather information had thrown my carefully-timed Sunday morning schedule into disarray. Instead of walking briskly to the choir room, slipping into a robe, taking a few seconds to pat my hair and gather up my music, I was forced to hurry—in high heels—down a crowded hall choked with a cheerfully chattering congregation.

Halfway there, I had to restrain myself from pushing a sweet, white-haired senior citizen over her walker, but I managed, smiling all the way.

The choir room was reproachfully empty as I snatched my robe from its hanger and my music from its cubicle and dashed into the choir loft, panting. Everyone was polite as I slid past them to my seat in the alto section, but I earned a

tiny disapproving wrinkle of the brow from the choir direc-
tor. Raising his arms, he signaled the first chords of the opening anthem and I joined in, gratefully if breathlessly,

> *"All hail the power of Jesus' name,*
> *Let angels prostrate fall..."*

I sang from my heart, caught up in the magnificent thought
of all creation in joyous praise of God. The hymns, as much as
any sermon, always spoke to me in church. There were times
when the wisdom and truth of the words so moved me, I
would have to fight back tears.

The first congregational hymn was "Great Is Thy Faith-
fulness," my favorite. My heart soared. God was reassuring
me of His love, and that He had everything under control.
My gratitude to Him was overwhelming.

I felt the warning tickle of tears in my eyes and was reaching for the tissue I kept for emergencies in the front of my
hymnal when I glanced at the congregation. An usher was
escorting a latecomer down the aisle to a vacant spot on the
front pew.

It was Gil Dickensen.

Immediately, I dropped the tissue, but there was no need
to attempt the clumsy task of retrieving it, because my tears of
joy had dried up.

What's *he* doing here? I thought angrily.

Not in so many words, but by way of snide remark, sar-
castic comment, and glib editorial, Gil had long ago led me
and the entire community to believe he had no respect at all
for organized religion.

"Isn't that Gil Dickensen?" whispered Margery Berton
behind her choir folder. "What's *he* doing here?"

You could say that again. Probably just showing off his
new suit from Bailey's. It was navy blue and fit him well. It set

off his gray hair to good advantage, too. He did look nice, I had to admit.

Just then, his eye caught mine. He smiled. As I nodded coolly in return, the acrobat who had taken up residence in my chest did another double somersault. *Oh, no, you don't!* I told it.

With ostentatious care, I turned my attention to locating the music for the offertory special. It was an arrangement of "Sheep May Safely Graze and Pasture" from Bach's *Peasant Cantata*. Our choir was well-known for its quality, and I like to think we didn't disappoint that day.

Once again, I threw myself into the music, turning only the slightest of glances Gil-ward. No eye contact this time. He was staring at one of the stained glass windows, apparently lost in thought.

Not for one minute did I believe Vern's assessment of Gil's recent actions. I had known him, in one capacity or another, all his life, and a person didn't change overnight.

"*Sheep may safely graze and pasture,*" we sang.

And what about those kisses? They were meaningless, I told myself. It was all precisely as I suspected—a superficial flirtation.

"*...in a watchful shepherd's sight.*"

But hadn't he demonstrated his concern, sending Vern to watch over me and coming all the way to Burlington after Lily's accident?

He was simply using his reporter's instincts, I answered myself. As a suspect in Marguerite's murder, I'm a potential news story, no doubt about it. Vern's just one of his stringers, that's all.

"*Those who rule with wisdom guiding...*"

And what about his trip to Bailey's Menswear and acquisition of the Fields' admittedly charming house? It was just as I told Vern, an acute case of midlife crisis.

"...*bring to hearts a peace abiding...*"

And as for Statler's Jewelry Store—well, I was a bit too busy to think about it right now, thank you very much! I modulated my voice to the delicate ending of the piece.

"...*bless a land with hearts made free.*"

The final notes faded away and the choir sat slowly and reverently, tucking the song folders in the side receptacles and extracting Bibles in readiness for the Scripture reading.

I consulted the program for the sermon title: "Marriage— An Honorable Estate, Blessed by God." I made a point not to look in Gil's direction for the rest of the service.

After church, there was no way I was going to mill around in the midst of a neck-hugging, back-slapping crowd containing Gil Dickensen. I wasted no time pulling on my coat, then threading my way through the throng and onto the sidewalk.

I hurried. There were a few things I needed to do: call Lily as promised, find out if Marie had returned home yet, and try to locate Derek. Somewhere in there, I would also find time to prepare for Monday's classes.

If I was quick about it, I could also call Gil's apartment and catch Vern alone. He could bring Lily's car and, if he chose, accompany me on my errands. It would be especially good to have him along if I happened to find Derek.

Not that I believed for one moment the boy would intentionally hurt me, but I'd experienced first-hand how overwrought he could become, and after all, "the best-laid schemes o' mice and men gang aft agley," as Alec—or Robbie Burns— might say. Come to think of it, Alec knew something about extremes of emotion, too, I remembered.

"Wait a minute..." I stopped walking and looked around. I was standing on the corner of Jury and Elmore street, directly in front of Danny's Diner. I had been thinking so furiously, I'd overshot my house and ended up downtown.

I stood staring at the silver, lozenge-shaped building, watching steam rise from the exhaust chimney. It was cold out here and I could smell bacon frying. My stomach growled and my ever-present dull headache revved into overdrive again. Why not have a bite of lunch here? No reason at all.

As I opened the door, the strip of sleighbells attached to the doorknob jingled.

"Miss Prentice!" said Danny Dinardi, his bald head shining in the neon light. He was standing at the grill, pressing a hamburger with the back of his spatula. A row of bacon strips sizzled nearby. Just beyond, six perfectly browned slices of toast popped out of the toaster with a light metallic rattle.

The faces of the six patrons seated at the counter turned and smiled in unison. Danny waved his free hand expansively. "Come in and get warm! Shirley—pour the lady a cup of coffee. You here for lunch?"

"Soon as I make a couple of calls," I promised and headed for the pay phone on the wall. "It smells good in here. How about one of your famous BLT's?"

"Good choice! The best in the country!" he declared immodestly.

But he was right. "It's the tomatoes, you know," he explained, as he always did, to the admiring assembly. "I get 'em homegrown from a lady out in the country. This time of year, she keeps 'em wrapped in newspaper in her cellar." It was a familiar, oft-repeated story, varying only slightly with the seasons. I could have chanted it along with him.

I dialed Gil's number. "Come on! Come on!" I muttered, as the phone rang for the fifth time. "Gil'll be home any minute." On the next ring, I heard a click, then Gil's recorded voice, saying, "You have reached the—"

"What?" roared an outraged male voice, breaking into the

recording.

"Vern?" I ventured timidly.

"Amelia? Gosh, I'm sorry. You got me out of the shower. The furnace pooped out last night and it's c-colder than a— it's freezing in here. I didn't want to leave the hot water, but you kept ringing."

I explained my idea about Lily's car. "I'm at Danny's. If you come over right away, I'll treat you to lunch."

"I'm there! W-well, not exactly," he added, his chattering teeth clearly audible. "But just l-let me get out of this towel and into my parka. Tell Danny I want a chili cheeseburger!" he ordered and hung up.

I put more coins in the telephone and dialed Dennis O'Brien. He was out of his office. I told them I'd call back.

My sandwich and I arrived at our booth at the same time. I loved Danny's Diner! Bowing my head, I murmured a bliss-ful blessing, then carefully lifted half the sandwich and opened my mouth to receive the ambrosia.

"Amelia?"

A drop of tomato juice hit the front of my suit jacket at breast level. Reluctantly, I set down my sandwich and blotted the stain with a paper napkin.

"Hello, Judith," I said. "How are you?"

"Lovely. Didn't Pastor Broadhead give a lovely sermon? Apparently those nodules in his throat have healed completely." Nurse Dee was resplendent in a gray velvet toque and match-ing gray wool coat with velvet collar. Blue-gray eyes and gloves the exact shade of her hair completed the ensemble. Only the red patches on her cheeks broke up the monochromatic theme. "I thought he captured the essence of marriage, didn't you?"

I picked up another napkin and blotted again. "I'm afraid I wouldn't know..." I began.

"Oh, of course, I forgot—you've never married." Nurse

Dee, herself, was a widow. "May I sit down?"

I nodded, on my third napkin now, hoping against hope I could save my green wool suit. As it was, the stain would require the expert treatment of a dry cleaner, and even then, complete recovery would be iffy.

Oh well, I thought, crumpling the napkin. I've done all I can.

Nothing, neither Judith Dee nor an indelible tomato stain, would prevent me from enjoying my Danny's BLT.

"My, that looks good. I'll have the same, Shirley," Judith said, turning to the hovering waitress.

Danny's wife nodded impassively, replaced her pencil in her jeans pocket, and strolled away. It was common knowledge that Danny had all the personality in the family.

"Shirley Dinardi's an interesting woman," said Judith, leaning into the aisle and peering after the waitress. "Keeps all her emotions in, obviously. That's why she gets those shingles, of course." She clucked in pity.

It was a constant mystery to me where Judith got her medical information—her practice was limited to patching up public school students—and I had long wondered whether she didn't cross the line between simple, down-and-dirty gossip and a breach of professional ethics. Her information was usually reliable, I had to give her that. Maybe she was a good interviewer, like Gil. Or maybe she could just read minds.

She smiled at me. I squirmed inwardly and tried not to think of anything personal.

"Please, please," she said pleasantly, "enjoy your sandwich before it gets cold."

I relaxed.

Judith pulled off her gloves and eased her coat from her shoulders. Her dress was gray crepe, with a silver brooch on the collar. "Well, I see you got back from Vermont all right.

How is Mrs. Burns?"

My mouth was full, but I nodded and grunted to indicate that Lily was indeed still alive.

The sandwich was great.

The bacon was crisp and the tomatoes flavorful. Danny was generous with the mayonnaise on the gently toasted bread and the crisp Bibb lettuce added a definite, but not overbearing, textural counterbalance to the smoky flavor of the meat.

This was how a food critic from downstate had once described it, and though the review had convulsed the meat-and-potatoes crowd that made up Danny's clientele, he still displayed the framed magazine article proudly on his wall, next to a large crucifix and an autographed picture of Steve Allen.

"So she's better, then? I'm so glad."

With difficulty, I dragged my attention back to Judith Dee.

She leaned out in the aisle. "Shirley," she called, "bring me a hot chocolate with that, would you please?" She sat back in her seat and just as I took another bite, asked, "When will she be coming home?"

Chewing as rapidly as was ladylike, I shrugged wordlessly and bobbed my head from side to side.

It seemed to satisfy Judith. "I see." She reached across the table and lifted my bangs. "Your head looks much better. It's coming along nicely. Need any pain medication?"

I swallowed a gulp of Danny's wonderful coffee. A little too hot, but it helped clear the palate. In fact, it seared it. "No, thanks, Judith. A little Tylenol seems to do the trick." I reached in my purse, pulled out a tiny bottle, and tipped it on the table. Two tablets rolled out.

"Uh, oh. Looks like those are your last two. Here—" Judith rooted around in her handbag, which, of course, was gray leather. "I've got a couple of bottles of the hospital brand.

They're capsules, but you take two, just like the drugstore kind. Here. Go ahead, I've got plenty."

I swallowed my tablets, then tucked the bottle of Judith's capsules in my purse. She was so anxious to be of help, it seemed rude to refuse.

"Oh, good, here we are!" said Judith.

Unceremoniously, Shirley slid Judith's order on the table, following with the hot chocolate in a heavy cup with a chipped saucer. It was piping hot and there was a rapidly melting mountain of whipped cream on top. Nobody came to Danny's to admire the china, anyway.

The sleighbells on the door jangled. At the sight of Vern's tall frame, I called out to the taciturn Shirley, "We're going to need a chili cheeseburger over here."

Shirley nodded.

Vern stood looking down at me. "You forgot to order it, didn't you?" His hair was still damp.

"Yes. Sorry."

"Why, hello there!" Judith seemed delighted to see Vern. "Won't you join us?"

I moved over and Vern sat.

Shirley approached and stood, staring questioningly at Vern.

"What would you like to drink?" I translated.

"Chocolate milkshake," he told her.

I shivered. "Ice cream?"

Judith smiled indulgently. Between dainty bites of her sandwich and minute sips of cocoa, Judith inquired about the condition of Vern's leg.

He glanced down, having apparently forgotten the injury. "Uh, yeah, thanks. It's fine."

"It was miraculous the wound wasn't more serious. If you like, you can drop by my house and I can change the bandage for you."

"Uh. No, thanks. It's okay." Vern shrugged.

"Well, it's your choice, certainly, but you don't want it to become infected, do you?"

"No, I guess not. Maybe I'll come by later, if I have time."

"That will be fine. By the way, I'm a little curious," she ventured with a tiny smile. "Would you mind telling me just who or what it was you were chasing so hard at Peasemarsh?"

"I, uh, that is, we, thought we saw a friend of ours," he said and drummed on the table. He leaned into the aisle and said fretfully, "Where is that burger, anyhow?"

"Was it Marie LeBow?"

"Uh—" Vern glanced at me.

"Yes, that's right," I admitted. Obviously, Judith had heard me calling Marie's name outside the dressing rooms. "But he tripped before he could catch up with her, as you know."

Judith looked over each shoulder and leaned forward. "I heard she was terribly depressed over Marguerite's death."

"Well, actually—" Vern began.

I stepped on his foot with my high heel.

Vern made a tiny squeak in his throat, but got the message and clammed up. Judith had a way of worming the most personal information out of people. But not this time.

"Actually, it would be terribly strange if she weren't upset, don't you think?" I asked sadly. "Oh, look, Vern! Here's your burger."

With her usual grace, Shirley set the heavy plate before Vern and slapped a hand-scrawled pink check on the table, face down.

"Shirley..." I said. She turned around and stared. I held up the slip. "Could we have separate checks, please?"

Scowling, she snatched it from me and retired to re-figure what we owed. By the time she had returned with three slips and handed them around with the same quiet charm, Vern was finishing up, licking chili from his fingertips.

"Well," Judith said to me, retrieving her check and sliding out of the booth. "This has been so pleasant, Amelia. Let's do it again soon. And it was good to see you, too," she said to Vern as she pulled on her coat. "But don't forget to let me re-bandage that cut. President Coolidge's son neglected a wound," she said, her brows furrowing in concern, "and it killed him! Bye, now." She pulled her purse over her arm and headed down the aisle towards the exit.

"What's with *her*?" Vern asked as he slid out of the booth.

"That's just Judith," I told him. "She's a little eccentric, but she's harmless." I set a couple of dollars on the table for Shirley.

"And what's with the thing with stepping on my foot?" he said, lifting his large sneaker to show me the dirty imprint of my heel. "I bet that's what happened to Coolidge's son." He flexed his foot up and down and winced. "I'm going to have a bad bruise."

"I'm so sorry, Vern," I said. "It's just that I knew that if we told Judith anything about Marie, it would be all over town. You heard the woman."

"Well, I can see the Coolidge family has no secrets from her." Vern grinned.

"Here—hand me your check. I owe it to you, now."

"For an injury like this, I'd say you owed me dessert, too."

"Don't push your luck, buddy," I said and began to work my way down the now-crowded aisle to the cash register. "All right, how about some candy or gum or something? We've got lots to do this afternoon."

Vern settled for two Hershey bars, which he immediately consumed in the car. He also insisted on doing the driving, but I didn't mind. I needed to concentrate on the tasks at hand. "Head back to my house. I want to call Lily and Marie."

As we drove up my street, however, I changed my mind. "Go on, Vern. Don't stop. Go on, please."

"What's with you?" Vern asked, irritated. He glanced at my house and smiled. "Oh, *I* see. That's Gil's car. And there he is on the porch, ringing the doorbell, like a nice little newspaper editor. What did the poor guy do, anyway? Don't you *want* to become my Auntie Amelia?" Playfully, he laid his head on my shoulder, not an easy—or safe—thing to do while driving at thirty miles per hour.

"Sit up and behave yourself," I said sharply, trying not to laugh. "Can't we just be friends?"

"No!" he said with affected babyish petulance. "I want a commitment! I want stability. I want *an aunt!*"

I sighed. "Turn here. We'll run over to Marie's. I can call Lily from there, or what's a long distance card for? Really, Vern, you don't understand about Gil and me. We have a history and some of it is—"

"Then tell me. I can take it. I'm—" he glanced at his watch, "almost twenty-one. I read a lot. I've heard about looooove..." He moaned the word.

I had to laugh. "Cut it out!"

He settled back down and continued, "No, really. This thing has got Gil by the throat. He's hooked, you know. Okay, I know, I mixed a metaphor, but anyway, the whole time I've lived at his place—at least a couple months—he's been kind of, oh, I don't know, serious and well, sort of old. I mean, he's happy, he loves his work, don't get me wrong, but—when I came back to the apartment the other day and told him about this woman I'd met, well—"

At a stop light, Vern stretched his long arms and continued. "Mom told me about Gil's once being engaged. It was like a family legend. To hear her tell it, it was the romantic tragedy of the century."

"Carol was a dear friend," I said, nodding sadly.

"But nobody told me your *name*, see. Or maybe I didn't remember it," Vern said. "Anyway, I'd been ragging on Gil to find himself a woman. You know, just kidding around? And then the other day at lunch I told him about this really cute little teacher lady I drove in my cab."

"'Cute?' Is that what you called me?"

"Sure—it fits. Don't you think you're cute?"

"It never occurred to me. Go on."

"That was after I drove you the first time. And he says, 'I know her. We almost married once.' And I go, 'That's the one? Well, you were an idiot to let her go!'"

"Vern, you didn't."

"Sure, I did. Then, when I got the call to pick you up again a couple hours later, I knew it just had to be fate."

"Fate? Oh, Vern." I remembered. *Fate* and *small world* were words he had used.

I hadn't given them a second thought. After all, whoever heard of a matchmaking taxi driver?

"Anyway, after I drove you the second time, I stopped at the paper and talked to Gil some more. Finally, he goes, 'How do I make you shut up?' and I go, 'Get over to her place and give it one more chance and I'll never mention it again.' So he cleans up a little—you know, combs his hair and straightens his tie—and leaves."

"Just like that?"

"Sure. And when he got back that night—you kept him out a little bit late, you know—he was different. He didn't say much, but he was pumped!" He grinned sheepishly.

I wasn't sure what *pumped* meant, but judging by the context, it was something good. "Vern, I think you're reading a little too much into—"

"Hear me out, please. Next morning, he leaves me this note that says, 'Keep an eye out. Stick like glue.' He was worried about you after that thing with Marguerite. And sure enough...oops, here we are." He pulled up by the curb at Marie's house.

She was back, that was obvious. No longer was the leaf rake lying across the sidewalk, and the leaves themselves were gone from the lawn. Three large, neat black plastic lawn bags lined up on the curb gave evidence to where they were. Marie's small white sedan was parked in the same place as the other night. Behind it was her sister Valerie's battered but imposing maroon van, bearing Vermont license plates.

"She's back. Come on." I opened the car door.

Vern hesitated.

"Are you coming?" I said impatiently.

He emerged from the car, staring at me with an odd expression. "I don't think you heard *anything* I said." He slammed his door and leaned against it, arms folded.

"Vern," I said, coming around to his side. "Of course I heard it, every word. I just don't put the same interpretation on it you do. Gil and I—"

He waved his hands impatiently. "I know, I know. You told me. Well, from now on, I quit. You're on your own. I'm history. Come on, let's do this thing." He neatly sidestepped my attempt to give him a friendly pat on the arm and stalked up Marie's walk. Upon reaching the porch, he stood scowling at my much slower progress.

I was still wearing my church shoes.

"Tell me again why we're supposed to be here," he grumbled as I plodded up the two steps to the front door.

"We've come to formally offer our condolences. It's traditional to bring food. I wish I'd thought to stop at the Food Basket for some fruit or something." I pressed the doorbell.

This time, it was answered immediately.

"Miss Prentice." Hester Swanson, attired as usual in an apron, was also wearing a self-conscious expression. She spoke in a half-whisper. "Come in. Marie will be so glad to see you." Her questioning glance at Vern prompted a hushed introduction.

She ushered us into the house. I tried to disguise a limp. Why didn't more people follow the Japanese custom of removing shoes at the front door, I wondered. Right now, it seemed like a wonderful idea.

I could smell coffee and something else—pie? beef roast? There were muffled voices coming from somewhere in Marie's tiny bungalow, but the living room was deserted. "Everybody's in the kitchen," Hester explained.

We followed her down a dark and abbreviated hallway lined with framed pictures of Marguerite from babyhood to recent past. This wasn't going to be an easy visit.

"Miss Prentice!" Marie embraced me as I entered the tiny kitchen. Her face was white and puffy and her eyes were red, as might be expected. "Thank you for coming. This is Marguerite's teacher," she explained to the gathered handful seated around the tiny, white-painted kitchen table.

"We were just eating," said a small, wrinkled man with long white hair and Marie's eyes. He thrust empty plates at Vern and me. "Come on, sit down—Pierre, go get some of them chairs from the front room," he instructed a slightly built teenager. "I'm Jack Garneau, Marie's father," he explained. He gestured toward a tiny black-clad figure in the corner. "That's her *maman* over in the recliner there. Yvonne, this is Miss Prentice, the lady Marie's been telling us about."

Maman Yvonne, lying back in a worn plastic recliner, was in no condition to speak. She raised her head. Her pain-filled eyes met mine and she nodded. She held a large handkerchief to her mouth with a miniscule arthritic hand. I returned the nod, solemnly.

"That's Father Frontenac with her," he added, indicating the young man seated on a stool next to the recliner, holding Yvonne's other hand. The priest smiled at me kindly, then turned back to the old lady, whispering to her in French.

"You've met Valerie, I think," said Jack. Marie's sister blinked at me, stone-faced. She folded her arms over her ample chest and leaned back in her chair.

Jack continued the introductions. "This here's Valerie's boy, Pierre, and that's the Mister over there." Valerie's sleepy-looking husband acknowledged me with a faint smile. He was holding a glass of red wine.

"Mrs. Swanson's been helping out, too." Marie's father waved his hand vaguely. Hester dipped in a near-curtsey.

Vern hastened to assist Pierre with the chairs and shortly we were seated at the tightly-packed table. The kitchen was hot and the table covered with the unappealing evidence of a half-finished meal, but my feet were grateful for the rest. I slid out of my shoes.

I declined the offer of food or wine, citing my recent lunch.

"Coffee, then," insisted Jack Garneau, setting a steaming cup before me.

Vern, who had consumed a half-pound hamburger, a quart of milkshake and two Hershey bars in the last hour, filled his plate to overflowing from the fragrant array that covered every surface in the kitchen.

"This pie is great," he said, chewing a gargantuan bite, then washing it down with a gulp of wine.

"Oh, that's *tortiere*, Canadian meat pie," Hester Swanson put in proudly. "I made it from Marie's recipe. There's beef and pork, and heavy cream. The piecrust is made extra rich, with real butter. Have all you want. I made plenty."

"It was good of you, Hester," Marie said automatically. She picked up her fork, poked at her food, then put it back down.

Valerie snorted and squirmed in her hard wooden chair. "Supposed to be for Christmas," she muttered, "not funerals."

"It don't matter, Val," said her husband. "It's the thought that counts." She slid a sharp look his way, and he retired into contemplation of his wineglass.

"Funeral's at ten AM on Tuesday, Miss Prentice," Marie said, clearly trying to change the subject. "Our Lady of Victory Chapel. We got people coming from all over: downstate, Vermont, Quebec," she said, giving the Canadian province the French pronunciation, "ka-*beck*." The potentially long list of mourners seemed to give her a certain quiet satisfaction.

"I'll be there, too, Marie," I assured her. "Marguerite was special."

Jack Garneau squinted, reached in his back pocket to fetch a huge handkerchief, and blew his nose loudly. "That's true," he agreed, "she was, for sure." He drained his wine glass and poured himself another.

"You get the package?" Marie asked me suddenly.

"Not yet. It'll probably come tomorrow."

"If it don't, you tell me," she said.

What could she do, I wondered, but assured her I would.

"Mrs. Burns okay?" Marie asked.

"Yes, she'll be fine. They're keeping her in the hospital a little longer, just to make sure."

"Terrible thing, that was. Falling in the water like that. Scary." Marie stared into the middle distance. She was trying to be the courteous hostess, but she was clearly on automatic pilot.

The table settled into a contemplative silence, broken only

by the gentle voice of Father Frontenac, murmuring the rosary with *Maman* Yvonne.

I sipped coffee and watched Vern eat. The size of his bites was extraordinary. All at once, Valerie heaved herself out of her chair and trudged wordlessly from the room. Her husband pantomimed the smoking process to Jack Garneau. The two men excused themselves and stepped out onto the back porch.

"Guess I can clear this away now," said Hester, picking up Jack's nearly full plate. "Marie, you're almost out of wine. Soon's I clear up, I'll pick up some more for tomorrow."

"Thanks, Hester," said Marie listlessly. "Excuse me a minute." She followed her sister down the hall.

Young Pierre and I sat silently as Hester bustled around, clearing the table. There seemed to be nothing to say. Vern continued to eat.

From down the hall came the sounds of an argument. Marie's voice, muffled, protested in response to Valerie's alto growl.

"*Mais c'est son père!*" I heard Valerie shout.

Then Marie, sobbing.

"Father—" Pierre called apprehensively.

"I'm coming." The priest jumped from his seat next to *Maman* Yvonne and dashed down the hall with the boy.

Hester opened the back door. Cold air and cigarette smoke swept in. The men looked startled.

"There's a problem," she told them. "You better see about it."

Jack and Valerie's husband tossed their cigarettes aside and dashed into the room. Following the raised voices, they continued down the hall.

"I need to go to the store," Hester announced as she untied her apron. Pulling on her coat, she was out the back door before I could make any reply.

The arguing down the hall continued.

I tried not to listen. Most of it was in rapid French—too rapid for me to understand—but the tone of the voices told much of the story: Valerie was outraged over something and seemed to blame Marie, who was becoming more distraught by the second. It was apparent from Father Frontenac's calm, deep tones he was trying to diffuse the situation, but wasn't making any headway.

I looked over at *Maman* Yvonne. She remained in the recliner, her eyes shut tight, her small gnarled hands gripping a rosary and handkerchief to her chest. Her thin legs, encased in black stockings and ending in matching orthopedic shoes, were propped on the chair's footrest. It was an undignified position, but probably good for the circulation. Her feet shook slightly, I noticed. In fact, her whole body was trembling.

Without bothering to get back into my high heels, I rose from my seat and took the priest's place beside the old lady. Lightly, I laid my hand over hers. Her eyes popped open, she blinked several times, then her mouth curved slightly in the faintest of smiles. Tears trickled down the deep creases along her eyes. She took my hand in one of hers and squeezed tightly, then closed her eyes again.

Vern and I looked at each other across the kitchen.

The arguing continued. The beads of the old lady's rosary pressed into my skin. The kitchen clock, a yellow plastic cat with a waving tail, said two-twenty. I tried to time my breathing with the movement of the tail.

Breathe innn, four swings.

Breathe ouuut, four swings.

I looked down at *Maman* Yvonne. She had stopped trembling, but still had my hand in a desperate grip.

Vern scraped the remains of his second lunch into a trash

can, then placed the plate in the sink. The hall door stood open, and the sounds of the argument were clearly audible. With a look at me, he gently closed it. Then, retrieving an old newspaper stacked for recycling, he carried it over to the table and began reading.

The muffled voices continued for several more minutes, then ended with a sharp retort and the slamming of a door. In the silence of the kitchen, I heard a soft, regular snore and realized that the feeling had returned to my hand and *Maman* Yvonne had fallen asleep. Sheepishly, one by one, the men returned to the kitchen.

I managed to hush them with gestures towards *Maman* Yvonne. Clean wine glasses were distributed and filled. There was no sign of Marie or Valerie.

"Marie's lying down and Valerie's left," Father Frontenac whispered to me as he returned. "It's a bad thing, all this. As you probably heard, there's an awful lot of bitterness over the past. Marguerite had been trying to help in the healing process, but...well. Tragic." He sighed.

"How's she doing?" He smiled down at the old lady. His face was rounded and almost bald, like a baby's, with the same expression of innocent friendliness. With exquisite care, he pried the crooked old fingers from mine and gently replaced it with his plump one.

Maman Yvonne stirred slightly, but continued snoring.

"Thank you for coming," the priest whispered. "I'm glad you were here. They need their friends right now."

I patted him on the arm and backed away.

Quietly, we said our good-byes to the trio at the table.

Jack Garneau insisted on escorting us to the door. "The girls—always, they fight. Valerie the most, though. She always hated Étienne—Marguerite's father, you know?—and she's mad as the devil he's not here. It's Marie's fault, she says.

If Marguerite had her father, she'd be alive." He drew in a long breath through his teeth. "Ahhhh, the things they say. It's no good." He shook his head. "I try to tell her, you don't say this stuff. Not now. But she don't listen. Poor Marie…"

"Do you know where to find Marguerite's father?"

"No. Not for twenty year." He stood staring into the distance. "Little Marguerite, she always loved her daddy. But she never really had one. *Pauvre petite…*" His face crumpled. Energetic and outgoing as he seemed, Jack Garneau was fully as old as his frail wife and, at this moment, he looked it. Blinking frantically, he regained his composure. "It's real good of you to come, real good. Marie—she'll be okay. She's a good girl, that one."

"Mr. Garneau," I said. It was a bad time, but I might never have another chance. "Did you ever hear of something called 'UDJ?'"

He wiped his nose on a handkerchief and replaced it in his pants pocket. "No, never. What is it?"

"I'm not sure, but if you have the chance, will you ask the people in your family? It might help the police."

"Sure. Sure. What's it again?"

I told him.

He repeated the letters. "Funny. But I'll do it."

"If anyone knows anything, please have them call me."

"I will." Jack seemed distracted. It was past time for us to leave. "Thanks again for coming." He closed the door gently behind us.

"You forgot to make that phone call to Mrs. Burns," Vern reminded me as we climbed into the car. "Don't worry, it's safe to go home now. I'm sure the coast is clear," he added.

"Now you listen just a minute—" I began, but stopped suddenly, laying my hand on Vern's arm as he started the ignition.

"What is it?"

"Look at who's come to visit."

Derek Standish was jogging down the walk. He jumped the steps easily in one leap and rang the doorbell. Swaying impatiently, he massaged his knuckles.

I could almost hear them cracking.

"Who is it?" Vern asked.

I explained rapidly, my eyes glued to Derek's white jacket. "What d'you think he's doing here?"

I squeezed Vern's arm. "Shhhh! Watch!"

With growing anxiety, I watched Jack Garneau answer the door and regard the tall boy with a questioning expression. Derek was talking rapidly, waving his hands as he spoke. Was he going to hurt the old man?

I reached for the door handle. "Vern, I think—"

Just then, Jack's short arms reached around Derek's solid middle. His small brown hands patted the boy's massive back as Derek bent over him and shook with sobs. Gently, the old man escorted the drooping figure of Derek Standish into the house.

I relaxed. "It's okay, Vern. Let's go home." Now I was sure I was right not to tell who had waylaid me in the parking deck. People mourned in different ways. Apparently, anger was how Derek expressed his grief. At least, that was my none-too-expert psychological opinion. "I can call Lily. She's probably thinking we fell in the lake, too."

Chapter Thirteen

"Sam, is it my imagination or are you a little bit thinner?"

The individual in question ignored me and continued to wolf down a carefully measured serving of SlimKitty for Mature Cats.

"Lily's been away almost two whole days. No more sour cream, huh, fella?" I scratched him gently behind one ear. "Where'd that catnip toy go? Surely you're not that hungry, are you?"

He stopped eating long enough to throw me a resentful glance, then resumed.

I had been snubbed, but now that I was back at home and out of those high-heeled instruments of torture, I didn't mind so much. They may have been designed for playing basketball, but basketball games only last a couple of hours and two full days in a row had been too much for my feet.

When Vern dropped me off, I had promised to think over all he'd told me about Gil, but that could wait. It was 3:30

and after what had transpired lately, I felt I deserved to spend at least a fraction of the Day of Rest resting.

I looked at the stove. A cup of herbal tea would be nice, but it took too much effort. "A nap. Now that's the ticket," I told Sam. "I'll have tea later."

Clearly, Sam agreed. Having just finished his after-meal wash-up, he had already claimed his favorite spot in the middle of the rag rug. Rather than make the laborious trudge up the stairs to my bedroom, I lay on the tapestry settee in the front parlor, pulling Mother's crocheted afghan over my shoulders. "I think I'll just stretch out a minute," I said, remembering her quaint term for a nap.

A light wind blew the tips of the maples just outside the tall windows, sending multi-colored gusts of leaves flying past. In a little less than two weeks, Halloween would rear its some-times-ugly head, and I would be swamped by hoards of el-ementary school ghouls in pre-printed dime store costumes. Hopping up every two minutes to distribute candy was a nui-sance, but my parents had loved it, especially Mother.

Even in her last illness, she had insisted on holding court in her wheelchair on the front porch, swathed in blankets. "And who are you? Cinderella?" she'd ask a tiny child. "How beautiful you look!" or "What a scary ghost!" Her words weren't particularly original, but her joy was genuine, and the kids knew it, even the rowdy ones whose only costume besides street clothes was a mask and a pillowcase to bear away the goodies. They all, to a ghoul, favored her with a shy smile and a sincere "Happy Halloween!" as her bony, shaking hand dropped candy into each open bag. Though the evening air became nippy and the trick-or-treaters thinned, she had in-sisted on remaining outside until nearly eleven.

"Thank you, darling," she'd whispered to me through lips blue with cold, but smiling. "It was wonderful. All those children." The effort had totally exhausted her, and she'd slept solidly for the next two days. "It was worth it, though," she'd said when she awoke, her eyes shining with the memory.

She knew it was her last Halloween. She didn't even make it to Christmas. After she died, I'd put her still-wrapped presents in the attic.

A tear trickled onto the upholstery. What made me think of Mother just now? Of course, she had been in the forefront of my thoughts until December of last year, but I'd been determined to put the memories of her last agony behind me.

"I hate it that you'll be alone," she'd whispered to me a month before her death. "When your dad died, I had you, but now you'll be left alone."

"Don't worry," I said as brightly as I could, "I'll have Barbara." We had long ago dispensed with the polite fiction of her recovery.

"Barbara's place is in Florida with her family." Her frown was deeper than in her moment of deepest pain. "Besides, you know what I mean—alone. 'It is not good that man should be alone,'" she quoted. "'I will make him a helper fit for him.'"

In spite of myself, I laughed. "Mother, doesn't it also say somewhere: 'To the unmarried and the widows I say that it is well for them to remain single as I do'?"

She smiled back. "Corinthians." She patted my hand. "But you're no St. Paul, that's for sure. I'll just have to pray about it." She'd closed her eyes and drifted off to sleep.

The next day, she'd rallied incredibly, sitting up, joking, and polishing off a bowl of soup with crackers. The joy in her face was unmistakable. "Everything's going to be all right, darling," she'd told me breathlessly as Sam purred in her lap. "God's given me a peace about it. I asked Him for a sort of Christmas present." She would say no more, only, "Everything's going to be all right." She repeated the phrase like a motto in the ensuing weeks. They had been her last words.

"Oh, Mother," I said, sniffing into a tissue. "I *am* alone. And I miss you and Dad so much." My father had seemed indestructible, like a force of nature. My sense of security had been badly eroded at his death. Mother had possessed the gift of delight. Some twinkling sense of joy had faded away when she did. Life was so different without them.

Sam hopped up on the settee and nudged insistently for a place. "Come on up, you old cat." I hugged him and lifted him so he faced me, nose to nose. "Did Mother tell you to comfort me when I needed it? Was that your assignment?" It made sense. I hadn't really cried until the night of Marguerite's death. And Sam had been there for me.

Believe what you like, Sam's look said. He wriggled out of my grip and bounded away.

"Speaking of assignment," I said, "I've got a lesson plan to prepare." Reluctantly, I pulled myself up from the settee. My feet were still sore from the high heels.

The telephone rang and I answered it.

"Hello. My name is Burns. You don't probably don't remember me, but once upon a time, we were friends."

"Oh, Lily, I'm so sorry. I was just about to—"

"Don't even bother to make up excuses. You forgot."

"I forgot. I've been doing that a lot lately. Please forgive me."

"As long as you admit it," Lily said.

"You sound better."

"Well, that's because I *am* better," she said brightly. A little too brightly. "And I have a mutual friend sitting right here who will tell you so. Come here, say hello to Amelia," she ordered. I heard rustling.

"It's true, Miss Amelia. She's all right," said Alec. "Fit as a fiddle!"

"...and ready to be checked out!" Lily finished with a laugh, taking back the phone.

"Now? Today?" I looked around for my shoes. "Just give me a couple of hours—"

"No need, dear. Arrangements have already been made. Right, Alec?" Her silvery laughter rang out again.

"*Alec's* taking you? I thought you said he stepped off a box of fishsticks," I pointed out suspiciously.

"And I meant every word, Amelia, dear."

She was up to something, all right. "Lily, what's going on?"

"Amelia," she continued silkily, "*Al*-ec brought me a present—did you know that? It was *can*-dy. One of those *samplers*. So sweet!"

Oh, boy, now I knew. Flowers were the gift of choice for Lily. For reasons known only to herself, she had always considered a gift of candy extremely *déclassé*. I, on the other hand, would have been delighted. Poor Alec.

"We've had the most *fas*-cinating talk." Lily bit off her words in a manner I recognized. I only hoped Alec hadn't perceived the depth of her irritation.

"After I thanked him for saving my life—because that's what he did, you know—I told him *all about* my ordeal in the water. Amelia, did you know I actually *heard* something while I was going under for the last time?"

"Lily, what have you done?" I didn't like her tone at all. She was entirely too pleased with herself.

"It went like this—Weeeooooo! Weeeoooo! I saw something, too—a kind of big shadow in the water. Of course, I thought I must have been hallucinating, but Alec thinks differently." I could *hear* her eyelashes batting.

"I'll just *bet* he does! Lily, he's trying to conduct scientific research. You could set his work back years."

"Oh, I certainly hope so!" she squealed girlishly.

I called Lily a name, a bad one. It was beneath me, but I was under duress.

"As usual, you hit the nail on the head, darling Amelia. But don't you worry about a thing. Alec and I have everything under control. Bye!"

I could really use that tea now. As I filled the kettle, I considered warning Alec about Lily. Could I frame it in terms subtle enough to spare the man's feelings? I didn't think so.

"Alec, please remember to take what Lily says with a grain of salt," I tried experimentally. "She has such a vivid imagination."

If Alec had an ounce of perception—and I was pretty sure he had—he'd see through that one in a second.

What if I just said, "Alec, Lily is just pretending to like you. She thinks you're a fraud. She really can't stand you." Whew! It would take a pretty strong ego to withstand that.

All at once, I remembered Alec in the elevator, his eyes wild in outrage, his hairy hands crumpling the corner of the candy box. I shuddered. It's *Lily* I'd better warn, I resolved. Then, I headed for my desk and my lesson plans.

By the time the tea kettle whistled, I had it all worked out: I would play my audio recording of *As You Like It*, performed by the Shakespeare Company of Stratford, Ontario. The students could follow along in the text while they listened. This was one of my favorite lessons. Shakespeare wrote words to be spoken aloud rather than read silently. I hoped they would come alive for my students.

It would involve making over a hundred copies of one particular scene. This time, though, I would go to school early and take my chances in the teacher's workroom.

I poured hot water over the teabag and looked out the kitchen window. Dusk would fall in the next hour, and there was a light wind. I pulled on a sweater and carried my mug of tea outside, holding the door open for Sam, who seemed to need fresh air, too.

The wide front porch wrapped around the front half of our—my house. I looked out over our—my yard. It was all mine, now. I frowned at the tall clump of evergreen bushes that sheltered this end of the porch from the cold wind. Sally Jennings was right. They did look sick. And the leaves needed raking again.

I inhaled the steam from my tea—orange and spices. The warmth of it trickled inside of me and at least for now I was impervious to the cold.

It would get much colder later, though, I reminded myself. Time to call the oil company. In just one standard North Country winter, the furnace in the basement consumed hundreds of gallons of fuel oil.

I glanced over at the old porch swing. It was way past time to put it in the cellar for the winter, but it was where I did my best thinking, and one more swing would do me good.

A simple wooden affair painted yellow to match the house, it was suspended from chains connected to the ceiling above. For the past twelve years, Sam and I had operated under a time-share agreement. If either one of us reached the swing first, the other would stay off. There was no negotiation about this. Sam had made that abundantly clear.

I scanned the darkening front yard. There was no sign of the cat. Sam must be off somewhere, perhaps sitting wistfully on Lily's back stoop, enjoying memories of sour cream.

Mug firmly in hand, I made my move, but my assumption of Sam's whereabouts had been mistaken.

Out of nowhere—most likely the nearby brown bushes—Sam leaped from below and made a lightning dash for the swing, his form reminiscent of his days as a young tom.

"Oh, Sam!" I said, annoyed. I knew that haste was useless. Fat as he was, he had animal speed on his side.

What followed seemed almost part of Sam's magnificent leap. When he landed, the swing arced towards the house, but one corner on Sam's end simply detached from its support chain and dumped him on the floor.

"*Sam!*"

At the same moment, the cat gave an unearthly yowl and literally disappeared from the porch in a gray streak. There was a rattle as the chain pulled itself from the support above, depositing rungs in an untidy pile on the floor. The swing, hanging by its other chain, rocked and spiraled, the wood of the seat scraping the porch.

"What happened?" said someone coming up the front steps behind me. I turned to face Steve Tréchère.

"Miss Prentice? You are all right?" said Louis Jourdan's face in that devastating accent.

"My cat had a little mishap," I said, indicating the swing. "I just hope he's not hurt."

"He looked fine when he went by me," he said. "I'm sure he'll be okay. Your swing broke, though," he said, picking up the metal screw that held the chain to the chair. "It came loose, I think."

"I was going to put it away for the winter, anyway."

"You could have been injured," he pointed out, frowning, "but for the cat, eh?" He smiled and dropped the hardware, dusting off his hands. "Miss Prentice, may I disturb you a little bit? There are some things I want to discuss."

"No disturbance at all. I was just having some tea. Come in and I'll pour you a cup."

"That would be nice." He didn't speak as he followed me into the kitchen, only looked around with interest. He was dressed more casually today, in a lambskin shearling coat, plaid shirt, and pleated Docker pants. Not exactly a Louis Jourdan outfit, but very attractive, anyway.

"No sugar, please." He didn't sit right away, but explored the kitchen, surveying the countertops and running his finger along the cabinets.

"And this room? For storage?" he asked, pulling open a door.

"Yes. The pantry. And that's the breakfast room."

"It's pretty old-fashioned," he observed.

"It's supposed to be. It's the original kitchen—1888—with the addition of electric appliances, of course," I said and took a seat at the kitchen table. "But it's not for sale, Mr. Tréchère," I said firmly.

He waved his hand in the air and nodded. "But Mrs. Jennings—Sally—said..." He made one of those pleasant French grimaces.

"I'm sorry, but I've tried to tell her many times."

He pulled out a kitchen chair and joined me at the table. "It's all right. I understand. It's a charming house. You live here a long time, eh?"

"All my life."

"All alone?" he asked, lifting his mug to sip.

"Yes. Well, since my mother died last year."

"Very sad. But you are a teacher, I think?"

All these questions were beginning to make me nervous. It was like an interview. Or an interrogation. "Yes. High school English."

"This girl. The one who—died. She was your student?" He frowned.

"Marguerite?" I nodded. "She graduated two years ago. She was a sweet girl."

"You were close to her, eh?"

"Not any more than any other student. But I liked her."

Two can play this interrogation game, Buster. Now it's your turn.
"You knew her, too, I believe?"

He stared. His face held no expression at all.

I went on. "I mean, you knew her socially, someone told me. Had lunch together, things like that?" I stirred more sugar into my tea and tried to keep my tone light.

"Well, yes...I met her once..." He ran his finger around the rim of his mug.

I sat silent, letting him squirm. *I don't believe you,* I thought.

"Very briefly, you understand. But she seemed very nice, as you said." He waved his hand dismissively. "This is a sad subject, isn't it, Miss Prentice? Perhaps you will permit me to explain what I wanted to do with your very lovely house?"

I gave up. Some tough interrogator I was. "Please."

"I wanted a—what's it called? Not a hotel. A bed and breakfast, that's it. I would call it Chez Prentice."

A bed and breakfast. Why had I never thought of it?

He leaned forward. "I see you like the idea, eh?"

"It has a lot of possibilities," I admitted.

"I have a reason for this." He drank deeply from his mug and said, "There is a woman. I have loved her for many years, but I don't know if she returns this love." He looked across at me with real pain in his eyes.

What *is* this? Here I am, talking real estate with a handsome, sinister Frenchman and all of a sudden he turns into a Teenager in Love. What was it with middle-aged men and *l'amour* lately?

"She is very proud, this woman. She has a hard life but she also has pride and I know she will take nothing from me." His finger traced the grain on the surface of the wood table. "But I think she might work for me. This is how I will get close to her..." He trailed off, staring into his mug of tea.

"And this woman would run the bed and breakfast?"

He patted the table. His diamond ring sparkled. "Exactly. And this is the perfect house."

"There are six bedrooms upstairs, but just one bathroom on each floor."

He nodded. "Ah. Of course, small changes are needed."

He left the table and strode into the next room. "But look—over there, I would put the reception. And here, the dining."

He moved to the staircase and put his foot on the first step. "May I?"

I smiled and shrugged. "Certainly. Go ahead."

At first, I was careful to keep a safe distance between us. However, in the space of the next five minutes, as we explored my house, I completely forgot that Steve Tréchère might be a murderer. With just a few words and a couple of articulate gestures, he had me visualizing a thriving inn, filled to capacity with happy tourists, eager to spend their money. He hummed with enthusiasm, like an engine, full of ideas about the place.

"And no televisions in the bedrooms," he said firmly as we descended the stairs.

"Of course," I said, "it's more peaceful that way."

He nodded. "More peaceful. And more cheap!"

"Well, anyway, as I said, Mr. Tréchère, I'm afraid it's not for sale."

"I understand. But..." He smiled slightly and tilted his head. His brown eyes twinkled eagerly.

Had he looked at Marguerite that way? Her poor little romantic heart would have melted to a puddle. But his other lady love seems to be able to resist him. *What does this other woman know about you, Steve?*

He reached in his jacket and pulled out a handful of business cards. "I'll be at the Lakeside Hotel for two more days, then back to Montreal. Please think about it. Here's my address and telephone. Uh, oh..."

Cards cascaded out of his hand and across the hall floor. "Always somebody gives me a card. I have too many. I need a case for them," he complained as we searched the floor for the last of the cards.

"There are many other houses in the area," I told him at the door. "I'm sure you'll find the perfect one for your lady."

He shook his head. "Not so perfect as Chez Prentice," he said. "Goodbye."

"Good-bye," I said. "*Bonne chance.*"

His eyes widened in pleased surprise. "*Merci. À bientôt.*"

I closed the door and looked at the card he gave me. An elegant, stylized logo in silver, his name, Montreal address, and phone number.

"I can't imagine I'll ever need this," I told Sam, who had reappeared at my feet. "But you never know. Right now, I'm hungry."

I was headed for the kitchen when I spotted something white peeking out from under the edge of Grandmother Prentice's oriental rug. It was another of Steve Tréchère's business cards. "Well, now we have an extra, Sam," I said. "One for the refrigerator door, and one for—" I turned over the second card. Three capital letters were written in ballpoint across the back:

"UDJ" and a question mark.

Chapter Fourteen

"Upheaval."

"Danger."

"Jeopardy."

I tried out another trio of words that might fit those letters.

"What's the use, Sam? Maybe it means nothing. A coincidence. That could be it, couldn't it?"

The cat was curled up on the kitchen rug. He lifted his head, blinked at me twice, and resumed his curled position.

"No, I don't think so, either." I sighed and looked around me. There were crumpled papers all over the table, where I had written phrases, then given up on them in disgust. I unfolded one.

"Underdeveloped Derivative Juveniles." One of my more interesting attempts.

"Derek and Steve Tréchère—what do they have in common? They both knew Marguerite and this..." I tapped

Tréchère's business card with my fingernail. "UDJ."

What did it mean? Did I dare ask either one of them? Or should I just give this information to the police? Would they take me seriously? Probably not. Maybe I could tell Dennis, but maybe I'd already gotten him in enough trouble.

"Uh, oh, Sam," I said, "I did it again. I forgot to call back about the carjacking." I went to the phone. I would tell Dennis everything.

I'd missed him again.

"Could you tell me when he's expected back? Oh. In that case, would you ask him to call Amelia Prentice?" I couldn't see myself trying to explain the situation to anybody else.

"Ugh. This place is a mess," I told Sam.

As I gathered up the crumpled papers and put them in the trash can, my eyes fell on the stack of mail I had brought in yesterday. There were several bills, I remembered. Might as well pay them and mail them off tomorrow.

"Power bill," I recited, shuffling the stack, "Book of the Month Club, Frasier's Florist—Oh, goodness, I'll need to order some flowers for Marguerite's funeral first chance I get tomorrow." I made a mental note as I pulled out a peach-colored slip from the handful. "Attempted delivery," the slip said. The sender was listed as M. LeBow.

"Marguerite's journal!" I told Sam.

The slip informed me that the package would be waiting at the post office during regular business hours.

"Drat that wretched tiny mailbox!" I said, not for the first time. "That does it—I'm buying a bigger one tomorrow!"

The telephone rang.

"Amelia," Vern said breathlessly, "I just called 911, but I think I need more help. I mean, she does, and he does, and you're the only woman I know—I mean, awwww," he moaned. "You gotta come over here, right now!"

"Vern, calm down and tell me what's going on." I heard a clunk and a rustle. "Vern? Vern!"

"Sorry, I dropped the phone while I was pulling up my jeans."

"You *what*? Vern, where are you?"

"I'm at Mrs. Dee's house. She shot this guy. You know, what's-his-name? She shot him, Amelia. He's bleedin' and I think she's havin' a heart attack or something. You gotta come, Amelia, please!" I had never heard Vern like this, desperate and childlike.

"Steady, Vern. I'll be right there. Just hold on."

As I hung up, I realized a hard fact: I had no readily available car. I was willing to walk, even run, over to Judith Dee's house, but it would take much too long.

"No time to stand on ceremony," I mumbled and dialed Gil's number. His answering machine took an inordinate amount of time getting to the point

Finally: *Beep.*

"Gil, it's Amelia. I've had a call from Vern and he's in some kind of trouble. I'm going to try at the paper—"

"Amelia? What is it?"Gil's voice, breaking in, was brisk.

"Just come, Gil. My house. I'll explain when you get here!"

I had no sooner pulled on my coat and locked the front door than Gil's car slid to a halt at the curb.

Before he could get out, I hopped in. "Judith Dee's house. On Mason. Do you know it?"

He did and pulled out into the street immediately. "Now, tell me what's happened."

I repeated Vern's message as best I could remember. "I think she must have had a prowler. I have no idea what Vern was doing there. He sounded so awful, like a terrified little boy."

"In some ways, he is," said Gil. He took a corner at an outrageous speed and just missed running a red light, but I kept my mouth shut, for once.

As we stopped in front of Judith's handsome clapboard ranch house, a fire truck, an emergency vehicle, and two police cars pulled in the driveway. Two policemen beat us to the door.

Vern let them in. The lights were on in the house. Even at a distance, I could see that there was blood on his light gray sweatshirt.

"Vern!" I cried.

"You'll have to stay back, folks," another policemen said as he stepped in our path. "This is a crime scene."

Paramedics, with two stretchers, ran inside.

"My nephew's in there, officer!" Gil protested.

"Sorry." With a shrug, the man was gone.

"What do we do?" I asked Gil, whose eyebrows were tightly knotted.

"I'm not sure." He swung his gaze all about, then returned it to my face. "I don't know."

"So we wait here."

"I guess so." He pulled a portable telephone from his breast pocket. While he alerted his office of an incoming story, I leaned against the hood of Gil's car and prayed silently.

Judith's living room drapes were open, and we could observe some of the activity from our vantage point by the curb. While paramedics came in and out with equipment, kneeling over someone unseen on the floor, a policeman sat next to Vern on a couch near the picture window and interviewed him.

The boy looked tired and shook his head frequently. The officer wrote in a notebook. He seemed to have an endless list of questions. At one point, a paramedic approached and gave Vern a cursory examination. Apparently, no treatment was needed.

I sighed my relief and pointed this out to Gil, who was still conferring on his phone.

Neighbors had begun to assemble in curious clusters up and down the street. A dog stood on the driveway next door and barked incessantly at the strangers.

I was surprised to see a discreet "For Sale" sign next to Judith's driveway, bearing the handsome logo of Jennings Real Estate. My old classmate was everywhere, it seemed.

A stiff breeze blew through Judith's shrubbery. Where *was* Judith, anyway? Vern said she'd had a heart attack. I shivered.

Gil, having finished his call, replaced the telephone in his pocket, slid over next to me, and put his arm around my shoulders. I leaned into him and closed my eyes. For some minutes, we stood in the middle of this anxious scene, silently taking strength from each other.

The front door opened and a paramedic backed out carrying an IV bag. He was followed closely by a stretcher containing Judith Dee.

I ran forward. Due to substantial interference from a policeman, I was only able to catch a glimpse of her face, gray as her hair, and eyes clenched shut.

Another stretcher was being rolled out. Another IV bag. I stood on tiptoe. The patient's large feet extended beyond the end of the stretcher. An attendant was hunched over the head, blocking my view. An arm in a bloodstained white jacket sleeve flopped out from underneath the blanket and someone gently tucked it back in.

Judith had shot Derek Standish.

The ambulance doors slammed shut. As it screamed away in the direction of the hospital, Vern emerged, wrapped in a blanket.

A policeman spoke with him before consigning him to our care. "We may have a few more questions later. We'll call if we do."

Vern nodded wearily and stumbled in our direction. "Hi," he said.

"Hi, pal," said Gil. "Ready to go home?"

Vern gave a shuddering sigh. "Ready."

There was a tap on my shoulder. A weary-looking Toby House said, "Miss Prentice, you're looking a lot better."

"Thanks to you, Toby. How is Mrs. Dee?"

"She's going to be fine. A bit shocky. It's that big kid we're worried about. He's got a bad head wound." He nodded in Vern's direction. "*He's* fine, though. A few bruises. Just needs some rest. Probably ought to take tomorrow off."

I had more questions, lots of them, but Toby said, "Look, I gotta go. I'm glad to see you're better. Eye-bay, Entice-pray." He patted me on the shoulder and ran to join his colleagues.

"Thank you, Obee-tay," I whispered.

At my insistence, Vern came to my house.

"I've got five empty bedrooms," I called to Gil as he climbed into Vern's car. "Real ones, with real beds. What kind of rest will he get on a camp cot in your kitchen?"

Gil smiled, nodded, and drove off in the direction of Jury Street.

"What will people say?" Vern asked quietly from the passenger's seat of Lily's car. "There might be a scandal." The mischief in his voice cheered me no end.

"I'll take my chances," I said, reaching over to squeeze his hand.

"Maybe Gil could chaperone." He winked at me.

"You're tired, Vern," I protested a half-hour later. "Just eat your soup and go to sleep. You can tell us all about it tomorrow." I had tucked him in the big bed in my sister's old room.

"She's right, pal," Gil piped up from the rocker in the corner.

Vern drained the last of his chicken soup and replaced it on his tray. "No, I want to tell you now."

He tried to pull down the too-short sleeves of Dad's old silk pajamas, gave up, and lay back, pulling the quilt around his shoulders. "But listen carefully, 'cause I'm only going to tell this once more tonight." He yawned.

I perched on the corner of the bed. I heard the old rocker creak as Gil leaned forward. "We're listening."

"Amelia, you remember when Mrs. Dee offered to re-bandage my leg at lunch? I mean, not really *at* lunch, but later, at her house?"

I nodded.

"Well, it started getting a little sore tonight and I thought, what the heck? So I went over there. She was real nice about it. Took me into the kitchen and got the bandages and medicine ready—by the way, did you know that the mayor has an ulcer?—but I forgot I'd have to take off my pants for her to work on my knee."

"She fixed it at Peasemarsh, didn't she?" Gil asked dryly. "Didn't you drop your drawers there?"

"Hush," I said. "His pants were torn then."

"Right, and of course I didn't want to let her cut up my only other pair of clean jeans. It was kind of funny, really. We both were a little embarrassed, so I offered to go home and come back in some cutoffs, but she said it was too much trouble. She went and got an old bathrobe of her husband's—did you notice this is the second time in one day I've borrowed a dead man's clothes?—then she told me to take my pants off and put it on. And she left the room to give me some privacy."

Gil smirked. "How discreet of her."

"Honest, Gil, she's a nice person. While I was changing, the doorbell rang. The kitchen door was shut, but it's a small house and I could hear everything."

"Derek Standish," I said.

"Right. And he was drunk. At least he sounded drunk. He talked kind of low, so I didn't get worried right away, but then he started talking about who killed Marguerite. And that it was her."

"She," I said, too quietly to be heard.

Gil leaned forward in his chair. "He said Judith killed Marguerite?"

"Yeah. Stupid, huh? He was drunk. Anyway, I was there in the kitchen in that old bathrobe, trying to decide whether to come out right then or call the police first. I took the robe off and started to pull on my jeans, but then I heard a crash, so I ran out there in my sweatshirt and underpants."

"Oh, man," Gil said, and laughed.

Vern grinned slightly. "Yeah. It's funny to tell now. It was good I went out there, though, because he had his hands around her throat."

"Oh, no!" I cried.

"I mean, it was like a TV show or something. I didn't know what to do. Of course, I'm tall, but he was way too big to pull off her, so I grabbed his hands and pulled back his pinkies." He demonstrated on his own hand.

I felt weak.

"Did that work?" Gil asked.

Vern smiled. "Well, kinda. Besides, I think it startled him to find somebody else there. He looked at me standing there in my underwear, and let go of her. Then he went for me."

"Oh, Vern," I gasped.

"I ran around the furniture a little, but he has these long arms and he grabbed hold of the back of my sweatshirt. I thought I was dead. And then, boom!"

"She shot him?" Gil asked.

Vern nodded. "I'd forgotten all about her, but she must've pulled the gun out from somewhere. Well, Derek fell, and I fell, and when I got up, he didn't. There was blood all over us. She was standing there with that gun in her hand, staring at me, and for a second, I thought she was going to shoot me, too."

"Poor Vern," I said.

"Then she fell, too. Keeled right over and dropped the gun."

"Fainted," I said.

"That's what I thought at first, but I wasn't sure. So I called 911 and then I called you." He yawned again.

"That's enough for now." I slid off the bed. "Vern, we're going to let you get some sleep."

Vern reached for my hand. "Wait. There's something else. The whole time Derek was choking her, he kept shouting something. It wouldn't have meant anything to me, except that you mentioned it yesterday."

Gil shook his head. "What are you talking about?"

"I think I know." I stared at Vern. "'UDJ.'"

"Yup," he said, his eyes drooping, "that's it."

Chapter Fifteen

"Okay," Gil said as we descended the staircase, "what's with this UPS stuff?"

"UDJ."

"Whatever."

"Let me reheat some of that chicken soup, and I'll tell you all about it. I'm hungry, aren't you?"

"I will be," he said, pulling out his cell phone, "as soon as I call the paper."

We finished off the rest of the soup and half of another can. While we ate, I told him about the carjacking, identifying Derek as the intruder.

"Obviously, those letters meant something to Derek."

Gil's reaction mirrored his nephew's. "And you didn't see fit to tell all this to the police?"

"Don't wave that spoon at me, Gil Dickensen. I just didn't think that Derek would—"

"You got that right. You didn't think. Doesn't it occur

to you that if you'd turned him in right away, he might not be in the hospital now?"

"So now you're psychic? Don't make me feel any worse than I do already, please."

He reached across the table, pulled a fresh stack of saltines from the box, and tore it open. "Okay, I'll concede you couldn't know he'd go for Mrs. Dee or that she'd have a gun. Where'd he get the idea she'd killed Marguerite, anyway?"

"I can't imagine. This morning, I did overhear some kids saying Derek had threatened to 'get' whoever killed Marguerite."

"And Miss Prentice, in her infinite wisdom, still saw no reason to go to the authorities."

"I've tried to call Dennis, twice," I protested. I tasted a spoonful of my soup. It was getting cold, fast.

Gil popped an entire saltine in his mouth and chewed. Then he picked up his soup bowl and drained it. I now knew where Vern had learned his manners. "Ahh," he said, "just like Mother used to open and heat up."

I put down my spoon and moved my bowl aside. It was time to clear the air. "Gil, what's going on?"

"What do you mean?"

"The other day, you said I'd 'thrown a spell' over Vern. I'm beginning to think Vern has thrown a spell over you."

He wiped his mouth with his napkin, crumpled it, and dropped it in his empty bowl. "Meaning?" His gaze was direct and disconcerting.

The acrobat inside me was getting restless. "Meaning..." I cleared the table and put the dishes in the sink. It gave me time to frame my words carefully. "Have you or have you not maxed out your charge account at Bailey's Menswear?"

"What if I have?" He leaned back in his chair and folded his arms. "I needed a little spiffing up." He adjusted the collar of his new and very handsome sport shirt.

"I'll take that as a yes." I swept cracker crumbs off the table and into my palm, willing my hands not to shake. "Next question: have you really put a down payment on a certain cottage by the lake?" I dumped the crumbs in my empty soup bowl.

""I'm considering it. I've been throwing away my money on rent for years. It'll be a better investment. Besides, it has a yard for Vern to play in." There was a familiar twitching at the corners of his mouth.

I took a deep breath. "Right. And now for question number three: What were you doing at Statler's Jewelry store?"

He stood abruptly. "That Vern! I'm going to finish what the Standish kid started!" He stood and whirled dramatically, giving me just enough time to reach him before he headed for the stairs. I couldn't help it. I was laughing as I tugged on his shirt.

"Gil, cut it out! Sit back down here. We've got to talk."

He obeyed.

"Look, I don't know what's going on with you, but Vern seems to think it involves me. *Does* it involve me?"

He folded his arms again. "Maybe."

"All right, then. In that case, I think we need to understand each other."

"God knows I've tried," Gil said, smiling.

"You see, that's just what I mean, speaking of God. You were at my church this morning."

"You want me to apologize, or what?"

"It's just that, knowing how you feel about religion—"

"And now *you're* psychic? How could you possibly know the state of my soul? Didn't it occur to you that I might want to learn more? Aren't you supposed to welcome me with a fatted calf or something instead of sneering?"

"I wasn't sneering. It's just that you were so abrupt." I had a flash of insight. "That's it! That's what it is about you that drives me crazy: you keep doing things so abruptly, without thinking."

Gil looked injured. "I like to call it spontaneous. Besides, how do you know I don't put a lot of thought into what I do? Kinder people might call me decisive."

"Gil, decisive, spontaneous, whatever, you just never give a person any warning, any hint about what you've got in mind. You just decide. Twenty years ago, you up and decided we were getting married. Boom, without warning. You took me off guard."

"So you told me at the time," he mumbled.

"And here you show up at my house out of nowhere on Friday and turn into Romeo, wanting to neck at any given opportunity—"

"You didn't seem to mind. Not at first, anyway."

"That's just it, Gil. I didn't—don't mind." I laughed shakily. "If you just weren't so cotton-pickin' *abrupt.*"

Gil had been sitting forward, his elbows on the table. He looked at me a long time, sighed, and said, "I see."

I shook myself free of his gaze and looked down at the paper napkin I had been holding. It was in shreds. "Well, anyway, that's how I feel."

I just couldn't look at him any more. The chair legs scraped loudly against the floor as I got up. I walked to the kitchen sink and stood there, staring at my reflection in the window above Mother's collection of humorous salt shakers. My face looked like it had been drawn in chalk on a blackboard.

Gil's face appeared behind me. "Amelia," he said, "it's true. I am impulsive. I do go on instinct, and it's served me well in the past, but that's the newspaper business. This time, I want to do things properly."

Gently, he turned me around, took my hand, and led me to the front parlor. "It seems more proper in here, somehow." He sat beside me on Mother's antique loveseat, my hand in his. "Amelia, you're right. I have made some big decisions in the last few days. But you're wrong about one thing: I do put in a lot of thought."

I opened my mouth to speak, then shut it.

"I've been living alone for a long time, and it's not—good."

"*It is not good that man should be alone*—'" I quoted.

"What?"

"Nothing. Sorry I interrupted."

"Amelia, I want you to have the time you needed twenty years ago—to decide."

"And what you want me to think about is..."

"Whether you will marry me." He compressed his lips nervously. I looked into his eyes, which didn't avoid mine. I couldn't detect a trace of the old mockery in his expression. What I saw was anxiety and, I thought, sadness.

"And you are asking me this because..." I prompted shamelessly.

"Because I love you," he pronounced as gravely as a diagnosis of terminal disease. "I always have."

I put my arms around his neck and kissed him.

It was a good kiss and I was rather proud of it, considering the limited opportunity I'd had to practice. "No," I said softly.

There was a moment of shocked silence as he gathered himself. His eyes widened and he shrugged, but he didn't let me go. "Okay," he said casually. He bent down and kissed me back. "Live in sin, then?" he said, whispering against my lips.

I leaned back and traced a finger around his mouth. "How about this: we take our time. We date. We court. We keep company. We get to know each other. And then, if you still want to, you ask me again." I held up my finger sternly. "The first question, not the second!"

The tension in the air was dispersed.

Gil smiled. "Sounds reasonable."

We sealed the bargain.

"Now I'm going to have to stop avoiding you all the time," I told him some minutes later.

"And I you. Why do they call this thing a loveseat, anyway?" Gil grumbled. "You can't *do* anything on it."

I slapped him playfully on the chest. "I mean it. We've been antagonistic for so long, it's going to take some adjustment."

"Just how long is this adjustment supposed to take?" he asked, holding my hand to his cheek.

I stroked his face. It was a nice one, with lots of pleasant places to kiss. A slight roughness was beginning to form on his chin and cheeks. I ran my fingers across them, enjoying the texture. "As long as it takes," I whispered.

"Well, Miss Prentice," he groaned, lifting himself from the seat and pulling me to my feet. "If you really meant what you said about the 'living in sin' thing, I'd better be getting home."

We found his jacket and I walked him to the door.

"Take care of my nephew." He kissed the tip of my nose. "He needs you, you know."

I was surprised. "Me?"

"He still misses his mother. You're the closest he's come to having one in a long time. You've been good for him."

"Right. As long as I don't get him shot or something."

"And don't forget—tell O'Brien!" he said, tapping my nose.

"I'm trying," I said meekly.

"Just do it. Promise?"

I did, and he left.

It was embarrassing how wonderful I felt. Dear, sweet

Marguerite LeBow was dead. Judith Dee had been attacked, and poor, mixed-up Derek Standish might not pull through. On top of that, Vern lay upstairs, prostrate from the evening's trauma. I knew all this, and yet I couldn't quench the desire to sing.

"'You're just too good to be true...'" I crooned as I washed the dishes, remembering a song Gil and I had once danced to.

I heard a rustling noise at the back door. I squinted at the window, but there was nothing but blackness outside. Frantically, I grabbed the first thing that came to hand with which to hit the intruder—a large jar of mayonnaise—then jerked the back door open.

"I'm baaack!" said Lily Burns.

Chapter Sixteen

"Thanks, but that's not my brand," said Lily as she strolled into the kitchen. "I like Miracle Whip myself." She took the jar from me.

I hugged her. "You're looking well. Are you?"

"I'm in 'amazingly good health for a woman my age,' to quote a pimply-faced adolescent who pretended to be a doctor," she said, opening my refrigerator and replacing the mayonnaise inside. "Where do you keep the ground coffee these days? I'm longing for a cup."

"I'm out," I said, handing her a jar of instant and a spoon. "I haven't had time to go to the store."

"Just don't get between me and that microwave," she said, running water in a mug. "I'm going to fix myself a cup, we're going to sit at that table, and you're going to tell me everything that's been going on. And I mean everything."

So she did and I did.

Telling her lasted through three cups of coffee and two

slices of buttered toast, which Lily prepared herself, all the while listening intently. Of course, I left out the part about Gil and me, especially when she flatly refused to discuss her treatment of the Professor.

She was especially interested in Steve Tréchère and his plans for a bed and breakfast. "Did he say who this woman was?" she asked, pulling out her old leather cigarette case and extracting a small bag of jelly beans. She popped a green one in her mouth and offered me the bag.

I shook my head. "No, just that he's loved her for a long time. But he hasn't met you yet. Would you like an introduction?" I added coyly. "He's very attractive."

Lily patted her hair. She cocked an eyebrow mischievously and tossed down another jelly bean. An orange one. "Well, anybody with a nickname like 'The Millionaire from Montreal' can't be all bad." She chewed vigorously.

"Was that Mae West or Marilyn Monroe?"

"Neither. It was Lily Burns." Her face turned suddenly serious. "Tell me more about this UDJ thing."

"I've told you all I know."

"I just thought of something. It might not be initials. Couldn't it be a code of some sort?"

"UDJ. Udy-jay. Lily! It's pig Latin! For Judy!" I jumped from my chair. "Judy. Judith Dee, maybe? Lily, of course!"

"Now don't go jumping to conclusions, Amelia. That's pretty silly."

"But it's just the sort of thing Marguerite would do! And Derek must have figured it out. That's why he tried to kill Judith!"

"Amelia, the boy's been blundering around all over the place. He had *you* figured for the killer once. He could be wrong about her, too."

"That makes sense, of course. But think about this: Marguerite tried to volunteer to go undercover to expose drug activity. The police turned her down, but what if she decided to conduct her own investigation?"

Lily frowned. "That's a silly, dangerous thing to do."

"What do I keep telling you? Marguerite was sweet, but she was just silly enough to do something dangerous, especially if she felt strongly about it." I picked up the empty plates and carried them to the sink. "You know, the more I think about it, the more it makes sense. It would explain the journal, too."

"What do you mean?"

"Marie said Marguerite wanted me to have it, if anything happened to her. She may have been keeping a record of her investigation. It would be just like her."

"It might explain her letter to Alec," Lily said thoughtfully and dipped into her jelly bean bag, pulling out a pink one. "He told me all about it on the drive home. She accused him of 'corruption of minors,' whatever that means. He took it as a slam against the validity of his work. Made him furious." She chewed rapidly and swallowed.

"Isn't that what you were doing?" I pointed out.

"No, of course not. Alec said that he's used to skepticism. It's the idea that his work might be actually harmful to young people that set him off." She explored her bag of candy with her index finger.

"It would upset me, too," I conceded, wondering at Lily's familiar tone when she mentioned Alec's name. Could he be getting through to her after all?

"Where did the Standish boy hear about UDJ, then?" Lily asked, getting back to the main subject. "Yuk. Licorice." She tossed the offending black jelly bean on the table.

"From Marguerite, of course. He was infatuated with her. She must have dropped hints about her suspicions, including

UDJ."

"And when she was killed, he decided to find out about UDJ."

"Poor Derek," I said, remembering that limp arm hanging from the stretcher.

Lily looked up suddenly. "Could he have been the one who tossed me in the drink?"

I considered the idea. "He did have a job on the ferryboat. What do you remember about it?"

Lily squinted in mental effort. "I was walking towards the car. It was raining and there was a lot of wind, so I was hunched over. Something sort of rushed me. Everything happened so fast. I felt myself falling...then...then..." She sighed. "I'm sorry. Everything goes black from there."

"What about 'Woooo-eeee' and the dark shadow in the water?" I asked wickedly.

Lily slid her eyes sideways. "Oh, yeah. That's right. I remember that, too."

I sighed. "Lily, you're hopeless. Still, this Derek thing makes all the sense in the world. At the hospital, he asked about you and said something about making a mistake. You know, I think we may have figured out this thing!"

"So basically you think Judith Dee was dealing drugs and Marguerite found out about it," Lily said, setting down her bag of candy and ticking the statements off on her fingers. "She wrote an 'I saw what you did' letter to the people she suspected. Judith took the bait and killed the poor kid."

I started pacing in my excitement. "And Derek, who obviously had a crush on Marguerite, takes it on himself to go after the murderer. Think about it—a school nurse—what better way to distribute drugs? She's in contact with young people on a regular basis. She can—oh!" I cried.

"What is it?"

"She gave me some pain capsules for my head. I have them in my purse." Hurrying to the front hall, I located my purse and found the small, unmarked bottle and held it up. Lily took it and tipped out the capsules.

"They look pretty standard, but what do I know? You haven't taken any?"

"No, thank goodness, but Judith was insistent I keep them."

Lily handed back the pills, yawning. "Well, I can't say I'm a hundred percent sold on your theory, but you better call Dennis O'Brien and tell him about it anyway, just to be on the safe side." She put her hand to her chest. "Whew! I'm exhausted all of a sudden." She retrieved her jelly beans, walked to the back door, and paused, hand on the doorknob. "You know, the only thing that makes me think there may be something to all this is when Derek Standish accused Judith Dee of murder—"

"She shot him," I finished for her.

She pointed her finger at me like a pistol. "Exactly."

Her navigation of my backyard was slow and cautious. "It's so dark out here," she complained loudly. "I thought you had lights or something." I looked up at the motion-sensing lights. None of them was working. I clicked on the porch light.

"Thanks," I heard her call.

I watched until I saw her silhouetted by her own back porch light. After Lily left, I called the police station again and asked for Dennis. He still wasn't there. I called his home, and Dorothy, after apologizing profusely for the way my babysitting career was terminated, told me he was still out, working on an investigation. I left messages for him to call me back at both places. Then I went to bed.

Chapter Seventeen

The next morning went so smoothly, I found myself almost forgetting the strain of the last few days. Vern was still sleeping like a little boy in a storybook when I left. I put a note for him on the bathroom mirror:

Washed your sweatshirt & jeans (hanging in closet.) Fix a big breakfast & be lazy. Dr.'s orders, Amelia.

The teacher's workroom was deserted when I arrived, and I finished all the copying, collating, and stapling early enough to enjoy a cup of the first coffee out of the big percolator in the teacher's lounge. My classes actually enjoyed hearing Shakespeare read aloud by trained actors and laughed in at least some of the right places.

"Why don't they do this stuff in the Drama Club?" Hardy Patschke asked. "It would be awesome."

"You could suggest it, Hardy. I know we did *Midsummer Night's Dream* when I was a sophomore here."

"Didn't know it was written then, Miss Prentice."

There was an apprehensive hum as the class waited for my reaction.

"Good try, Hardy, but not up to your usual standard," I commented dryly. "You seem to be slipping."

I spotted several smiles of agreement.

Hardy was undaunted. "Don't worry, I'll do better next time," he promised with a grin that displayed his new braces, loyally tinted in the school colors.

All in all, it was a good day, except for a weird encounter with Judith Dee in the hall after lunch. "I'm tougher than I look," she told me when I expressed amazement at seeing her. "Takes more than that to get me down!" she added. Gingerly, she touched the high turtleneck of her sweater. "They tell me the boy who attacked me is still in a coma." She took my hand. "I don't wish him any harm..."

I'll just bet you don't, I thought.

"...but if dear Vern hadn't been there, well..." She shook her head, a faraway look in her eye. "I just wish I knew where Derek got such a notion about me."

I didn't enlighten her. I was finding it difficult to stand there and talk calmly.

"They asked me where I got the gun," she said. "It was my husband's, Amelia. He got it in the army. I never used it before. Never needed to." She looked at me with dancing gray eyes. "It was self-defense, pure and simple. That's what I told them. Vern will tell you—ask him! Self-defense, pure and simple." She kept rubbing one hand with the other.

Out, damned spot, I thought. "I'm sure it was, Judith. I'm sure it was."

I hurried off to call Dennis again. He was still unavailable.

"I thought you'd never get here!" Vern said as I walked through my front door.

"Fine, thanks, how are you?" I said, hanging up my coat.

"What's the matter?"

"Why don't you get an answering machine? I must have taken a dozen messages." He had a handful of paper scraps in one hand and a half-eaten sandwich in the other. "It's onion and mayo; want me to make you one?" he asked, noticing my gaze.

"Ecch! No, thank you," I said, reaching for the message slips. "O'Brien. WCB," I read.

"That's 'will call back.'" He took another bite of sandwich and some mayonnaise fell on his sweatshirt. "Oh, rats!"

I could sympathize. I reminded myself to take my suit to the cleaners. "Marie LeBow. CH?"

Vern licked his fingers. "Call her. Alec called, too, asking about me, but I handled that one for you."

"Jack Garneau. re: UDJ. DCH."

"Don't call him, 'cause I talked to him. He remembered me. He said he asked around and nobody ever heard of those letters."

I looked at the next slip. "SJ?"

"Sally Jennings."

"Good. That's one I can tear up," I said, and proceeded to do so.

"I don't know. She asked if you were going to Marguerite's funeral."

"Why? She didn't know Marguerite. At least, I don't think so. Oh, wait. I think I know. She's going to try to persuade Marie to sell her house, I'll bet."

"Wow, that's cold," said Vern.

"No, that's Sally," I said. "My father was no sooner buried than she was over here, pressuring my mother to sell this place. You saw her in action yourself the other night. She still hasn't given up. Oops, someone's at the door."

When I answered it, Vern took one look from behind me,

burst out laughing, and quickly retired to the safety of the kitchen.

It was Sally Jennings. "Amelia. Hi. Me again. May I come in?" Without waiting for an answer, she proceeded inside. "Who was that?"

"Just a houseguest. Pay him no attention." I led her to the parlor. She sat on Mother's loveseat and I took a Victorian rocker across from her. "Sally, I talked with Steve Tréchère—"

"I know, Amelia. He was very taken with you. Very taken. He still hasn't given up his dream of turning this place into a bed and breakfast. He said you discussed the possibility, right?"

"Well, yes, but—"

"Well, then, you can see what an *incredible* idea it is. If Steve Tréchère and his friends keep investing, it could mean a turn-around for this town. He said you liked the idea. You did, didn't you?" she wheedled. There was a desperate air about her I had never seen before.

"Well, I—"

I heard the telephone ring. "I'll get it," Vern called from the kitchen.

Sally mistook my hesitation for agreement. "I know, I know. When he told me his plans for the place, well, I was just blown away, too! Anyway—"

Vern stuck his head in. "Amelia. Phone for you. It's urgent."

"Excuse me, Sally." *Thank you*, I mouthed to Vern as I passed.

Ever the hero, he stepped into the parlor and proceeded to make small talk with Sally. "Hi, remember me? We met the other night in the yard. By the way, did you know that this place has termites? Big ones. Talk about a dump! It's practically falling apart. And it's haunted! Oh, yes! Many's the night old Ebenezer Prentice walks..."

It was Dennis O'Brien returning my call. Briefly, he apologized for his rude behavior the other day. "I can't explain myself completely, just yet, Miss Prentice, but it was inexcusable, the way I behaved."

"Don't worry about it, Dennis. I know you had good reason." As succinctly as possible, I told him about Derek and the carjacking and everything else that had transpired since. Last of all, I told him about the letters UDJ and my theory about them.

"I think Marguerite's journal may say something about it...no, it's still at the Post Office. I have a slip for it here and I'm going to pick it up in a few minutes. I'll bring it right over to the station."

I heard the front door closing.

Vern sauntered into the kitchen and flashed me the high sign. He had gotten rid of Sally. What a guy!

There was another knock on the door. Vern spun on his heel and headed for the door.

I returned my attention to the telephone. "Yes, I know. You're absolutely right. I should have called much earlier. I'm so terribly sorry...Yes. I think it should tell you a lot. I'll bring it in right away." I hung up.

"Miss Prentice?" said a voice behind me.

I turned. "Mrs. Swanson." What was *she* doing here? "Please, call me Amelia."

Vern stood behind her. He shrugged helplessly.

"'N' I'm Hester, remember?" She smirked and darted her eyes around the kitchen. "Um, Amelia," she began. Her eye was caught by the row of salt shakers on the windowsill. "Hey, cute." She picked up a pair and examined them. "'Specially this little maid and butler."

Behind her, Vern frowned and tapped his watch.

"Hester?" I began. "I'm afraid that we have—"

There was another knock on the front door.

"Now what?" Vern whined under his breath.

It was Judith Dee, bearing a huge box of chocolates. "I just had to drop by and thank my rescuer," she said breathlessly, handing the gift to him.

From the way his face lit up, I could tell that Vern didn't share Lily's negative opinion of candy as a gift. "You didn't need to do this," he said, pulling off the gift wrap and opening the box. "A sampler. Wow, thank you! Nobody ever gave me one of these before. Here," he said, holding out the box to me. "Amelia?"

"Not right now, thanks, Vern." I had been standing transfixed through all this. What should I do? Would Judith actually have the audacity to try to harm him? In an Agatha Christie novel, I remembered, a murderer used a hypodermic needle to inject poison into soft chocolates.

"Mrs. Dee? I hate to eat alone," he said. "Oh, and, er— Hester?"

"Hm?" Hester, who had wandered in from the kitchen, was leafing through a new magazine from the stack of mail on a side table. "No, thanks."

"Well, maybe this little coated almond," Judith said, reaching for her selection and popping it in her mouth. "Well, I just wanted to thank you," she said, picking up her purse and heading for the door.

Why was she so anxious to leave? Did she want to be gone before anything happened?

Vern followed her, holding the huge open box on one arm. "It was awful nice of you," he said, his hand poised over a large coconut-filled.

"Go ahead," said Judith. "Take one. Don't mind me."

I had to do something. *Think fast, Amelia!*

"Was that Sam out there on the porch?" I said. "Here,

kitty, kitty!" Rushing past Vern towards the door, I elbowed his arm and knocked the candy box into the air. Chocolates, jellies, and sugared nuts flew through the air, rained on our heads, then rolled to inconvenient places all over the first floor and the lower landing of the staircase.

"Oops," I said insincerely.

The four of us, including a highly amused Hester, scrambled after the candies, piling them willy-nilly into the box. As I repeated polite apologies, I caught Vern shooting me an injured glare. Judith promised to replace the box with a brand-new one.

By that time, I thought, *he will have been warned.*

Judith left hastily, still dusting powdered sugar off her shoes.

"Why did you do that?" Vern whispered angrily, crawling after a peanut cluster that had lodged itself under a piano leg in the parlor. "You practically slugged me!" He dropped the candy in the box. "Are you some kind of health food nut or something?"

"Look, folks," Hester said, her hand on the front door knob, "I gotta go. I'll call you later." Pulling the heavy door open, she scurried across the front porch and was gone.

"What was all *that* about?" Vern stood in the open doorway, his hands full of dusty chocolates, as cold gusts swirled around him.

"Never mind." I pulled him inside and closed and locked the front door. "Just listen—" While Vern discarded the candy, I explained my theory about UDJ. By the time he'd rinsed his hands, I'd finished and obtained his complete forgiveness.

"Remember, I don't have any concrete proof of this," I cautioned, handing him a paper towel.

"But you've told Detective O'Brien, right?"

"Yes, though I'm not sure he took me very seriously."

"Don't worry. They'll follow every lead they get," he said. "At least, that's what they do on 'Law and Order,'" he added sheepishly. He glanced out a front window. "Oh, no! Another one!"

I looked out. Sure enough, reenacting the scene in which Gaston realizes he loves Gigi, Steve Tréchère was bounding up the porch steps. Almost jauntily, he knocked on the door.

"Miss Prentice," he said as I opened the door, "I see you have disposed of the broken swing."

I looked out the door. Sure enough, it was gone.

Vern tapped me on the shoulder and whispered, "I took care of it. Back porch."

I stepped back to make way for him. "Won't you come in?"

"*Merci.* I wanted to talk with you one more time about what we discussed the other night." Strolling forward, he gazed up the staircase and gestured. "Can't you see it? Wouldn't it be marvelous? Guests occupying all those charming rooms up-stairs. Perhaps a bride, descending here..."

For a second, we were all three caught up in Steve Tréchère's vision. I hated to break the spell. "But Mr. Tréchère, it's still not for sale."

"Ah!" He held up a finger. "That's true! But perhaps, and you understand that I say, perhaps—no pressure, of course—perhaps we could become *business partners*!"

He'd done it again: come up with a fascinating idea and sprung it on me out of nowhere. Why, I wondered, did I find this trait so enchanting in Steve Tréchère and so irritating in Gil Dickensen?

"Well," I said, "if you'll just let me think it over..."

"Of course! Take your time! We can discuss it later. I will check back with you later, eh?"

"Well, what do you know about that?" Vern said as we

stood on the porch and watched Steve Tréchère drive away.

"I don't know, Vern," I said. I looked at my watch. "Hey! It's quarter to five! Better get to the Post Office, or we'll have to wait another day to get the journal!"

"Right. Let's get going. The slip is right here on the table." He walked into the entrance hall and stood looking at the table. "Uh, oh."

"What—'Uh, oh?' I don't like the sound of that!"

"I don't like *saying* it. Amelia, it was right here. That slip!" A panicky tone, not unlike that of last night, crept into Vern's voice. "I swear! I saw it there when you came in the door!" He crawled around on his hands and knees. "Maybe it fell down under here..." He found another chocolate, which he tossed aside with an annoyed grunt.

"Don't worry," I said, "we'll just run over to the Post Office and I can show them my driver's license. Hurry! They close in a half hour!"

"I'm sorry, ma'am, but we're real busy," the man at the Post Office window protested, gesturing at the long line behind us. "Like I told you, the package was already picked up. See? Signed for and everything." He held out the slip, containing an illegible scrawl that in no way resembled my own. "There's so many people come through here, I can't remember everybody picking up a package," he said plaintively. There was nothing we could do but leave.

"Which one of them was it?" Vern said as he started the car.

"You're thinking the same thing I am?"

"Sure. That slip didn't just walk away. One of them took it."

"It could have gotten blown away somewhere. There was

a lot of activity in that hall."

"Okay, then—who picked up the package?"

"Good point."

"And we both know who it was."

We spoke together: "UDJ!"

I felt sick. This one simple thing to accomplish, and I had failed. "Well, I better call the police station and let Dennis know." I didn't want to call Dennis. I wanted someone to hold me and tell me things were going to be all right. I wanted it to be Gil.

He couldn't have read my mind, yet Vern said, "How about we check in with Gil first?"

"Sure," I agreed casually.

They were as busy at the newspaper as at the Post Office. Gil stepped into the newspaper's minuscule reception area just long enough to inform us of that fact and to give me a chaste peck on the cheek.

"Was that too randy?" he whispered in my ear.

"It was borderline, but acceptable," I whispered back.

Vern's eyes were enormous. "Wow! It's like that, is it?"

"Amelia, you tell him what it's like, please. Run along now, kids." Gil fairly pushed us out the door.

"Call you later," he said to me, closing his office door.

Vern blocked my exit. "Why didn't you tell me?"

I pushed past him and descended the stairs. "There's not that much to tell, Vern. We're just going to, um, date for a while and see what happens."

Vern was beaming as he held the car door open for me. "Works for me!" He looked at the car clock. "Can you call O'Brien from home? I gotta run."

"You're not going to stay another night?"

"No, thanks. I've got to go to class tomorrow and I promised to make up the time I missed over the weekend by driving for Marcel tonight."

The atmosphere on the way home was considerably cheerier than before. I attributed it to Gil's kiss. "Got just enough time to grab a burger and punch in," Vern said to me at the curb. He patted my hand. "We'll get to the bottom of this thing, Amelia, don't worry. And just to be on the safe side, why don't you throw those chocolates away for me." He winked and sped off.

I called Dennis O'Brien. The officer who answered told me he was gone again, so I left a message: "Someone else picked up the journal. Call me for details. Amelia."

It was a good thing Vern hadn't stayed longer. I made a quick inventory: in addition to bed linens, the boy had used seven towels, three washcloths, five plates, eight spoons, a fork, three table knives, a coffee cup, two saucepans, numerous slices of bread and half a jar of mayonnaise. Most of these items or their remains were still sitting in the kitchen sink. I had no idea where he found the onion.

Not that I begrudged him these things. In fact, I enjoyed his company. But it had taken me this long to get used to living alone and I rather liked it.

The telephone rang. "Amelia," said Sally Jennings, "I'm glad I caught you."

"Steve Tréchère came by again after you did, Sally. I told him I'd think about his idea."

"Isn't it fabulous?" she gushed. "But that's not the only thing I wanted to talk about. It's Gil."

"Gil who?"

"Don't be coy with me, Amelia. I've known you since fifth grade. It doesn't take a rocket scientist to know that you and Gil have become an item."

"Apparently it doesn't," I said dryly.

The implication was lost on her. "And that he's been looking at the Field place on the lake."

"You're handling that sale, too? You're some busy lady, Sally."

"You have to be, Amelia, in this market. Did you know closings have decreased by fifty percent in the last four years alone?"

Whatever that meant, it sounded bad, so I said, "That's a shame."

"Anyway, you can do me a favor."

This sounded interesting. The Super Sally I remembered from our high school days was so self-contained, she didn't need favors from anybody, least of all me.

"What is it?"

"Would you come take a look at the Field house and see if you like it? Gil is still undecided about it—"

"I heard he made a down payment."

"No such luck. He's just considering it. But if he knew you liked it, well..."

I could feel my face getting hot. It was embarrassing to be so transparent in front of the entire town. My first impulse was to turn Sally down flat, coolly and with poise. My second, however, was quite the opposite. I had always wanted to see the inside of that place.

"Sure, Sally. When?"

"Why, right now!"

I was surprised, but it was only six-thirty and it couldn't hurt to check out what Gil considered a dream house. "I'll be ready in five minutes," I said.

It occurred to me that Lily would enjoy coming along, but when I called her, I got the answering machine. "This is just to let you know that you're about to miss a little trip with Sally Jennings and me to see the Field place," I told it. "Pick up if you're there, Lily."

There was no answer.

"Well, I've got to run. I'll tell you all about it tomorrow."

Chapter Eighteen

I was waiting on the porch when Sally pulled up.

"You're driving a different car," I observed as I climbed inside the dark van.

"Company vehicle," she said, waving at the rows of seats behind us. "It'll carry nine people in a pinch. Air conditioning vents on each row, duplicate speakers. I like to listen to oldies. Do you mind?" She punched a button on the radio.

"...sorry now?" whined Connie Francis. "Whose heart is achin'..."

"Of course not." I buckled my seat belt firmly. What I *did* mind was if she'd had a couple of martinis with Barry before picking me up. I'd seldom seen her this nervous.

"All righty! We're off!" Sally said brightly. She pulled out into the street without a hitch and I began to relax.

"Exactly how far is this house from town, Sally?"

"A little over seven miles, but it's good road all the way and it has that gorgeous view across the lake. If it's not foggy, you can see the Green Mountains."

"It sounds beautiful."

"I know you're going to love it. Speaking of love, how did this thing with Gil Dickensen get started?" Her blonde hair had fallen over one eye. She turned the other on me, brow arched.

I felt my face heating up, but I kept my voice casual. "Oh, you know, he was an old beau—"

"A *beau*! Isn't that cute?" She shook back her hair and returned her attention to the road.

"Yeah, well, that's what people are saying about me these days," I said, remembering Vern. "Supposedly, I'm 'cute.'"

"...goin' to the chapel and we're gonna get married..." sang the radio.

Sally patted my arm with her kid glove. "But you are, Amelia. Cute, I mean. You still have a nice figure and almost no gray hair. And everybody in high school always envied that wonderful clear complexion."

Nice of her to admit that we went to high school in the same decade. Too bad there was no witness to this. "Fat lot of good my complexion did me at the Prom," I thought, then realized that I had spoken aloud.

"But everybody loved your cousin," Sally said, repeating the ancient, well-meaning litany that had so humiliated me as a teenager. "He was *such* a good dancer."

"Yes, well—" I began, but Sally put her hand back on my arm.

"Shhh! Listen."

It was a news bulletin. "...in the murder of 21-year old Marguerite LeBow. Police have arrested Judith Dee, 60, of 488 Mason Street. Dee's house is the site of a recent shooting incident in which 16-year-old Derek Standish was gravely injured. Reports indicate that while conducting a search of the

Dee house, police found an unknown quantity of illegal drugs. Stay tuned to this station for more information as it becomes available."

Then Jay and the Americans resumed singing about what could happen only in America.

"Wow! Judith Dee! Who'd've thought? You know her from school, don't you, Amelia? Did you have any idea?"

"Derek Standish did. He said that Judith was UDJ. Then she shot him."

"She was *what*?" Sally seemed surprised.

"It was a kind of clue that Marguerite left. UDJ: pig Latin for Judy, see?"

Sally laughed. "No kidding! Pig Latin? How idiotic. That's *great!*" She seemed inordinately amused.

"Still—Derek knew, didn't he?" I observed sagely and sat back to listen to Tommy James and the Shondelles declare musically that they thought we were alone now.

"We're almost there," Sally said a few minutes later as we turned down a narrow unpaved road.

"Not many neighbors," I commented.

"Wonderful, isn't it? All this privacy," Sally said, turning down a gravel driveway and pulling into an open-ended barn structure that served as a carport. I hopped out of the van and walked around to the front of the house.

In the dim moonlight, the Field cottage took on a dark blue tint. The white picket fence Vern had mentioned wasn't white at all. It was unpainted wood, but straight and charming and lined with low, plump bushes. We navigated the flagstone walk carefully.

Sally, I noticed, was elegantly casual in designer jeans and sneakers. I hadn't had time to change from my standard classroom uniform of mid-length skirt, white blouse and cardigan sweater, but fortunately I was back to wearing flat shoes again.

The night was cold, so we were both wearing our heavy winter coats.

"You can see the exterior is all cedar shake," Sally said as she turned the key. "They put it on four years ago. Up until then, it was plain log. One story, four fireplaces." She opened the door. "It was tough luck for the Fields, getting the place all fixed up, then being transferred."

"Have they moved out already?"

Sally nodded. "They left for Japan a week ago. They took all the furniture they wanted, so the rest of it comes with the house."

As we stepped inside, Sally snapped on the light. We were standing in a narrow hallway with hardwood floors and paneled walls. A rack of deer horns hung to my right, and a pair of snowshoes were fastened to the wall with a nail on the left. We proceeded down the hall and into a cozy room with a worn, slipcovered sofa facing a stone fireplace. Right away, I wanted to light a fire and curl up with a book.

"Jacob Field—that's Mike's great-grandfather—built the house. This room was built first," Sally said. "It was just a one-room lakeside camp then." She pointed to a wooden carving above the fireplace: 1890.

"Then they kept adding rooms, one by one. The kitchen is here," she continued, indicating a slate-topped counter on the left. Behind it was a stainless steel sink, a large refrigerator, and an Aga stove. "Completely remodeled two years ago," she said proudly. "Well, what do you think so far?"

I looked around me. The style of the Field home was rustic, even primitive, evoking the woods and nature, vastly different from *chez* Prentice.

"I love it!" I said, and meant it. This house spoke to me of peace and welcome and joy. This house was mine. I wanted to live here. With Gil. "I love it," I said again, becoming more sure with each passing moment.

Sally smiled. "Really? I'm so glad. It's not the Prentice mansion, of course, but it's snug." She waved her hand at the passageway to the right. "The rooms back there are charming, but what you really *must* see," she said insistently, pushing me along, "is this."

We turned a corner.

"A screened porch. And a deck. How perfect!" I said, stepping outside. The cold wind off the lake hit my face like a slap. "Whew!"

Sally proceeded to the edge of the deck and pointed. "And a rowboat! Comes with the house, of course," she said, galloping down the wooden steps to the rocky shoreline.

I followed, crunching unsteadily across the uneven surface.

"Look," Sally said, sweeping her arm toward the water.

The inky surface of Lake Champlain was calm tonight, and the long reflection of the round moon cast a silvery, net-like shimmer on the surface.

"Isn't this beautiful?"

"Yes," I gasped. It was really cold. My breath came in foggy puffs.

The sky was dark, but not so dark as the Green Mountains silhouetted in the distance. A tiny light, blinking regularly, moved slowly across the sky.

"The Burlington airport's over there. Come on," she said, untying the rowboat and stepping into it. She held out her hand. "There's something else I want to show you."

I moved back. "No, thanks, it's too cold. Besides, I'm not much of a rowboat person."

"You're kidding. You mean you're still scared of the water?"

"We can't all be athletes, Sally," I said huffily, clapping my arms in the cold.

"I know, but flunking the swimming test," she said with a laugh, "in front of the entire senior class? That's got to be some kind of record." Her voice had taken on a derisive tone I hadn't heard in years. "I didn't know a human body could sink to the bottom like that—like a rock. But you did—right to the bottom of the Y pool!"

I drew myself up haughtily. "Thank you very much for reminding me, Sally. Anyway, I think I'll skip the boat ride." I turned back toward the house and mounted the first step.

"No, you won't."

I turned. Sally was still standing half out, half in the boat. By the half-light from the house, I could see that she held a small gun, pointed in my direction.

"Well, *you* look ridiculous," I said curtly. It was true. I had seen a woman in a James Bond movie strike that very same pose. She wasn't as warmly dressed, of course, but she had the same cool, disdainful look on her face. The acrobat inside my chest started auditioning for Barnum and Bailey. I tried to ignore him. "What kind of a toy have you got there?"

"If you don't want to see a demonstration of this *toy*," Sally said, "you'll join me in this boat."

This time, *I* was the rocket scientist who figured out the situation: Sally was not what she had seemed, and it behooved me to cooperate with her for the time being. None too steadily, I scrambled aboard and took a seat in the stern.

Sally pushed us loose of the rocks and hopped lightly aboard, still holding that ridiculously tiny gun.

"What do you call that thing? I mean, a beretta or something?" I asked, curiosity getting the better of shock.

Sally tilted her head and examined the gun. "You know, I never thought to ask. It was a gift from a friend. It fits nicely in my coat pocket and is quite easy to use."

She held it up and pulled the trigger. There was a loud noise that caused me to jump, rocking the boat. A stone on the shore leaped. "And I have good aim," she added unnecessarily.

With one oar, Sally maneuvered the boat around until the bow faced the lake. She then turned to me. "Row," she instructed, gesturing towards the oars with the gun, "that way." She pointed east, toward Vermont.

I set my purse in the bottom of the boat and rowed. A little crookedly at first, but I gradually got the hang of it.

It seemed to me I was entitled to a few answers. "Sally," I asked in my sternest teacher's voice, "what's going on here?"

Sally pulled something from her jacket pocket and held it up. Her gold bracelet with its disc bangle gleamed in the moonlight. "Recognize this?"

"What about your bracelet?" I asked, leaning forward to examine it.

"Don't give me that. I've seen you staring at it every time I wear it. Trying to read the initials, of course. Marguerite figured it all out before you did, you know. She noticed it once when we were doing business together, so to speak. Asked me what the initials stood for. And like a fool, I told her. Row!" she ordered, and replaced the bracelet in her pocket.

My steel-trap mind clicked into place at last. "The monogram. Ursula Dodd Jennings," I said, remembering her maiden name. "*UDJ.*"

"Right," she said. "Keep rowing."

I rowed. My shoulders hurt, but I kept on. "But I thought...I mean, they arrested Judith."

"Yes, thanks to a little something I stashed in her garage. You were on the wrong track, but you'd have figured it out, eventually. I know that." She leaned forward. "I heard your telephone conference with the police today. Your nephew tried to divert my attention, but I have excellent hearing."

"He's not—" I began, but stopped myself. If my heart was any judge, Vern already was my nephew.

"Yes, he's not very bright, is he?" she finished for me, switching gun hands to zip her jacket higher. "He never saw me take that little pink slip."

"Oh," I said, nodding with her, "and *you're* the drug dealer Marguerite was after."

"You wanna know something funny?" she asked conversationally. "I'd quit. I'd actually finished with that whole business."

My eyes had long since adjusted to the dim light. I watched the gun sag slightly in her grip. Did I have time to grab it?

Her hand tightened.

No, I didn't. *Dear Lord in Heaven, help me!*

"I told you about the real estate market. Ever since they jerked the air base out of here. Whoever thought they'd take away a military base that's been here since 1812?"

"Who indeed?" I shrugged and kept rowing. At least it was helping me keep warm. I looked out across the water. There was a thin, metallic buzz in the distance. A boat. Too far away to do *me* any good.

"Things have been tough for Barry and I, thanks to you."

I forgot to be frightened.

"*What do you mean?*" I squawked and stopped rowing in outrage. She had made a number of errors in grammar so far, but I decided to let them pass.

"I'll tell you," she said steadily. All at once, she looked past me towards the New York shore and said, "Jennings Village."

"Beg pardon?" I said with ludicrous, parentally-programmed courtesy.

"*Jennings Village—a commercial pedestrian mall of upscale*

shops and restaurants in charming Victorian homes," she quoted. "That's what the brochure says, anyway. I've got a thousand of 'em printed up. And every one of those shops and restaurants paying rent to the UDJ Corporation."

As she talked, she held the gun with both hands, pointed at the bottom of the boat. Better not disturb her now. If she shot out a hole, this thing would surely sink, and that didn't bear thinking about.

"It's been my dream for years. I've been buying houses on Jury Street since '89, you know."

"You couldn't have! There are people *living* in them."

She laughed. "Rentals, Amelia. All rentals. Of course, part of the lease is to keep it confidential. But they're all up next year and if everything goes according to plan, my contacts in the city council will see that Jury Street is closed off, at taxpayer expense, thank you very much!"

"But—but—" I spluttered. "Why didn't you *tell* us what you wanted to do?"

Sally snorted. "Yeah, right. And let the prices go through the roof. I paid top dollar as it was. Bought all eleven houses with my own money. But I ran out." With a wave of the gun, she gestured for me to start rowing again.

I complied, though my shoulder muscles screamed in protest. "Ran out?"

"Of money, of course. I went everywhere I could. Begged everybody I knew. No luck."

"So you decided to deal drugs?"

"Don't say it like that! They ought to legalize them anyway!"

So that was how she rationalized it.

"And once I got enough money, I'd already quit."

"But then Marguerite—"

Her laughter was mirthless. "That's right, then along comes

self-righteous little Marguerite LeBow. Of course, I was on to
her right away. Marguerite the narc! What a joke!" She snorted.
"Using all those TV clichés and pretending to need the stuff.
It was *pathetic*. I have some friends, Amelia. Business acquaintances. Of course, it's nobody *you* would know," she said mock-
ingly, "but when I told them a problem had come up, they
gave me this *little* pill." She spoke in a baby-talk voice and
held up thumb and forefinger to indicate how tiny the pill
had been. "You're supposed to put it in food, but I had a better idea. She took allergy medicine, you know that?"

I shook my head. I'd been learning a lot about Marguerite
in the past few days. I continued to row. My back ached. I
could see the lights of our town over Sally's shoulder. There
were people there. My friends. And police. But we were rowing away from them. The lake was wide, and they were too far
away to hear us.

Lord? Are You listening?

"That's right," Sally continued, "prescription capsules. In
her purse. I just opened a capsule, dumped out some of the
powder, and stuck in the pill."

"What kind of pill?"

"I forget. Some kind of spy stuff. Who cares? When she
took it, I was nowhere near the place."

But *I* was. "Sally, even if she had turned you in, it wasn't
that serious. They aren't that hard on drug charges these days,"
I continued, making up criminal statutes as I went along. "You
probably would have gotten, um, probation. You didn't need
to *kill* her!"

Sally's face registered mild surprise. "Are you kidding? Do
you realize what would happen to Jennings Realty—and
Jennings Village—if even a hint of that came out?" She shook
her head. "No. I worked too hard to have somebody like Marguerite LeBow spoil it." She spoke the name with disgust.

I shivered, but not entirely from the cold.

Sally gazed philosophically across the lake. The breeze rippled her hair. Her profile looked almost noble. "You can see how it was, can't you, Amelia?" she asked mildly.

"Yes, Sally," I said with breathless sarcasm, not believing the direction this conversation was taking, "sure I can." I continued to row.

Suddenly, she turned back towards me. Obviously, she'd missed the irony in my tone. "Listen, we've been friends, haven't we? Ever since grade school? You're an honest person. A religious person. Swear to me, before God, that this'll go no further, and we'll row back to the Fields' place and forget all about it. How about it?"

I could see her eyes, open wide and staring sincerely into mine.

I shipped the oars once again. "I swear not to tell, and we'll go home?" I wanted to get the finer points of this little contract straight.

Dear God, I prayed desperately, *is this how You're going to rescue me?*

She nodded vigorously. "Yes. Just swear. I know you'll keep your word."

I believed she was serious. "Well, okay, I, er—" I began.

"You *swear?*" she asked eagerly. There was a broad smile on her face.

I'll do it. Then, when we get back to town, I'll just call Dennis O'Brien and—

"Before God? Nobody ever has to know," she added reassuringly, "just us." Her teeth glinted in the moonlight. Perhaps this was how she'd become a Gold Star Member of the Million Seller's Club.

Marguerite's earnest face popped into my mind. "It's just so, so—*evil!*" she'd said.

Tears began to fill my eyes. *You were right, Marguerite. Evil is the only word for it.* Without thinking, I slowly shook my head. "I can't."

"I *knew* you'd say that," Sally said with a laugh. "I was lying anyway, you know." She held the gun in both hands, pointed at me, and said evenly, "Stand up, Amelia."

"N-no!"

"I'll shoot you. You know I will." Her tone was light, matter-of-fact.

I folded my arms and frowned ferociously. Being shot sounded preferable to going in that water. It was a brave front, but I couldn't control the tears of rage and panic flowing down my cheeks.

"Oh, come on! You can't think I'm *happy* about this. Without you around, I don't suppose Gil will want to buy the Field house."

"Sally, please don't," I begged through a sob.

"Do you think your sister would sell me your house? She is your heir, isn't she?" She waved the gun. "Stand up," she repeated.

I remained where I was, shivering in the icy breeze. The boat bobbed gently on the sleeping lake. I could hear the dull buzz of another motor in the distance. If only they knew what was happening here! What would Sally do if I screamed?

"You're stubborn—you know that? Like with your house. I gave you the works—loose boards, dead bushes, the broken swing, even cut the wires on your doorbell and your security lights. Twice as much as I did to the Scolari house. You weren't going to sell, even if the place collapsed around your head."

"But—"

"Stand *up*, Amelia."

"But how—"

There was a loud explosion, and I felt my face being jerked

violently to one side.

"There. I pierced your ear for you. Care to try for the other one?"

I put my left hand to my face. Blood, gleaming black in the moonlight, was streaming down my neck. Slowly, trembling, leaning first to one side, then the other, I stood, quite literally rocking the boat..

"Now, step off."

"No! You rotten—" Vile, hateful, blasphemous names for her bubbled up from my throat. I swallowed them. I was determined that *those* wouldn't be my last words on earth.

Sally sighed impatiently. "Come on! I haven't got all night."

"NO!" I shouted. The boat rocked again, and I grabbed desperately at the sides to balance myself. I could feel the warm blood dripping down my neck and wondered absently if I could ever get the stain out of my blouse.

Sally extended her long arm and brought the gun close to my face, guiding me upright and saying in mocking singsong, "Come on, Amelia, just pretend you're at the Y."

I heard my own voice moaning, high-pitched and animal with misery. "NO!"

Sally fired again, this time in the air, but I flinched, moving my head to one side, and it was just enough to send me wheeling overboard.

I didn't even hear the splash. There seemed to be pressure everywhere. On my chest, on my eyes. A muffled ache pressed ever harder into my ears. And it was so cold.

Flapping my arms, I managed to propel myself upward and break the surface for a few precious seconds. With the fingertips of one hand, I grabbed the side of the rowboat, but Sally was right there, peeling my fingers away.

"Give it up, Amelia!" she growled. "Let go. They're all gone. Your parents, your cat—" She hit my hand with something hard.

I gave a strangled yelp and let go.

Sally began to row away.

I sank again. I struggled and sank even further. My saturated wool coat was weighing me down. My straight skirt seemed to bind my legs. I held my breath until my chest began to explode.

Was this what it was like to drown? *Oh, Gil! Why didn't I marry you? Oh, Gil...* I flailed frantically.

I'm dying, dear Lord. Into thy hands I commend my spirit...I'll be seeing Mother...and Dad...and my baby sister Amy who died when she was born...

Frigid lake water shot into my sinuses and exploded behind my eyes.

My last thought would be one of mild irritation. Drowning *hurt* lots more than I'd been led to believe.

Chapter Nineteen

Pretty soon now, I'll be going down a long tunnel, with a light at the end.

Just then, my feet hit something solid.

It was impossible. Even as the top of my head seemed about to blow off, I felt myself rising, slowly, steadily. My head and shoulders were suddenly above the water, in the frigid air. I gasped and hacked, snorted and gulped oxygen greedily. There was a steady roaring in my ears that wouldn't go away.

I looked down. Somewhere below in the black water, my feet still stood on the solid something that kept almost half of me above the surface. Could there be a sand bar in the middle of the lake? I turned and found my nose inches from the side of a vibrating boat. The name painted on the side was "Sweet Afton."

I heard a voice above me. "Praise be! Look what I've found! Hang on, Miss Amelia!" I looked up into the grinning, hairy face of Alexander Alexander.

A life preserver came flying over the side. I grabbed it and clung, but still the blessed, firm surface remained steady beneath my tiptoes.

The Professor climbed down a rope ladder, gripped my arm firmly, and hauled me up, soon assisted by another pair of eager hands.

"Heere ye come! Up ye go!" I heard him say.

Just before I was hauled over the side, I looked down and saw a dark, smooth shape undulate along the surface, then disappear smoothly into the black waves.

A blanket was thrown over me. I heard someone say, "She'll freeze out here. Let's get her inside."

"Lily, no," I croaked feebly, "please, wait." With every ounce of strength I had left, I pulled myself to a standing position at the side of Alec's boat, leaned over, and lost the meager contents of my stomach. It was just as well that I hadn't had dinner.

"Hoo, boy! Thar she blows!" I heard Lily shout behind me.

I straightened up and attempted to regain my dignity. "Don't be crude," I snapped at her, swabbing my mouth with a corner of blanket.

"Poor bairn," Alec said, patting my back.

"She'll be all right," Lily said. She leaned near my face and smiled. "And she hasn't been a bairn for at least forty years."

"Shut up," I said, "your hair looks terrible." It did, too, all blown to one side and coming loose from its moorings in the stiffening lake breeze.

She laughed. "You see, Alec? I told you she'd be ungrateful. Come on, dear, let's get you into the cabin. You're turning blue." She pushed me unceremoniously through a door and into a tiny room full of intimidating, blinking instruments of every description.

I took a deep breath. "Lily, it was Sally Jennings. She killed Marguerite and tried to kill me. She might go after Marie. We've got to call Dennis or somebody!"

"Consider it done, dear lady," Alec said behind me. Expertly, he stepped forward, pressed buttons, turned knobs, and spoke urgently into a microphone. Much of the exchange was in some kind of mystifying code. Once, he paused to ask me for a detail: "...and was last seen—Miss Amelia, where was she last seen?"

"In a rowboat on the lake near the Field camp. She can't have gone far."

Alec nodded. He started whistling a hymn through his teeth.

My mind supplied the words: *Rescue the perishing, care for the dying! Snatch them in pity from sin and the grave.* Alec always had an appropriate song for every occasion.

While he worked, Lily deposited me in one of the two seats and reached for a thermos bottle. "My hair does look pretty bad," she admitted, examining her reflection in the silvery end of the thermos. "Maybe I should have stopped at Gladys's Beauty Spot for a wash and set before I arranged to *have...you...rescued!*" She leaned down towards me, speaking the last few words with particular emphasis.

"Thank you for saving me, Lily," I said meekly.

"That's better." She poured steaming liquid into the thermos cup and handed it to me. "Here, sip this slowly. It's cocoa and brandy—Alec's recipe. Purely medicinal. Trust me, you'll like it." She reached into a pocket of her jacket, pulled out a rubbery black stick, and took a bite out of it.

I leaned forward and sniffed. "What's that you're eating? Licorice? You hate licorice!"

"I know, but Alec told me it makes a good substitute for cigarettes. Supposedly, it tastes like tar and nicotine." An involuntary shudder ran across her face. "It's working—I think."

"There," Alec said, putting down the microphone. "That's done. Now, we'll head home." He went outside to the controls. We heard the engine roar. The boat swayed as he turned the wheel and accelerated.

I was still sopping wet, but getting warmer. I took a sip of the concoction. Not bad. I took another. My mind was clearing and I began to have questions. "Lily, how did you—"

"How did I know you were going to need me?"

I nodded and took another sip.

"As soon as I heard your phone message, I knew you shouldn't be alone with Sally. We expected to meet you at the Field house, but then we heard shots. A few minutes later, we spotted you."

"But they've arrested Judith. How did *you* know it was Sally?"

Lily took the other seat and swung it in my direction. "That UDJ thing stunk to high heaven, and I just couldn't swallow Judith as the killer. And I can't swallow this, either," she added as she spat a wad of chewed licorice into her palm and looked balefully around for an appropriate receptacle.

"Sorry, I can't help you," I said. "My tissues were in my purse and I left that in Sally's rowboat."

She glared at the black goo. "How can anybody actually eat this stuff?" She glanced around the tiny cabin and her expression brightened. "Ahah! I know just the place for it." She stepped through a small door marked "Head" and emerged wiping her hands on a paper towel. "Where were we?" She resumed her seat.

"You were telling me about your brilliant deductions." I wrapped my hands around my cup. "Why couldn't you swallow Judith as a killer?"

Lily spun gently in her seat. "Because I know her better

than you do. A hundred years ago, our husbands were buddies. She gives me a pain a pill can't reach, but believe it or not, she's a truly soft-hearted gal. To her, those school kids are her children. Even all that personal medical stuff she spouts is really just her way of showing she cares. Now Sally, on the other hand..."

"Is always pushing the envelope," I put in proudly. Another Hardy Patschke expression.

"You could put it that way. What I was going to say was, she's obsessive. She started out as a nobody, you know, and made herself into a somebody. And not the old-fashioned way, either. Remember how she got elected head cheerleader? She literally stuffed the ballot boxes!"

"Lily, how do you know all this?"

"Well, I was on the yearbook staff and I always kept up with what was going on in school, remember?"

"I remember." It was hard to believe, but Lily was actually less of a gossip now than in high school.

"But I didn't remember everything." Lily shook her head. "I forgot all about Sally's real first name. It was supposed to be a deep, dark secret, but of course, it wasn't. I learned about it when she begged us to change her name in the yearbook."

"And you did?"

"Sure, why not? We shortened Elm DeWitt's name, too. From Elmer."

"Is *that* his real name?" I asked, astonished, picturing our distinguished District Attorney.

"Didn't you know that? You think he was named for a tree? Anyway, about an hour after I got home, I remembered what it was about UDJ that bothered me. You know the rest." She looked intently at me and frowned. "Are you all right?" she asked, gently pushing soggy hair off my face. "You look pale."

I winced. "Ouch! Easy. That's where Sally shot me." I touched my ear and my hand came away clean. The cold lake water must have washed away most of the blood.

"She *what*?" She leaned forward and lifted my hair. "Let me see that!" She gently examined my ear. I heard her breath hissing between her teeth. "Oh, Amelia," she whispered, "I hope they catch her. I hope they catch her and I hope she *fries*," she added, hissing the last word. Her breath still smelled of licorice.

"Don't forget she did much worse to Marguerite," I said, "and if it wasn't for me, she wouldn't have known about the journal. That's why it's vital we catch her before she goes after Marie—oh!" I cried. I turned to Alec. "Oh, please—could we go back to the Field place? I think I know where the journal might be. Sally was in a rowboat. We can probably still beat her back there and find it. It might be proof of something."

Alec said nothing, only saluted with two fingers and turned the wheel. What a nice man he is, I thought.

Lily beamed at him. I shot her a quizzical glance, which she answered by sticking out her black tongue at me.

We arrived back at the Field place rapidly. The lights in the house were still on, but there seemed to be no sign of Sally.

"Don't you move!" Lily ordered. "You're still wet. You go out in this cold and you'll freeze solid. Where do you think the journal is?"

"Try her van. In the carport around front. And be careful. Sally may be back at any minute, and she's got a gun!"

Alec reached into a small cupboard and pulled out a rifle. "So have I, m'dear," he said grimly. "So've I." With a courtliness that was a pleasure to watch, he assisted Lily down the ladder and into the shallow water. "Stay inside, Miss Amelia. If you hear anything, just hide. We won't let her near you."

He gripped the rifle meaningfully.

I believed him. I stayed in the cabin, trying to make sense of Alec's gadgets and screens until the suspense became too much for me. In one of the cupboards, I found a waterproof slicker with a hood and put it on. Crouching carefully, I sneaked out onto the deck and peered over the side. I could hear Alec and Lily talking to one another on shore and occasionally I saw them silhouetted in the bright lights of the house. I turned my gaze out onto the silvery surface of the lake, where a mist was rising.

I crouched there for some time, keeping watch. Despite Alec's orders, I had decided to call out a warning at the first sign of the rowboat's approach. The lake's surface remained placid, ruffled only slightly by gusts of cold wind. The lights of the house were reflected out over the water. In the distance, I saw a flock of white birds ascend to the skies like a snowy cloud and fly away, calling to each other hoarsely.

Where *was* Sally? Surely she would have had time to row back by now. I whispered my question to the silent lake, which only continued to gently rock the Sweet Afton.

Lily and Alec returned just as I began shivering uncontrollably. Lily scolded and Alec chided as they hustled me back into the warmth of the cabin.

"Go!" I said between chattering teeth, "G-get going! Sh-she'll be back any m-minute!"

Alec saluted. "Will do." He gunned the motor and we were off.

Lily sat beside me with a secret smile on her face. "Don't you want to see what we found?" she asked coyly, and pulled a sealed, padded manila envelope from inside her coat.

It was addressed to me.

On the ride home in Alec's truck, Lily and I read Marguerite's journal. Of course, we fully intended to turn it over to the police once we got to town, but it was evidence and there was no telling when we'd get to see it again. And, by golly, as Lily pointed out, Marguerite had meant it for me!

"Journal of Marguerite Angelique LeBow," said the title page.

"Lovely handwriting," Lily remarked. "Why, Amelia, you only gave her a C," she said, pointing to a red letter in the corner.

"She didn't follow directions," I explained. "She added quotes. It was supposed to be all her own writing." How stupid and arbitrary that seemed now. Why *shouldn't* she have put meaningful quotes in her own personal journal?

I turned the pages in the thick black-and-white marbleized notebook until I came to the end of the assignment.

A full page had been devoted to my critique of her work in red ink. I winced at the brisk impersonality of my comments. I had been tired when I corrected the journals, but there was really no excuse for my harshness. It made me feel thankful and humble that Marguerite had forgiven me this.

The next page was touchingly entitled, "Private, Top Secret, Eyes Only."

I had only the vaguest idea what "Eyes Only" meant. No doubt Marguerite had borrowed the term from a spy novel.

Once she had completed the school assignment, it was clear that Marguerite felt free to make the journal truly her own. Very few entries bore dates. For a full fifteen pages, in a variety of colored inks, she rambled philosophically on a wide array of subjects: the meaning of life, the existence of God, the opposite sex, money, injustice, evil, fear, and forgiveness, among many others, covering both sides of the pages and bearing down hard with her pen. Even though her handwriting became hard to decipher in the heat of her enthusiasm, I could see how passionately idealistic she was. Sometimes she pasted newspaper clippings in among her thoughts.

"In spite of everything, I still believe that people are really good at heart—Anne Frank," Lily read aloud, her finger tracing the words.

Here and there, she illustrated her ideas with tiny doodles and figures. Most frequently, a stick-figure angel would insert a comment in a cartoon-style balloon.

"Be not overcome with evil, but overcome evil with good—Romans 12:21," said the angel, and, in another place, "One man with courage makes a majority—Andrew Jackson." There were many more such notations.

At the center of the book was a tasseled bookmark bearing Kipling's poem, *If.*

For the next few pages, Marguerite seemed taken with Kahlil Gibran, then a fascination with Shakespeare's sonnets took over.

Abruptly, the rambling entries stopped. A new title page read, "Unofficial Investigative Journal," and numerical dates crisply marked each short entry.

"Bingo," said Lily. "The police wouldn't listen to her, so she went undercover on her own."

"Oh, Marguerite," I breathed, "how I wish you hadn't."

The journal entries began to tell a story:

"8/10/01—Informed known drug users that I was interested in making a score."

"'Making a score?' Where'd she get this stuff?"

"TV, most likely." I turned a page.

Lily pointed at a pair of names. "Look, those must be the 'drug users.' Do you know them?"

"I sure do," I said grimly, "and I'm not surprised." They were former students.

"8/21/01—Spent $280 from savings account on cocaine. Expensive! Evidence stored in mattress. (Remember to ask

about reimburse.) Contact wouldn't reveal name of source—
yet. Will keep trying."

I looked at Lily. "That's how she got the reputation of
being involved in drugs."

Lily frowned. "Because she *was*. Poor idiot kid."

After several similar entries, it became apparent that Marguerite was having difficulty getting any more information.
She was reduced to speculation, which she wrote in a unique
code of her own.

> Chief Suspects:
> Gray Lady—near kids, can get drugs, too
>   sweet to be real
> Fisherman—near kids, moves around a lot,
>   foreigner
> UDJ—moves around a lot, mean, has lots of
> $$$
> Mustache—unsuspected, near kids, mean..."

Lily laughed. "'Fisherman!' That's gotta be you, Alec!"

From the driver's seat of his truck, Alec sniffed. "So I was
a suspect, eh? Maybe that's why she wrote me that terrible
letter."

"And 'Mustache.' Do you suppose that could be Gerard
Berghauser?" I said. "I wonder if he got a letter, too. Gray
Lady's obvious. That's Judith."

There was another list.

> People I Can Trust:
> Miss Amelia Prentice
> Father Frontenac
> Derek Standish
> My Mom

Lily laid a hand over mine. "Oh, Amelia, look.'"

The last name was underlined:

<u>My Dad</u>.

I looked at Lily. We were both blinking back tears.

"Here." Lily handed me a tissue from her pocket and took one for herself.

After a good blow, I said, "Her grandfather told me Marguerite had never stopped loving her father." Eagerly, I turned the next page. "But, it's blank!" I turned more. "It's all blank from here on out! She must have died before she could write more. Lily, this isn't evidence. It's probably useless to Dennis." I closed the book. "We'll give it to him anyway and see what he can make of it," I said with a sigh and replaced the journal in the envelope.

We traveled the rest of the way into town in silence. As Alec pulled up in front of my house, we heard a loud, insistent honking from behind, and Gil's car came careening around us, screeching to a halt at the curb.

Gil leaped from the car, ran to the truck, and jerked open the door. "Where is she?" he asked Lily, helping her down. She gestured to me in the cab, and Gil reached out his arms.

"Come here," he said.

Damp, shivering, and tear-soaked, I fell into his arms, and he carried me up the steps onto the porch. "I heard a police report on my scanner. They said you'd been attacked," he said, slightly out of breath.

Lily had stepped ahead of him, found my extra key taped to the bottom of the mailbox, and unlocked the door. "Here," she ordered, "take her upstairs."

I felt a little like Scarlett O'Hara as Gil swept me up the staircase and into my bedroom, but the illusion ended as he dumped me on the bed and bent over, heaving from the exertion.

"Good work. Now, get out," Lily said, and ushered him to the door. "Go down with Alec and put on some water to boil."

Gil shot her a quizzical glance.

"For coffee. For coffee. All she has is instant,"she pointed
out. "And there's whiskey under the kitchen sink behind the
Brillo pads,"she added. "She uses it for coughs. Have some."
She shut the bedroom door firmly.

Twenty minutes later, I descended under my own speed,
freshly showered and clad modestly in a long flannel nightgown, terrycloth robe, and fuzzy slippers. My wound, once
cleaned, turned out to be a small nick along the top of my ear
and a graze on my scalp. Disfiguring, certainly, but not grotesque. A couple of standard, skin-toned bandages covered
the damage. Lily insisted she knew a plastic surgeon who could
repair it all in no time.

Alec and Gil were sitting companionably in the parlor,
nursing juice glasses of whiskey.

"Miss Amelia, you look enchanting,"said Alec, rising, "like
a beautiful child."

Suddenly embarrassed, I avoided eye contact with Gil.

"I told her it's more than she wears teaching," Lily said.

"Amelia,"Gil began conversationally, "Alec and I were looking for your cat."

Forgetting all about the modesty issue, I stood stock-still,
experiencing again my ordeal in the lake: *Sally, beating on my
fingers, growling, "They're all gone! Your parents, your cat—"*

"My cat! Oh, dear Lord!" I dashed for the kitchen. "Oh,
please! Sam! Sam!"

There was no sign of him near his bowl, which I always
kept full of dry cat food. I opened the back door and looked
around. Vern had leaned the broken porch swing against the
house, and I spotted movement underneath it. There was a
faint whimper. I jerked the swing to one side and knelt beside
Sam, who lay listlessly on the floor, his round stomach pro-

truding, not even bothering to curl up in his customary ball.

"Oh, Sam," I cried. "What did Sally do to you?"

Sam blinked slowly, once.

"Lily! Look how bloated he is! He's been poisoned! Oh, Sam—"

Lily didn't waste time lamenting. "Give him here." She scooped Sam up in her arms. "Come on, Alec, we're taking him to the vet! Amelia, you call ahead and tell them we're coming."

I was glad Gil was there. "You've got to stop blaming yourself, Amelia," he insisted after I made the call. "You didn't poison the cat."

I paced. "No, but I never really liked him. That makes it worse. Poor old Sam."

"Sit down over here." He patted the place next to him on the loveseat invitingly.

"I can't. I'm too strung out. Oh, Gil, would you do me a favor?" I grabbed the padded envelope from the hall table and gave it to him. "Would you take this to the police station? I'm not even sure if it's legal for us to have it."

"They won't arrest me, will they?" he asked, smiling. He wrapped his arms around me and spoke into my hair. "Okay, but promise me you'll go right to bed and try not to worry. All the really bad part's over."

"Oh, Gil," I sighed, "I hope you're right."

Chapter Twenty

I slept surprisingly well that night. "Maybe the bad part *is* over," I told myself as I stretched. The sun glittered through the stained-glass window panels as I came down the stairs. I began my morning chores cheerfully and had located the box of cat food and bent over Sam's still-full bowl, ready to refill it, when I remembered.

"Oh, Sam," I sighed, "be all right!" The veterinarian hadn't found any evidence of poison, but he was keeping him under observation.

Last night, Dennis had interrogated me over the phone on the condition that I come into the station the following afternoon. I had already lined up a substitute at school and made plans to attend Marguerite's funeral Mass at ten. There was no reason to change them, despite last night's excitement. I listened to the radio and searched the newspaper for some new information about Sally, but aside from a cursory statement that she was being sought to help the police in their investigation and an announcement that Judith would be released this morning, there was nothing.

I walked to the church. It was a long way, but the exercise would do me good, and I had some thinking to do. My eyes drank in the bright colors as the autumn leaves fell around me, but my mind was far away, flailing helplessly in the black waters of the lake.

I had come close, extremely close, to dying last night. I was of two minds about that. On one hand, once I became reconciled to the inevitable out there in the cold water, I had actually found myself looking forward to the experience. If one believed as I did, the process of death was fearsome, but the destination was not. On the other hand, I had also had regrets. So many that my mind couldn't enunciate them in those decisive few seconds. All the missed opportunities! Not marrying Gil being chief among them. That was a mistake I intended to rectify as soon as possible.

"And that house!" I said aloud, and laughed. I wondered if the Field house would still be for sale. I—well, "lusted" was not too strong a word—I lusted after that house. Surely it could be sold through another agency. Surely Gil could buy it. Surely we could live there. My heart lifted at the thought. Soon, I resolved, I would find a special, uninterrupted time to tell Gil and see his reaction.

And there was more. I turned my mind to the *très* attractive Steve Tréchère. I liked his idea. A bed and breakfast would be the ideal way to put Dad and Mother's house to use. I could see Mother's face, eagerly preparing for company. She had loved company, and now with any luck the house would always be full of guests. I thought about the special woman he had in mind to operate the place and hoped fervently she would accept his offer. I even had an idea of who she was.

I saw a large, dark van go down the street and wondered

vaguely where Sally had gone. It was strange, but I wasn't afraid of her now. Sally clearly had a strong sense of self-preservation, and I had no doubt that she'd decided that discretion was called for now. I wished I could have told Dennis more about those mysterious friends of hers.

I'd been thinking furiously for ten blocks. As I approached the church, I looked at my watch. A full hour early. There were very few cars in the lot across the street and none at the curb near the entrance. As I stood uncertainly, wondering what to do, a side door opened, and Father Frontenac stepped out, accompanied by Steve Tréchère. The two men spoke in low, friendly tones and, as they reached the sidewalk, shook hands warmly. All at once, they saw me and froze. The priest glanced uncertainly at Tréchère, then smiled at me.

"Miss Prentice. You're a little early, as you can see. Come right on in." He held the heavy door open for me.

"In a few minutes, thanks, Father. I need to have a word with Mr. Tréchère."

Tréchère's faint nod indicated assent, and the priest retired, looking, I thought, a little guilty.

"I've been thinking about your business proposition," I said. "I like it."

The tense expression in his face relaxed. "Oh, that's very good. I believe that we can come to a good agreement."

"Why don't you come by my house tomorrow afternoon, say four? And we can plan," I suggested. "You will be here in town tomorrow, won't you?"

"Of course!" he smiled vaguely and moved slightly away, as if to leave.

"Aren't you staying for the Mass?"

He looked distracted. "What? You mean this?" He waved his hands in the direction of the church. "No, I must be on my way. You will excuse me?"

"But you'll be back. I know that much."

He blinked furiously and frowned at me. "What, be back? For what?"

I stepped forward and gently laid my hand on his arm. "For your daughter's funeral, Étienne," I said softly. "*Étienne*, French for Stephen, father of *Marguerite*, French for daisy."

He stared.

His dark eyes filled with tears, and he waved his gloved hand in an irritated gesture. He said nothing.

"It's a cruel thing to find her and then lose her again," I said. "But you did find her, didn't you? And she did know that you loved her."

His chin trembled and he nodded. "I shall always be grateful to God for that," he whispered.

"Does Marie know it's you?"

He shook his head. "Marguerite and Father Anthony were trying to help me. To break it to her gently, you know. She's still mad at me. The whole family is."

"Except for your daughter."

His face broke. "Except her," he mouthed, "but I didn't know about this other thing, the drug thing. If I had..." A dark expression crossed his face.

This man could be a dangerous enemy. It gave me a certain guilty satisfaction that when and if Sally Jennings ever turned up, I'd have to take a number.

"But Marguerite..." His face lightened slightly at the memory of his daughter. "It was wonderful finding her again. She was *aimable*, so...full of plans and secrets. I laughed with her, but I didn't pay much attention to what she said about *her* plans. There was something about this UDJ thing. I saw her, you know—spoke with her in the library—it must have been just a few minutes before—before—she died. We were supposed to meet. I waited for hours. Then I drove back to the library and all the emergency trucks and police cars were there. If only I..." Grief overtook him again. "Oh, *mon Dieu!*" He waved one gloved hand helplessly.

I snatched it in mid-air and held it firmly. "Whatever happens, please know this," I said steadily. "Your daughter loved you all her life. Even when you weren't there. Marie saw to that."

He nodded silently as he struggled for composure.

I continued holding on to his hand. "And it's my belief that you'll see her again—someday."

He looked at me through a watery smile. "Mine, too," he said in a whisper. "Thank you." He pulled his hand from mine and gestured in the direction of the street. "I must...I mean, excuse me, please." He turned and walked rapidly towards a dark car parked nearby.

I found a seat in the sanctuary and spent the rest of the hour praying for Marie and Étienne.

Father Frontenac performed the service with sweet dignity. There were few flowers. Marie had requested that donations be made to the church instead, but a huge basket of daisies—marguerites—stood at one end of the casket.

"Nobody knows who it's from," I heard a woman whisper.

Halfway through the service, I glanced up at the empty balcony. Étienne LeBow's grave face stared down. I detected a faint nod, returned it, and turned back to the prayer book.

Chapter Twenty-One

"Leave it to you to have your wedding in the middle of the Christmas season, Amelia," Lily whined as she helped Marie LeBow carry poinsettias into the soon-to-be-opened bed and breakfast, Chez Prentice.

"I had to, Lily," I said. "This way, Gil and I can go on our honeymoon and I won't have to miss any school."

"Well, I think it's romantic," declared Marie LeBow, shutting the big front door firmly. "There. That's all of 'em. No, Mrs. Burns, we're putting these in the dining room, next to the tree. Gotta keep 'em out of the draft."

"Got the food under control, Marie?" I asked.

"Oh, sure, piece of cake, you might say," she said, and dimpled. "By the way, speakin' of cake, Val's just finished with it in the kitchen. Wanna see?"

"Of course!"

Valerie's wide, round face was glistening with a combination of heat and excitement as she backed away to show us her handiwork. "Turned out real good, if I say so myself," she declared. She pushed hair out of her face with the back of her wrist and wiped her hands on her apron.

"It's exquisite!" I said. "Valerie, I had no idea you were so talented!"

"Oooh! Can I have a taste?" asked Lily, reaching, but one of Valerie's blistering do-it-and-die looks restrained her.

My wedding cake was a small one, as wedding cakes go, but it was a work of art. Every surface was covered with tiny, lifelike flowers: pink rosebuds, delicate violets, lilies of the valley, tiny scrolling vines of ivy. The cake was a riot of discreet pastels, blending perfectly with the pale pink poinsettias that would bank the cake table.

"'Exquisite,' that's the word I was thinkin' of," said Marie. "There now, didn't I tell you, Val? Amelia'd come up with a ten-dollar word for your cake."

Val nodded and beamed at her sister. "You sure did!"

Marie turned to me confidentially. "Val's always been good at bakin'; that's why I'm gonna get her to make all our bread 'n muffins 'n things. Her boy can bring 'em across the lake every couple days or so."

"Sounds good. And now that you've lined up Hester Swanson as the regular cook, you're set."

Marie consulted a clip-board. "Looks like it, if we can keep from killin' each other," she murmured dryly. Ever since agreeing to take over management of the B&B, she had shown an amazing aptitude for organization, making shrewd and frugal use of the generous advance Étienne had invested. "If they get the upstairs bathrooms done on schedule, we can open just like we planned on New Year's Day. You think this Tréchère guy'll come to the grand opening? I'd like to meet him sometime."

"Um, I think so. But you'll meet him sooner than that. In

fact, I know for sure he'll be at the wedding tomorrow."

"That's good," Marie said. She had come a long way in the last seven weeks. The complicated work of remodeling Chez Prentice had helped direct her attention away from her grief.

Against my unsolicited advice, Étienne had seen fit not to intrude on Marie's recovery, but had insisted on being the silent partner, at least for the time being. As time went by and Marie became stronger, I began to see the wisdom of his forbearance. Approaching her when she was at her most vulnerable would have been unfair, somehow.

The doorbell rang. "Marie!" I said. "It's fixed! You're turning Chez Prentice into a showplace!"

Marie smiled modestly and scribbled something else on her clipboard.

Lily answered the door, stepping back in surprise at the sight of Dennis O'Brien.

"Miss Prentice, can I speak with you? Privately?"

"Of course, Dennis." While Lily and Marie gaped, I led him into Dad's old study, now converted into Marie's office, and directed him to take a seat. "How about some coffee? We've modernized our kitchen, you know."

He smiled. "No, thanks, Miss Prentice. I can't stay but a minute. What I want to tell you will probably be in the news before tonight, but after everything, I thought you deserved to hear it from me." He ran an embarrassed hand through his thick hair and continued, "They've found the rowboat. The Fields' rowboat, although I guess you might call it your rowboat now."

I leaned forward. "And Sally?"

He shook his head. "Still no sign. They found the boat capsized over on the Vermont side. It must have drifted all this time. Surprisingly, it's in pretty good shape. Want me to see that you get it back?"

"No, thank you, Dennis," I said quickly, then paused. "No, I take that back. I promised Gil I'd take a swimming course at the Y. We might have a use for it yet."

Dennis smiled at me. "Hey, way to go, Miss Prentice. Put the bad stuff behind you."

"Still, I can't help thinking about Sally." That was an understatement. I'd had half-a-dozen disturbing nightmares since the whole thing happened. "Do you think she's just hiding?"

He shrugged. "We're still looking into it, but I don't think so. That water was pretty cold, and even if Mrs. Jennings was as good a swimmer as you say, she still couldn't have lasted long if the boat turned over. What's puzzling is how that might have happened. The lake was calm that night."

"So you're saying we'll never know what happened."

"No," he said, "I'm not saying that for publication, anyway, but that's probably the way it's going to turn out."

"And Barry won't be prosecuted."

"There's no proof he had anything to do with his wife's crime, Miss Prentice. But he has closed up the business and left town, you know."

I nodded. "Yes. He's at Betty Ford out in California."

Dennis chuckled as he stood. "Now how did you know that?"

"I have a reliable informant—and her initials are Lily Burns." I turned to a more serious subject. "Dennis, what's going to happen to Derek Standish?"

Dennis paused, his hand on the doorknob. "Well, since Mrs. Dee won't press charges, that pretty much takes him off the hook from our end. As far as rehab goes, I don't know much about it. Last I heard, he was learning how to talk again."

We sighed together.

"I don't suppose you found my purse in that boat?"

He shrugged and shook his head.

"Oh, well, I already replaced the credit cards and things. I just hated to lose that purse. It was my mother's." I escorted him out. "Please tell Dorothy how much I appreciated the fish slice," I told him at the front door.

"The what?"

"It's a piece of silverware. Your wedding gift. I told her once that it's what all the characters in PG Wodehouse gave as wedding presents, and she remembered."

"She'll be glad you liked it. She hunted all over the county. I just didn't know what you called the thing. This wedding is big news in our house, you know. Meaghan's pretty excited about tomorrow."

"She'll be a perfect flower girl. She proved it at the rehearsal yesterday."

"She did that," he admitted. "And tell Gil that having that rehearsal dinner at Danny's Diner was a terrific idea. Great fun. Well, see you tomorrow." He galloped down the steps just as Father Frontenac was mounting them. They exchanged greetings and I let the priest inside.

"It's time, huh?" I said.

He nodded. "Now or never. Where's Marie?" he asked, looking around nervously,

"Out in the kitchen, I think," I told him. "Where's Étienne?"

He jerked his head in the direction of a dark car, parked out front. "I've got to talk to Marie first, though."

"Marie!" I called. "Could you come into the office a minute?"

The hour that followed was difficult for me as I endeavored to ignore the closed door of the study and what was happening behind it. I tried to keep busy. I helped Valerie stow the wedding cake in the new restaurant-size refrigerator. I dried while Lily washed the cake-making utensils. I repolished Mother's silver candlesticks and counted the already-counted crystal goblets that stood in waiting formation on the buffet table in the dining room.

At last, Father Frontenac emerged, his eyes bright. "Tell him to come in," he said tersely and disappeared back into the study.

The man who responded to my beckoning gesture was not the self-assured Steve Tréchère, prosperous real estate mogul and Millionaire from Montreal. No longer did he bear the slightest resemblance to the jaunty Louis Jourdan. Even before he was halfway up the sidewalk, he had his hat in his hand. In the other hand, he carried a nosegay of pink baby roses. The desperate, anxious look in his eyes caused answering tears to spring into my own, and I mouthed a two-word prayer, "Please, God," as the study door closed behind him.

"What the bloody blue blazes is going on here?" Lily demanded behind me. She held two stemmed glasses in her hand and thrust one at me. "Here. It's ginger ale. I helped myself from the six cases you have out on the back porch. Marie says she got a good deal on it. Wasn't that your millionaire friend?" she asked, her eyes bright. She glanced in the hall mirror. "Oh, look at that! All my lipstick's worn off. Where's my purse?"

"Yes, that was Steve Tréchère, but I'm afraid I'm not at liberty to explain why he's here," I said stiffly.

"Well, excuse me all to the hot place!" said Lily, applying lipstick liberally. "There, that's better," she said, mashing her lips together as she gazed in the mirror. "Boy, I'm bushed. Come on, let's take a break."

She headed for the parlor and I followed, tossing uneasy glances over my shoulder at the hallway lest anyone should emerge from the office.

Lily pulled off her apron and wiped her face on it. "Whew!

That Valerie is a real slave driver. I'm glad I won't have to work here. And don't even get me started about Marie." She pulled a tiny box of toothpicks from her purse, extracted one with a delicate gesture, and began chewing. "Want one?" she offered. "Mint flavored. Best part is, no calories. I gained three pounds with those stupid jellybeans. And those carrot sticks were a nuisance. Somebody actually tried to light one for me in a dark restaurant the other night." She sighed. "Worst part is, I'd still give anything for one of those nasty, stinking coffin nails." She thrust the toothpick box forward. "Here, take one."

"No, thanks," I said, remembering my mother's strong aversion to the things. Still, Lily had managed to remain almost completely smokeless for two and a half months. Whatever works.

I took another sip of my ginger ale. "Lily, why are you here? You know Marie's got everything under control. You should be at home, resting up and getting your hair done for tomorrow."

"Don't worry, Amelia, I'm quite aware of my duties as Matron of Honor. My beauty will approach, but not exceed, that of the bride; I will patiently hold your bouquet during the ceremony; I will keep the groom's ring warmly and safely stashed in my ample—"

"No, Lily, what I mean is, why aren't you at home? You can't be having any fun here."

Lily leaned forward and looked in the direction of the study door. She batted her eyelashes. "Don't be too sure. No, really, Amelia, I'm just hanging out here to get away from my one-man fan club."

"But I thought you liked Alec."

She lay back and massaged her eyes with thumb and forefinger. Her toothpick bobbed rapidly in the corner of her mouth. "'Like' is such a strong word, Amelia. Tolerate, perhaps. Endure, certainly. But it's all become so tiresome."

I was reminded of Marlene Dietrich, languidly singing about how men cluster 'round her like moths around a flame. "You didn't seem to think it tiresome when he took you to see the road company of *Les Miserables*. Or night-clubbing in Montreal. Or—"

"Okay, we had a good time there for a while." She sat up. "But irregardless, all that whistling is starting to get to me. And besides, he overstepped the bounds of good taste!"

I was so astonished, I forgot to correct Lily's wording. Sweet, gentlemanly Alec, overcome with passion to the point of boorishness? I just couldn't picture it. "Lily!" I said breathlessly. "What did he do?"

She pulled her toothpick from the corner of her mouth and snapped it in half. "He proposed! Ring in the little velvet box, bended knee, the whole nine yards."

"And that offended you?"

"Not that, exactly, but Amelia, I just don't find him...that is, he just doesn't make me...he doesn't ring my chimes, okay?" She frowned. "Stop looking at me that way. It's not like you think. The guy has been such a perfect gentleman, he never even kissed me goodnight. All we've ever done is hold hands."

I sighed. "Poor Alec."

"I don't know why you keep sticking up for him all the time. If I didn't know better, I'd think Gil ought to be jealous."

I smiled but didn't answer. Lily was partly right. Alec and I had become closer friends ever since I had confided in him about my strange experience in the lake.

"You know, Alec," I'd told him cautiously, after we ran through the salient facts, "I think my experience was a little, um, different from Lily's."

Alec had stopped taking notes, raised one shaggy eyebrow,

and scratched his head with his pencil. "By that, I take it y'mean that yours isn't fiction?"

"What do you mean?"

"You know precisely what I mean." He laughed. "Don't look so surprised. She never fooled me with that 'woo-eee' business."

"But why—I mean, it's such a rotten trick—why do you—"

"Why do I pretend to believe her?" He turned to a blank page and began doodling in his notebook, sketching a cartoon. "Well, Miss Amelia, y'may have noticed that I have a bit of a soft spot for the lady." I watched his pencil move. He sketched a long dinosaur body with a curving tail. "And in the best tradition of unrequited lovers..." He added a long neck and topped it with a small, simpering face. "I take my opportunities where I can..." In the monster's flippers he put a tiny bow and arrow. "And in this way, you might say, my monster becomes..." He drew in a pair of ridiculously tiny wings and held the pad out to me. "...my own personal Cupid."

"Poor Alec," I said again, remembering the wistfulness in his eyes.

"Don't 'poor Alec' me, Amelia," Lily said. She located her coat on the parlor coatrack and pulled it on. "I've given that man some of the best weeks of my life. But don't worry. I'll let him down easy." She heaved her purse strap over her shoulder and headed for the door. "Gotta go. I'm getting my hair done at Gladys's."

I looked at the china clock on the mantelpiece. "Oh, gosh, so am I! And I'm already ten minutes late. May I ride with you?"

By the time I got back from the hairdresser's, everyone had left: Marie, Étienne, Valerie, Father Frontenac, the plumber. Everyone's car was gone from the newly-paved parking lot behind the house. Standing there now was a monstrous Winnebago with Florida plates.

I walked around to the front. A handsome, hand-painted sign declared that Chez Prentice was a "Victorian Bed and Breakfast." I ascended the front steps, which were now rock-solid. Workmen had repaired the porch swing and we had left it out for appearance's sake, despite the fact that it would be too cold out to enjoy swinging for the next few months.

A woman was sitting on it.

"Hello, Barb," I said, and joined her on the swing. "I saw your bus out back."

"Hello, yourself, Mel," said my sister, hugging me. "Frank's upstairs asleep. The trip wiped him out. Jacob and Trudy went out for pizza. The twins send their love, but they have finals at Auburn and couldn't make it. That lady who was working in the kitchen said you'd be back soon, so I thought I'd meet you."

I took her hand and squeezed it. "I'm glad you did. It was nice to find you here."

We sat in silence for a minute, swinging.

"Well, you're going to go through with it, then?"

I waited a few swings before answering. "Yes."

"You love him and everything?"

"Yes."

"Well. That's good. You'll be happy. Gil's a nice guy."

"Yes, he is. Mother always liked him."

"She did, didn't she? Wouldn't she just love this?" Barbara smiled, then shivered. "Darn! I forgot how cold it gets up here. I'm going inside."

"I'll stay a minute more," I said, adding, "I'm glad you came."

Barbara kissed my cheek. "So am I, baby sister."

Inside, all was in readiness for the reception. Poinsettias were everywhere. In the parlor, the Christmas tree, decked entirely in antique pastel blown-glass ornaments, smelled wonderful.

I cast an anxious glance at the now-empty office. What had happened to Marie and Étienne? I glanced at the telephone, but decided to wait. If the outcome had been a bad one, I just didn't want to know tonight. I moved on.

A protective sheet lay over the buffet table, and I knew that the refrigerator was filled with trays of tiny canapés. Above the door to the parlor, someone had hung a plump ball of mistletoe.

"Well, Mother," I whispered, "your prayer was answered. I'm not going to be alone any more. Boy, am I not going to be alone!"

The telephone rang.

"Hello, my darling," I answered.

"How do you *do* that!" said Gil.

"That's my secret."

"We're going to be married tomorrow. There should be no secrets between us. Come on, honey, give. Or is that what you say to everybody?"

"It's so simple, I'm surprised you haven't figured it out. Étienne bought one of those caller I.D. gadgets. It says your name right here."

"Are we being recorded, too?"

"No," I said and laughed. "Where's your best man?"

"Vern? He's out to dinner with his dad, but they'll be back soon, I think. I overheard them plotting with Alec to throw me a surprise bachelor party out here."

"Oh, no! They won't hurt you or anything, will they?" I had heard horror stories.

Gil laughed. "Don't worry. They're just going to have pizza and beer and a few ribald party favors. These things are pretty tame for a guy my age. Wait! I got someone here wants to say something to you."

I heard a deep, steady purr.

"Sam!" I cooed. "How are you? Is Daddy being good to you? Are you getting used to your new house?"

"Hey—save some of those sweet nothings for me," Gil interrupted. "He's okay, don't worry."

"I wouldn't have believed it, but I miss him, Gil. I wish I'd kept him here."

"You can't have him at the B&B, Amelia. There are all those health department regulations. And if you gave him to Lily, he'd probably eat himself into a semi-coma again, and you'd mistake it for poisoning."

"Wait a minute," I said sharply, "I beg to differ. Sally *did* poison his food through the cat door, remember? Sam was just too full of Lily's leftovers to eat it."

"Well, all I know is, you wasted a lot of guilt over it. This is the best answer. And once you're here..."

"But I miss *you*, too. Can't you come over and give me a good-night kiss?"

I heard him smile. "Much as I'd love to travel all those miles into town for sixty seconds of passion, I'd better pass. Besides, it's bad luck to see the bride and all that."

"I'm not superstitious," I declared petulantly.

"Well, I am, so good night, Love of My Life, and I'll see you tomorrow at two in the afternoon."

"It's a date," I whispered, and hung up.

Chapter Twenty-Two

When Valerie arrived the next morning, with her Sunday dress on a hanger and Sunday shoes in a box, she couldn't tell me anything about Marie. "She just called last night and said she had something to do. Didn't come back to the house all night. Told me to hold down the fort and I'd see her whenever." Valerie shrugged and patted my hand. "Don't you worry a bit. I've got it all under control." She began to tie on an apron. "You'll have to excuse me, though. I gotta finish makin' them canopies."

I tried not to speculate about whether this meant a happy reunion or a depressing need for Marie to be alone. I ran upstairs to finish my packing.

In the afternoon, Lily drove me to the church. She looked beautiful in her mint-green suit. "I did it, Amelia," she said gleefully as we got in her car. "I managed to avoid the Old Man of the Sea all last night. I didn't answer the phone at all, just turned off the ringer and went to sleep. Maybe he'll get the message."

I looked at myself in the car mirror. "Don't tell me these things, Lily. It makes me sad, and I'm determined to be happy today, no matter what. Is this lipstick too dark, do you think?"

"Oh, give it a rest, Amelia. You look gorgeous. That pale-pale pink suit is perfect. I have excellent taste, if I do say so myself." Lily had found my dress in a bridal catalog. "Here." She thrust a tiny zipper-lock plastic bag at me.

"What's this? What's in here?"

"An old penny, a new penny, a borrowed penny—you have to give that one back to me later—and a blue ribbon. Hide it under your bouquet. Or in your cleavage."

"Oh, Lily, I don't need—"

"Just humor me, okay?"

I was in a pale-pale pink fog once we reached the bride's room, an extra-large ladies' room with a few elderly plastic flower arrangements and color-coordinated boxes of tissue. There were people milling around me, but I hardly noticed them.

I stood in front of the mirror and stared at the woman there. She looked pretty good. Hair fixed, nice makeup, mani-cured nails, even earrings. Was she really getting married? I smiled at her. Of course she was! It seemed like the most logi-cal, inevitable thing in the world.

All at once, I realized everyone had gone. I heard music start somewhere. There was a knock at the door. I opened it.

Alec stood there, well-scrubbed and almost handsome in a new gray suit. "Oh, you look bonnie!" he said approvingly.

"So do you. What hymn are you whistling today, Alec?"

He scratched his head, and a tuft of hair escaped its care-ful, slicked-down position. "As a matter of fact, I've been tryin' to get 'Blest Be the Tie that Binds' out of m'haid all day," he said. "Funny, isn't it?"

"Not funny at all, Alec. It's perfect."

"Are ye ready then, Miss Amelia?" He held out his arm.

I kissed his cheek and took his elbow. "I'm ready."

Meaghan O'Brien and Lily had preceded us into the chapel and now it was our turn, mine and Alec's. Slowly, proudly, stepping to the music, we walked down the short aisle.

The chapel wasn't filled, but the first five or six rows were occupied. Everyone was standing and turned towards us, smiling. Through gaps in my pink cloud I recognized a few faces. Hardy Patschke crossed his eyes at me and I winked back. Judith Dee, dressed head to toe in blue lace, wiggled her gloved hand in our direction. Hester and Bert Swanson beamed. Valerie, now arrayed in her Sunday finery, was mopping her eyes with a tiny hanky while her husband and son looked on, embarrassed. Jack and *Maman* Yvonne Garneau nodded at me solemnly and pointed across the aisle.

I glanced to my left and stopped in my tracks. Étienne and Marie LeBow stood hand-in-hand. Marie held up her left hand and pointed to a wedding band. Father Frontenac was next to them, grinning and rolling his eyes. I gave them my biggest smile, and Alec and I finished our walk.

All at once, there I was, standing beside Gil Dickensen, promising to cleave only unto him, as long as we both shall live. I wasn't nervous at all. As I said, it seemed like the most natural, inevitable thing in the world.

"So you see, you won't need to throw your bouquet at me," Marie explained in my upstairs bedroom as I freshened up to leave on our honeymoon trip.

The reception had been a howling success. There had been just enough wedding cake. According to Marie's report, every canapé had been greedily consumed and the only beverage left was ginger ale, fortunately still cold from the back porch, because we had also run out of ice. Nevertheless, the festivities were still going strong. We could hear Dorothy O'Brien at the piano downstairs, playing Christmas carols while everybody sang.

"O come all ye faithful..."

Marie went on, "Father Anthony told us we're still married in the eyes of the Church irregardless, so we don't even have to get re-married. Of course, Val's not happy about it, but we'll change her mind, I know we will." I could see Marguerite's quavering intensity sparkling in her eyes. "Oh, Amelia, he's such a wonderful man! And I'm so glad he got to know his little girl," she finished in a husky whisper.

"I am, too, Marie," I said briskly, hurrying her out the door. "I'll see you downstairs, dear." If I listened to her any more, I would be a sodden mess before we started on our honeymoon.

I finished rearranging my hair and looked in the mirror. Not bad. Gladys had persuaded me to let it grow a little and designed a style that helped hide my mangled ear.

Gil didn't think it was mangled. "It just looks like somebody clipped it on top with a hole-puncher. My granddad used to do it all the time to his new calves."

"Are you ready to go?" my new husband asked as he emerged from the newly installed bathroom, wiping his hands on a towel. He grabbed me around the waist and pulled me down on the bed. "Or shall we start the honeymoon right here?" He kissed my neck.

"Gil," I said sternly as his hands began to work a kind of magic, "not on Hester's quilt." The Swansons had given us the prize-winning quilt as a wedding present.

"Mmm? Am I being a randy teenager again?" he whispered.

"Yes. But I like it." I put my arms around him.

"Hey, what's that noise?"

I sat up. "Wait a minute." I fished the plastic bag out of the front of my dress.

"One, two, three pennies, and a blue ribbon?" Gil said, examining it. "What's this?"

"Just something Lily gave me," I said, tossing it away. "I'll explain later."

After several minutes, we emerged at the top of the staircase and looked down on a cheerful, anticipatory crowd, made up largely of unattached females. I scanned the group and finally spotted Lily, in animated conversation with Marie LeBow near the parlor, studiously ignoring Alec.

I knew what I had to do. With the eager group of single women leaping for my flowers like a pack of hungry hounds at a hambone, I tossed the bouquet up and over their heads, landing it neatly in Lily's upraised, gesturing hands. There was a hearty, good-natured cheer, and Dorothy struck up "I'm Getting Married In the Morning" on the piano.

"Yesss!" I said and pumped my fist in the time-honored tradition of athletes. "Two points!"

Gil laughed and took my hand. "Come on, honey, let's go."

We descended in a blizzard of rice. Just as we reached the bottom step, a hand grabbed my elbow in a painful grip, yanked me to one side, and snarled in my ear, "I'll get you for this, Amelia!"

"I know you will, Lily, *irregardless.*" I laughed and winked at Alec, who, his arm around Lily's waist, was drawing her ever closer to the mistletoe and the inevitable.

The End

About the Author

Ellen Edwards Kennedy calls herself a "Southern-ized Yankee," which means she knows how to use "y'all" properly, but never drops her g's. Born in Alabama, she grew up in Miss Prentice's region of far northern New York State and lived with her husband and children across the South and West. She feels this has given her a deep love for these areas and a sharp ear for regional accents.

Through high school and college, she performed in summer stock and briefly nursed the vain dream of becoming a Broadway musical star, but settled for a career as an advertising copywriter. Her recent experiences as a high school substitute teacher make her uniquely qualified to translate obscure adolescent dialects into understandable English. She is a volunteer reader at the Triangle Reading Service, which provides audio literature to the visually impaired.

Ellen Kennedy is a member of Sisters in Crime, a graduate of Huntingdon College, a mother of two lovely grown-up daughters, a happily married wife of 25 years, and a born-again Christian. She is currently at work on a Miss Prentice sequel and a mystery set in small-town Texas. She and her husband live in North Carolina.

OTHER BOOKS BY
ST KITTS PRESS

The Voice He Loved by Laurel Schunk

"...a masterful tale that reaches into the inner workings of a bruised and battered psyche, while keeping the plot moving at a breathless pace."   —*The Charlotte Austin Review*
(www.charlotteaustinreviewltd.com,
reviewed by Nancy Mehl)

Black and Secret Midnight by Laurel Schunk

"Beth Anne's appealing child's-eye view of the world and the subtle Christian message should make this appealing to fans of Christian and mainstream mysteries."   —*Library Journal*

"Beth Anne is at times touchingly naive..."   —*Publishers Weekly*

"...a memorable picture of racism that is variously stark and nuanced."   —*Small Press Book Review*

"...a good look at racial relations in the south...with a mysterious twist."   —*The Pilot* (Southern Pines, NC)

"The story is so gripping that I worried [Beth Anne] would be killed before the end."
—*Murder: Past Tense* (The Hist. Mys. Apprec. Soc.)

"...Schunk's adult novels are serious, skillfully crafted works."
—*nwsbrfs* (Wichita Press Women, Inc.)

"...a light in the darkness and a novel to sink your teeth and your heart into." —*The Charlotte Austin Review* (www.charlotteaustinreviewltd.com, reviewed by Nancy Mehl)

Hyænas by Sandy Dengler

"Highly recommended." —*Library Journal*

"Dengler has crafted a masterpiece. *Hyaenas* proves that there are still new slants to the mystery genre."
—*The Charlotte Austin Review* (www.charlotteaustinreviewltd.com, reviewed by Nancy Mehl)

"*Hyænas* is both a terrific murder mystery and a work of unique, flawless written exploration of prehistoric antiquity."
—*Internet Bookwatch* (The Midwest Book Review)

Death in Exile by Laurel Schunk

"What could have been a straightforward Regency romance is elevated by apt social commentary in this offering from Schunk..."
—*Library Journal*

"Schunk is a good writer who has a good grasp of story and character." —*The Pilot* (Southern Pines, NC)

"This beautifully written Regency novel...will throw you into another time, and you won't want to leave."
—*The Charlotte Austin Review* (www.charlotteaustinreviewltd.com, reviewed by Nancy Mehl)

"Laurel Schunk is a masterful storyteller."
—*Murder: Past Tense* (The Hist. Mys. Apprec. Soc.)

Under the Wolf's Head by Kate Cameron

"The gardening tips seeded throughout the narrative are a clever ploy, echoing the inclusion of cooking tips in the ever-popular culinary mysteries..."   —*Publishers Weekly*

"Plenty of gardening filler and allusions to inept local law enforcement lighten the atmosphere, as do the often humorous sisterly 'fights' and the speedy prose."   —*Library Journal*

"You'll laugh at the sisters' relationship and grow to love the two women just as Callista's plants grow through her loving care."
—*GRIT: American Life & Traditions*

"Schunk in the past has tackled child abuse and racism; her first gardening mystery provides a message about ageism and the value placed on elderly lives..."   —*Norwich Bulletin* (Norwich, CT)

"Highly recommended."   —*The Charlotte Austin Review*
(www.charlotteaustinreviewltd.com,
reviewed by Nancy Mehl)

"*Under the Wolf's Head* is a wonderful new release by Kate Cameron."
—*About.com* (reviewed by Renie Dugwyler)

"...evokes in the reader an understanding of the atmosphere of a small town, where everyone is important and interesting."
—*The Bookdragon Review*
(www.bookdragonreview.com,
reviewed by Richard Royce)

"...a quick and pleasant read..."
—*nwsbrfs* (Wichita Press Women, Inc.)

Shaded Light by N.J. Lindquist

"...a cozy that will delight fans who appreciate solid, modern detection." —*Publishers Weekly*

"Detailed characterization, surprising relationships, and nefarious plot twists." —*Library Journal*

"A very good novel by an accomplished writer."
—*Rapport Magazine*

"This most enjoyable novel is written in the style of Agatha Christie...Follow the clues to a bang-up ending."
—*The Pilot* (Southern Pines, NC)

"...an admirable first outing for a pair of detectives readers will look forward to hearing from again." —*The Mystery Reader*
(reviewed by Jennifer Monahan Winberry)

"With any luck, we'll see more of Manziuk and Ryan in years to come." —*The Charlotte Austin Review*
(www.charlotteaustinreviewltd.com,
reviewed by PJ Nunn)

"This excellently plotted novel is the first in a projected series of Manziuk and Ryan mysteries." —*I Love a Mystery*

"Paul and [Jacquie] make a fabulous team as their divergent personalities harmoniously clash to the benefit of the reader."
—*Internet Bookwatch* (The Midwest Book Review)

"A cozy reminiscent of the best Agatha Christie had to offer."
—*Midwest Book Review* (reviewed by Leann Arndt)

The Heart of Matthew Jade by Ralph Allen

"...a compassionate view into religious, familial and romantic love..."
—*Publishers Weekly*

"Fabulous!" —Kevin Patrick, CNET Radio, San Francisco

"...an eye-opener. *The Heart of Matthew Jade* is a compelling novel that will stay with you long after you put it down."
—*The Charlotte Austin Review*
(www.charlotteaustinreviewltd.com,
reviewed by Nancy Mehl)

"...this novel's strength is in the behind the scenes glimpses of faith behind bars." —*The Bookdragon Review*
(www.bookdragonreview.com,
reviewed by Melanie C. Duncan)

A Clear North Light by Laurel Schunk

"Schunk solidly launches a new 'Lithuanian' trilogy, following one family's triumphs and tragedies through the generations."
—*Library Journal*

"...notable as much for its excellent character development as for its story line...Good reading..."—*nwsbrfs* (Wichita Press Women, Inc.)

"...dramatically illuminates the effect of deadly global politics on the private lives of all-too-human individuals caught up in events not of their making." —Gretchen Sprague,
author of *Maquette for Murder*

"...pulls one into an historical drama with excitement and moral persuasiveness as Petras fights and searches for faith, meaning, and love..." —James D. Yoder, author of *Lucy of the Trail of Tears*